RUNAWAY

A captivating historical saga

GRACE THOMPSON

JOFFE BOOKS

Revised edition 2022
Joffe Books, London
www.joffebooks.com

First published by Robert Hale Ltd.
in Great Britain in 2008

This paperback edition was first published
in Great Britain in 2022

Cover art by Jarmila Takač

ISBN: 978-1-80405-361-4

CHAPTER ONE

Faith Pryor was approaching her twenty-second birthday and on the following Saturday she planned a small party. She lived in a small bedsit so there couldn't be too many guests. She secretly hoped that this would be the occasion on which Nick would announce their engagement. St Valentine's Day, 14 February 1960, that would be a good day for a wedding. Just over a year from now.

She packed away the few ornaments she possessed, hiding them in drawers and cupboards. The room would be crowded; some might get broken, and besides, they would need every inch of space if the ten people she had invited all turned up. She had a small kitchen area and in it were the beginnings of the spread she planned. No cake; there was this small insistent hope that it would be an engagement cake instead of a birthday cake, and she could always knock up a sponge and decorate it if Nick hadn't said anything before Saturday.

Cooking was something she enjoyed and she went through the list of dishes she would prepare and a second list of ingredients she would have to buy with anticipated pleasure. Surely Nick would propose? His words were so close to what she dreamed of and he often told her he loved her. An engagement party would be a wonderful way to celebrate her birthday and end the years of loneliness. She added a few more items to her list; Saturday had to be special and this was no time to think of the cost.

She glanced at the clock. Tonight she and Nick were going out for a meal at a hotel a few miles away in the small South Wales seaside town of Barry. There was an hour before he was due to call. Putting aside her lists, she bathed and put on the beautiful new dress she had bought for her party. Tonight could be important and she wanted to look her best.

Looking at herself critically she saw what she privately referred to as a pleasantly plump young woman with hazel eyes that somehow matched the colour of her hair which she described as rusty brown. She brushed it up and piled it on her head, fastening it with grips. No time for anything more, and Nick liked it that way. At 7.30 p.m. she was sitting listening to the wireless and waiting to hear Nick arriving. At eight p.m. she gave up and pulled the clips from her hair, kicked off the high-heeled shoes put the new dress back on its hanger and gave a deep sigh. So Nick was letting her down. Not for the first time, she reminded herself sadly. At nine p.m. she made herself eggs on toast and at ten p.m. she went to bed.

At 7.30 a.m. the following morning, as she was gathering all she needed for the day's lessons at the school where she worked as a temporary teacher, there was a knock at the door. 'Hello, Nick,' she said as he stood there, head hanging low in mock shame. 'What happened this time?'

'You'd never believe it.'

'Try me.' She failed to raise a smile and instead walked back into her room and picked up her shoulder bag and briefcase.

'The damned car broke down. Clutch slipping again.'

'Nick, you only live fifteen minutes' walk away. You could have come and told me instead of leaving me waiting for you.'

'Did you wait long?'

'Till eight before giving up and making myself some food to make up for the dinner you promised me.'

'I'm sorry, love. What about tonight instead?'

Childishly she shook her head. 'I have lots of work to get ready for the exhibition. We're arranging an open day at the school. All the parents are coming and we have to make sure every child has something on display.' She didn't mention the party with her hope of its romantic end.

'You love your work, don't you?'

'Very much. I now have to decide whether I want it to be permanent.'

'And will you? Can you stop moving around and settle?'

'Do you think I should?' She smiled at him, hoping he might say something to persuade her it was the right thing to do. Even though he was not always reliable she wanted permanency at the school and with Nick, but he didn't say anything more. He kissed her lightly on the cheek and hurried off, leaving her feeling deflated, a not uncommon sensation where Nick Harris was concerned.

In an attempt to take her mind off growing doubts and disappointment she looked through the list of food she needed to buy for Saturday's party. She was determined that the evening would be a good one. And whatever happened afterwards, she had no ties. She was still free to walk away from here. Thank goodness she hadn't confided her hopes of an engagement to anyone, apart from a few vague hints. Yet the niggle of hope that he would surprise her with the offer of a ring still remained. She was aware that she was what some would call a waverer, a woman who needed to cover her every move, which was why she usually solved a problem when she was unable to make up her mind by running away.

Her contract would finish at the end of term; then, whatever happened, she would be able to move right away, start again, forget Nick and her foolish dreams. She would scuttle off as she had in the past, leaving her acquaintances to pick over the crumbs of her disappointment.

* * *

A few miles away, on the outskirts of the holiday resort of Barry, Ian Day was also thinking about a party. He and Tessa were planning to announce their engagement. They had been together since schooldays and Ian had bought a house, with the intention of living there with Tessa and his widowed mother, Vivienne. It was a large house and he had spent several months redecorating and adding modern improvements, mostly following Tessa's suggestions.

Last night he and Tessa had had a serious disagreement. She had told him she was going on holiday with a friend and he had protested that as they were saving for their wedding it was unreasonable. He looked around the spacious living room with its view over a garden that his mother had managed to tame, and wondered whether the engagement would happen as planned or whether he and Tessa needed time to make sure it was what they wanted and not something that had become an automatic acceptance of a future together. Perhaps growing up as close friends wasn't the best start for a marriage, simply the easiest.

* * *

Faith closed the gate as she went off for her day teaching the six-year-olds. Once she was in school, where people made demands on her time and the hours raced past, she would put aside her disappointment and enjoy her day with the children. As she walked she wondered seriously whether she really wanted to marry Nick. Was it her age and the desire to settle down more than love? Could she love someone who was so casual, so negligent of her feelings? And how could he treat her so if *he* loved *her*?

Mary Gould, a dinner lady at the school, caught up with her as she left that afternoon, struggling with a pile of books. 'Where were you last night? Your Nick was at the dance.'

'Oh, I didn't feel well, a chill, probably,' she lied, hoping her shock wasn't apparent.

'He seemed to be having a good time. Danced with someone he introduced as Tessa for most of the evening.

They seemed to know each other well and were acting like two people in love. Then after showing her off to us all he gave her a lift home.'

'The car was fixed then? It was giving some trouble with the clutch earlier.'

Mary Gould was in her fifties, her children were grown up and had moved away. Having been at home for the years of caring for them she had taken the job of dinner lady to fill some of the empty hours and, on her fiftieth birthday, her husband had presented her with a car. She used it to travel about, exploring and taking photographs. She had befriended Faith on her first day and they had occasionally spent an afternoon together, visiting interesting places, usually stopping at a café for a snack.

She reminded Faith of all she had missed by not growing up within a family as she constantly talked about her children and her mild, easy-going husband. If only she had been as fortunate how different her own life might have been, she thought. Sisters and brothers, parents, grandparents and cousins. Her lack of belonging was a constant ache.

'Want a lift?' Mary asked now. 'I stayed on to help with the stock-take.' With her arms filled with books, Faith willingly accepted. It was worth listening to Mary's unwittingly wounding chatter to save struggling with the slippery load.

With Mary's words echoing in her mind, Faith went home with her thoughts in tumult. After arranging to take her out, Nick had lied to her and gone dancing. She had been fooling herself. Lying to herself. How pathetic was that? Perhaps last night's disappointment had been a good thing. It was time to face facts; it was not the first time something like this had happened; he relied on charm to get away with treating her thoughtlessly — or worse. She had been acting like an idiot. This was the moment to face the truth and tell him goodbye.

The thought was painful. She had dreamed of having a home of her own after all the years of not belonging. Faith had no family at all, and had been fostered since a baby.

Meeting Nick, falling in love, had promised an end to all that lonely heartache. A home, a caring husband and children of her own. Children she would love and protect to compensate for her own miserable childhood. She knew she had wanted those things too much, it was time to admit her stupidity.

She had been denying the truth that was so apparent. She wasn't loved and perhaps never would be. People recognized that she had been damaged by her sad childhood. She tried too hard to please, grabbing at friendships in a way that put people off.

* * *

At lunch time a few days later, knowing Ian Day was working at home, Tessa went to see him. They were both uneasy after their recent argument but Tessa remained determined to take a holiday and use money they had saved for furnishings. Ian refused to agree but Tessa insisted on withdrawing her share of their savings and, angry and hurt, he drove to the bank and gave her half of their savings, more than she had contributed. He wondered whether this was the end of their engagement and hoped that before the day ended she would be back full of remorse to put things right.

When Tessa took the money and without a word hurried back to the shop where she worked, Ian drove to the house he had bought and wandered from room to room, wondering whether it would ever be the happy home he had envisaged for so long. An hour later he was staring at his friend, Harry Ford, in disbelief.

'No. Harry, it couldn't have been Tessa you saw. She hardly knows anyone round there and dancing isn't something we enjoy. Besides, last Saturday she was home nursing a heavy cold. She wasn't well enough to go out or she'd have been with me, working on our house.'

His friend shrugged. 'They looked pretty close to me and it was definitely your Tessa.'

He waited until Tessa would be home, then, leaving the shelves he was making for his and her future home, Ian got into the car and drove to where Tessa lived with her sisters and parents. The house was empty and he walked around the area disconsolately. After an hour he drove home and, in the hallway of the house in which he planned to start married life, there was a letter.

It was short but said all he needed to know. Tessa was leaving him and going to London with someone called Nick Harris.

His reaction to the shock of Tessa's deceit was to make up his mind to work every hour he could spare and get the house finished. The work would be completed by the date on which he and Tessa were to have married. It was a way of coping with the realization that everything he had been working towards had collapsed around him.

He concentrated on making a list of all he would need, calming himself until he could almost believe the letter hadn't arrived, or had been a joke.

* * *

In her bedsit, Faith stared at a similar letter, her mind refusing to take in its message. Nick wouldn't be at her birthday party, he had to go to London and he was taking a friend with him. The disappointment was tempered with a sense of relief, grateful for not having to spend the evening pretending everything was all right. Going with a friend? She was in no doubt that he was going with a woman. The woman he'd met at the dance after telling her the car had broken down? It really was time to face her situation and tell him goodbye. She felt a painful surge of self-dislike and regret. She had been too clingy, making him need to escape, having to lie to her, afraid she would cause him embarrassment.

She forced herself to concentrate on food for the friends who would be coming to wish her well on her birthday, but it wasn't easy to let go of a dream. For a moment she decided to cancel, tell everyone she was feeling ill, but no, she found it all too easy to walk away from problems and this was one she had to face.

But how? What would she tell her friends? They all knew Nick had been invited so how could she explain his absence? Easy enough for the casual friends who were coming, but she'd have to explain to those to whom she had asserted, with a secretive smile, that, no, they were nothing more than friends. They would know she had hoped for a future with him. They would soon know he had gone away, probably with someone called Tessa, someone she didn't even know.

She made a sponge cake and decorated it with lemon icing. No candles, no engagement announcement, just a simple cake representing nothing more than another birthday. Cheese straws, sausage rolls, sandwiches, salads, there was no joy in the preparations and she would be glad when the evening was over. There were nine people coming to her party. Nine people who would crowd into the small room and sit on the bed or on the floor, there being only one chair. They arrived within a few minutes of each other and brought flowers and small gifts and cards, which she put on one side to open later. They all worked at the school so there were no constrained moments and, as coats were discarded and wine offered, conversations and laughter quickly filled the air.

'In fact,' Faith admitted to Mary with a laugh, 'I'm hardly noticed, except to provide more food and drink!'

There was no escaping talk of Nick no matter how she tried to avoid it. She dismissed him with a laugh. 'We were never really serious,' she said airily. 'I don't think Nick is ready for a wife and family yet and despite all my wanderings I still haven't found a place that I feel is home.'

'Oh, I think they'll marry,' Mary said, revealing knowledge of the affair.

'There's romantic, him eloping with Tessa,' someone said and the shock of hearing what she had suspected was a harsh pain. Would they marry? How could he make such plans and still see me? she wondered. Then she realized, she had been nothing more than a shield to keep their secret.

'Where are you from?' someone asked later. 'Not from around here for sure. You don't have the same accent as us.'

'Difficult to answer.' Faith replied thoughtfully. 'I was born in London but I've lived in Wales practically all my life.' She didn't want to discuss her history any more than the romance of Nick and Tessa, so she stretched across to the small table and said brightly, 'Who's going to try my birthday cake?' Hands went up and the moment passed.

People began to drift away until only Mary Gould was left. As she began to clear the dishes she looked at Faith, aware of the sadness behind the light-brown eyes. 'You don't have to be on your own, you know. If you ever feel lonely you can come to my place any time you want to. My George is out most evenings, at the pub, putting the world to rights with the help of his friends, so I'd always be glad of your company.'

News of the elopement of Tessa and Nick quickly spread and as four and not three people were involved it was referred to as the eternal square. Faith hid her regrets well and joined in the gossip as though she were not one of the four.

* * *

In London Tessa and Nick found a small flat and Tessa quickly realized that the excitement and romance of being runaway lovers, defying convention, turning their backs on everything to be together, quickly faded amid the realities of finding work, paying rent and, for the most part, being broke. The hastily arranged wedding she had dreamed of was not part of Nick's plan. Despite her pleading, cajoling and displays of anger, it didn't happen. She sulked, blamed him for ruining her life. He told her to go back home.

'Too late,' she told him. 'I've written to my parents and yours telling them we're getting married next week.'

'You did what?'

'You can hardly expect me to walk away from Ian and my family for anything less than marriage.'

After hours of arguing, Nick eventually agreed and a register office ceremony was discussed. With diminished funds Tessa managed to find a dress and some shoes and a hat and, after separating for one night, made her way to the register office at the appointed time. After waiting for over an hour she went back to their flat where Nick was waiting for her.

'Sorry, but I don't think the time is right for us to marry,' he said as she began to shout and cry and hit him. He held her close. 'We're together and that's all that matters. When we have a decent place and decent jobs, then we'll have a proper wedding, not a cheap affair like today would have been. I want us to have everything perfect for the most important moment of our lives.'

* * *

To Faith's surprise, a few weeks later Nick reappeared. He moved back into his parents' house and a very subdued Tessa was with him. Faith had to face the gossips again. She dealt with it by using humour and distorting the truth. It was a joke, she knew all about it but had promised not to tell anyone. 'Very romantic,' she said brightly. 'Nick and Tessa have been seeing each other for weeks but no one knew except me. I was acting as their cover, their alibi when they needed one. It's been very exciting.' As she spoke she knew it was foolish to invent such a story, it was bound to fall about her ears. And it did.

The rumours began. All was not well with the couple. To Faith's dismay, Nick admitted he was unhappy and told everyone how he regretted leaving Faith so cruelly, that Tessa was too demanding and selfish.

One evening Faith opened the door to a very persuasive Nick who begged her to go back to him. 'I've already admitted I made a mistake leaving you for Tessa,' he said. 'I'm so ashamed at the way I treated you.'

Faith saw her lies coming back, mouthed maliciously by unkind acquaintances. Why hadn't she told the truth? She'd have been laughed at by some but others would have sympathized. Now she would be a joke. It wasn't something she could laugh off, not this time.

'No. Nick,' she said as he waited, looking suitably chastened. 'You've humiliated me for the last time.'

'But I've told my parents it's you I want. All right, I made a mistake, but we can't let it ruin our lives. Please Faith. Marry me, announce our engagement. That will get Tessa off my back if nothing else will.'

'Isn't she your wife? How do you plan to get out of that one, Nick?'

Allowing Tessa the face-saving lie he said, 'It was a mistake, we can get it annulled, or a divorce. We could tell everyone I was in the wrong and want to put it right. Tell everyone we're engaged. Please, Faith.'

'I see. You want me to announce our engagement, just until Tessa goes back to wherever she came from? Then what?'

'We could marry once I'm free,' he said, as though the thought had just occurred. 'Best to leave it a while and see how well we get on, though. Perhaps in a year or so? Next year perhaps?'

'No, Nick. Not next year or any year.' He was still blustering as she closed the door.

* * *

At school the following morning she was approached by several of her so-called friends. They made no effort to hide their amusement at the latest story. Only Mary was sympathetic. Older and wiser, she was aware of the pain Faith was suffering. 'Come on,' she coaxed. 'It will soon be forgotten. A bit of gossip like this is irresistible, if it had been someone else you'd have enjoyed it yourself, be fair. Give it a week and nothing more will be said.'

At the end of that terrible day Faith walked home by way of the back lanes to avoid seeing anyone else who wanted a laugh at her expense. Unfortunately some of the older pupils had gleaned the details too and their derogatory comments, as they followed her home, were just loud enough to be heard.

She reached home, dropped her bag and briefcase, then went out. Thank goodness the time during which she was 'temping' at the school was almost over. How right she had been to avoid taking a permanent position. It was time to move on once more. She tried to count her previous addresses and gave up after nine. The rest were guesses.

Try as she might she knew she would never be happy here now that Nick had made a laughing stock of her. Mary was right, it would die down, but the memory would be there and the occasional revival as newcomers were told was more than she could bear. She went to see her landlord and the following week, with her stint as temporary teacher in the infants class finished, she was on the train with a ticket in her purse for Barry, the seaside town where she had once spent a happy holiday: her only childhood holiday.

Her memories of that week were wonderful. Aged seven, oblivious to the war restrictions in force, she had been so excited as each day had dawned. Blue skies, friendly people, laughter and fun. Perhaps Barry Island with its golden beach and pleasure park, where every day was a holiday, was where she was meant to be.

She sat on the busy train, carrying her few possessions, and misery descended once more as she visualized many more years of this, moving on when things didn't work out as she hoped, new friends, a new school, then disappointment and off again.

She seemed unable to become a part of a group. Friends, all with large lively families had simply made her aware of her background and reminded her that she had always been alone. It had become automatic to accept loneliness, to being outside a group; an observer rather than a participant. That was how it would always be.

It was raining heavily as she left the railway station and she looked up at the relentless sky, the day as gloomy as her mood. This will probably be another broken dream, she thought with a sigh. Holidays aren't real, the memories wouldn't be the same as reality. The sun wouldn't always shine, the food wouldn't taste as delicious. The people wouldn't be as welcoming and friendly. She had been a child then. Now she was twenty-two and there wasn't a place to call home or a group of people to whom she truly belonged.

The happiness she remembered here in Barry was because it had been the first time she had been on holiday, the one time her foster-parents had relented and allowed her to go with them for their week's holiday instead of leaving her with carers. She had tried so hard to be good. Not asking for treats even when their daughter, Jane, was given them. She folded her clothes and went to bed when she was told, long before Jane, but they never took her again.

She knocked on the first house that displayed a 'room for rent' sign and without even asking to see it, she took it. At least she would have a base, somewhere to sit and consider her future.

The downstairs room was small and rather dark. But it overlooked the garden where there were overgrown trees and shrubs and with long grass where once there had been a lawn. Perfect for feeding and enjoying garden birds. She unpacked her miserably few possessions and examined the double bed. It was clean and, after testing, proved to be firm and comfortable. It would do until she decided what her next step would be. That seemed to be the story of her life. Moving from place to place looking for . . . she didn't know what. She just hoped that one day she would find it, that perfect place that would for ever be her home.

Her landlady was friendly and promised a good breakfast each morning. Faith would eat out during the day and Mrs Porter agreed to provide a sandwich and a drink for supper. She seemed to have been fortunate in her choice, although she hadn't actually made a choice. As so often in the past, she had taken the first available place and crossed her fingers for luck.

* * *

Ian Day was also moving. With Tessa married and never coming back he and his mother were leaving the rented house in which they had lived for many years, and were moving to the house he had planned to share with Tessa. He hoped that once the pain of his rejection had eased he would be happy there.

Vivienne Day watched her son and wondered if they were doing the right thing. Ghosts would be moving in with them, ghosts of disappointment and hurt. Would her son be able to forget and make this a happy place in which to live? She closed her eyes and offered up a prayer.

The house was almost finished. With Tessa an unenthusiastic helper, he had decorated all of the rooms himself and had fitted a smart cream-and-red kitchen. There was a small fridge in one corner and a cooker had been installed a few days earlier. Above the kitchen was a bathroom. He had worked long hours, often late into the night, to get the place ready for them to return to after their honeymoon in Cornwall. Everything he could see had been chosen to please Tessa. Living here was going to be hard, but the alternative was to sell it and let someone else move in.

'Half a dream is better than none,' he told his mother with a tight grimace that was an attempt at a smile. 'It's a nice house and I want us to be happy here.'

'Perhaps you and Tessa might . . .' Ian shook his head in reply and she said nothing more. After all, the girl was married and that had to be an end to any hope of a reconciliation.

* * *

Faith settled into her new home with ease. Mrs Porter relaxed the rules as she got to know her new lodger and they sometimes went to the pictures together and on mild winter days, they went for walks, coming home to enjoy a warming cup of tea in the cosy kitchen. With Faith's encouragement they began to tame the neglected garden, putting down food to encourage the birds.

There was a vacancy in the local school. A temporary one again, just for a few weeks while the regular teacher was recovering from an illness. Temporary suited her. She was still unsure whether she would stay. A month later, still working at the school with a hint of a permanent position, she learned it was Mrs Porter's birthday. Having gradually persuaded the lady to clear some of the tangle in the garden, she decided to buy a statue, a birdbath and a feeder, so they might both enjoy their feathered visitors.

Barry out of season, with many of the seaside shops closed and wind howling along the promenade on her few forays to the sandy bay was not what her memory had retained. Yet there was something very pleasant about joining the locals out with their dogs, stopping for a chat, complaining about the weather and looking forward to spring and summer. She was beginning to feel like a resident. Perhaps this time she might stay. She made enquiries about a place where she might buy the gifts she planned. Surely not all the shops were closed for the winter? The town had a busy life of its own, which was enhanced by summer visitors, but life went on when winter ruled and visitors stayed away.

She was told about Matt Hewitt who specialized in garden ornaments in stone, cement and wood. She called at his yard the following day to make enquiries. The workshop and yard was in an out-of-the-way place backing on to fields. She asked twice before she found it. Entering the yard, with its assorted statues and garden furniture, she wandered around the place looking for something that would please her landlady. There was plenty of choice and her gaze settled on a small cherub.

'Can I help?' a voice called and Matt Hewitt walked out from the small office. He was smiling and she could not resist smiling back. He was an attractive man; his hair and eyes were dark and he looked strong enough to lift a horse. His smile widened and brightened his penetrating eyes when he approached, warming her in a most unexpected way.

When she had explained what she wanted he led her into the shed, where he displayed his better pieces and began to tell her about projects on which he was presently engaged.

'I'm making a figure to be placed at the side of a pond,' he told her, leading her towards an inner room where it was evident that he did his finest work. The sculpted figure was of a beautiful young woman, her back bent, her fingers trailing in what would be the surface of the water but which was now some crumpled paper. Her hair fell to one side of her face, and her dress reached to a place above the knee, showing her perfect legs. It was elegant and utterly enchanting.

'She's beautiful,' Faith gasped. 'I've never seen anything lovelier. How can you bear to part with it?'

Matt laughed, showing clean, even teeth. He touched the figure, rubbing his hand along the girl's shoulder and down her long hair. 'It will be hard with this one, I admit, but I concentrate on the next, then the next.'

'I'm sorry,' Faith said, 'but I've wasted your time. I could never afford anything as lovely as this.'

'Don't worry, I have some smaller and less elaborate statues — and seats too. Gardens are for enjoying and you'd be surprised at how many people only go out in them to work. Buy your friend a seat.'

Walking through his displayed items more slowly, glancing at the price tickets, she decided he was right. Not only was a seat practical, the smaller statues that she could afford, including the cherub, were not carved but made from moulded cement, and anyway would have been too small for any impact. 'Thank you Mr Hewitt. This bench to seat two will be perfect.'

'Matt,' he corrected with a smile.

He delivered the seat and asked her out and she accepted. From the moment she had first seen Matt Hewitt, Nick had become nothing more than a faint shadow. She wondered about this, ashamed of the memory of waiting for Nick to propose. She was more than fickle, she was dishonest.

The first date was a bit unsettling. Matt was irritable and sharp with the waitress. She assumed that, in spite of his apparent confidence, he was anxious to please and impress her. The feeling was not exactly unpleasant, yet she felt a slight uneasiness. Surely he would relax when they knew each other better?

He took her back to meet his mother, offering to drive her home in the van he used for his work. Carol welcomed her and invited her inside for some tea. She was obviously pleased to meet her and from the way Matt introduced her she knew that he too was enjoying her company. The flattery gave her face an added glow and she was aware of a growing excitement. Matt looked at her with such obvious delight in his dark eyes that she felt more attractive, more confident. Before they parted at her door he said, 'My mother likes you and I want to see you again.'

'And if she had not?' she asked teasingly.

'I introduced you to show off and impress my mother, not please her. You are a lovely lady, Miss Faith Pryor. Nothing anyone said would stop me wanting to see you again and again.'

They began to meet with increasing regularity and it was soon apparent that Matt Hewitt would be an ardent lover. She was unsure, she harboured doubts about him letting her down but desire was strong, lovemaking promising an escape from loneliness at last. He wanted to spend every moment he could with her and she was flattered, and very much in love. For the next six weeks they were inseparable.

He lost his temper with a boy on a bicycle who rode along the pavement when they were walking back one evening and there were other instances of his impatience. His occasional bouts of temper worried her, although he never showed the slightest hint of anger towards her, his attitude being gentle, protective and caring. A young man whom he employed to help had been cuffed several times, a previous assistant had been chased from the yard after forgetting to pass on a message. These events she hadn't witnessed, but there were always people willing to spread gossip.

One evening she met the father of a pupil, who stopped her and asked about his son's progress. Matt came running up demanding to know what the man wanted and almost dragged Faith away before she could introduce them. Later she saw that the man had a bruise on his face and although he didn't explain she had the frightening feeling that Matt had struck him.

His mother Carol denied all the stories and said Matt was a reasonable man. 'Although he isn't a fool and not easily taken in by people trying to cheat him. He's fine as long as people behave correctly towards him,' she said, but Faith was not fully convinced.

Between their meetings her friendly landlady was kept abreast of the romance that was growing like a hothouse plant and she strongly approved of the handsome young man with his undoubted talent and his business.

Matt lived in the house adjoining the yard with his mother and Carol seemed as happy about their fast-growing relationship as Faith and Matt were. The house became Faith's second home and her landlady Mrs Porter visited with her as though they were one big family of friends. Determinedly putting aside her worries, Faith thought she couldn't be happier.

She just had to be careful not to stay and talk to anyone for too long. Jealousy was an unpleasant trait and one she found difficult to deal with when it reared its ugly head. Only Carol's reassurances stopped her from ending the relationship and moving on, that and the persistent dream of belonging.

Then Matt's increasing desire became a problem. She had fears of becoming pregnant, and no amount of persuasion on his part could change her mind, until he mentioned marriage. Her dream was about to come true, she would marry, have children and Matt's family would become hers too.

In May 1959, they made love for the first time in his mother's house while Carol and Mrs Porter were at the spring sales.

'Committed to each other we are. Now and for ever,' he murmured, but she was still afraid. He had been forceful and almost rough towards the end and she had succumbed as much from fear as from love. It made her unhappy and not a little frightened, but not having previous experience, she decided it must be the same for every woman, that magazine love stories were fantasies. Like her memories of Barry, where the sun always shone, they were not real life.

She spoke of her doubts to Mrs Porter, who encouraged Carol to talk about her son, delicately asking if there was a danger of violence.

'Matt is a wonderful son,' Carol told her. 'There has never been anything to make me feel anything else but proud. He would do anything necessary to make sure Faith is happy.'

Reassured, Mrs Porter told Faith there was nothing to fear. 'He's a wonderfully caring son and I always think that's a good reliable sign, don't you, dear?'

* * *

Six weeks later, in mid-June, Faith began to be anxious. A visit to a doctor confirmed her worries. She was expecting a child. Telling Matt was not something she relished. Would he lose his temper with her? Call her a cheat? Accuse her of trying to trap him like some women she had heard about? Fearing his anger she told Carol first and Carol burst into tears.

'Oh, Faith, dear! He'll be so delighted.' She eased the way by saying, 'Matt, Faith has something important to tell you,' then she slipped out of the room and stayed out for almost an hour.

She was right about Matt's reaction. He was thrilled and looked at her with such a loving look in those dark fascinating eyes that she forgot every doubt, until he said, 'You must move in with me so Mam and I can look after you. We have to get married straight away.' Then doubts crept back. The dream was far from perfect. She still found his affection tainted with a forcefulness that frightened her. There were still instances of unreasonable jealousy. Displays of temper when someone didn't please him were rare but alarming.

Carol added her pleading to Matt's and promised her a room of her own if that was what she wished. Carol decorated it prettily in pink and cream and in November, when, at six months she could no longer hide the truth, she regretfully left Mrs Porter's comfortable room and moved in with Matt and Carol. She refused to name a date for the wedding, promising that she would make a decision soon. Deep inside her was the ever present urge to run away again, but with a baby it was no longer possible. Running away was not a solution, not any more, even though the dream was beginning to turn sour. Love or fear, this time she had to stay and face what life had in store for her.

This was what she had dreamed of for so long: a husband a family, a child of her own. There was no doubt that he loved her. So he was quick-tempered and over protective. Wasn't that a price worth paying?

CHAPTER TWO

In the brief time during which Faith had worked at the local school she had become friendly with Winnie James and her three children, Jack who was eight, Bill aged six and Polly five. It was to Winnie that she confided her doubts about marrying Matt.

Winnie laughed. 'It's a bit late to change your mind, isn't it?' She patted her friend's bump and Faith agreed ruefully.

'I suppose I'm afraid because this time I won't be able to run away and that's what I usually do when things begin to worry me, or become difficult.'

'It'll be all right. Your little one will be a friend for my three one day. As they get older the age differences seem less. I can imagine our Polly being a real mother to him when he arrives.'

'More important, will I be a good mother? I don't think I have any natural nursing skills. After all, I didn't have any role models.'

'A lot of old "loll" if you ask me,' Winnie said. 'Loving your child isn't something you have to learn, it's as natural as closing your eyes when you want to sleep. I didn't even like dolls when I was growing up. I preferred cars!'

Despite Winnie's encouraging words Faith still had doubts. She had been squirrelling away her wages and guiltily accepting Matt and Carol's generosity regarding clothes and everything else the baby would need. Some instinct warned her that she might need an escape route as she always had in the past. Even a baby didn't cancel that thought out completely.

They didn't need to buy any furniture or other household items as they intended living 'through and through' with Carol, sharing everything in the house and having only a bedroom to call their own. That was a practical solution but not what Faith had imagined as the beginning of married life.

* * *

Faith watched like an anxious mother hen as the children walked in a 'crocodile' along the road from the park, heading back to school. She loved her work, but if Matt had his way she would have to leave her teaching career for at least a few years. Since meeting Matt Hewitt her life had changed beyond all her imaginings. It had given her what she had always dreamed of, a family of her own. Her sister, Joy, had been lost to her in 1939 when she had been one year old, the result of the mass evacuation of children from the large towns, and the confusions of World War II. She had heard nothing of her parents since that time and presumed they had been killed during the bombing of London. Constant searches for her sister had failed to find her.

She would still continue to search for Joy, even though hope was all but diminished. At least she now had Matt and in a few months she'd have the delight of a baby to enjoy and love and care for. Matt wanted this child so much and she had to believe he would be a good and loving father. If only she was as certain that he loved her, or, she admitted to her secret self, if she were certain that she loved Matt and wasn't just pretending because of her child and her desperate longing for a family.

As the procession of lively children reached the school gates the rest of the pupils were already coming out for playtime and she released the children, except the monitors, who helped her carry the sports equipment into the storeroom. Then she went to the staffroom for a welcome cup of tea.

On the following day, a Saturday, she and Matt were to marry but very few people were invited. A quiet marriage ceremony at the local register office was all she had arranged. Better not to make too much fuss, the dates of the wedding and the birth would be quoted often enough without increasing the number of people that knew.

She thought fleetingly of Nick Harris and wondered whether he and Tessa were happy. Had she clung to Nick because she had loved him? Or had he simply been an escape from continuing loneliness, a reason to stop running away? Was it the same with Matt? And did that make her incapable of true love?

It was half an hour after the children had gone home when Faith left the school. She had stayed behind to prepare some displays for the entrance hall. Walking home, her mind was still concentrating on the photographs and food from different nations which she had placed in front of a large world map with ribbons showing their origins, so she wasn't aware of the car approaching. It didn't actually hit her, but its closeness made her stumble and fall.

Before she could rise, several people ran to help her and one ran into a nearby shop and phoned for an ambulance. Protesting only weakly, she was taken to hospital. Matt and his mother were informed.

The doctor advised her to stay overnight to make sure both she and the baby were all right. She daren't reveal her relief when Carol accepted that they had to cancel the wedding.

When she came out of hospital she went straight to see her friend, Winnie.

'Faith! Are you sure you're all right? Shouldn't you be at home, resting?'

'I'm fine, really. I'd love a cup of tea, though.'

'Such a pity about the wedding. I'd bought flowers and buttonholes and now I can't even wear my new dress,' Winnie said in mock dismay. Glancing at her friend, aware of her doubts, she asked. 'How do you feel about cancelling the wedding? Will you rearrange it as soon as possible? Or have you decided to wait until after the baby's born? No one need know you didn't marry, if you don't want them to.'

'You'll think me wicked, but I can't help feeling relieved. A baby isn't the best reason to marry, whatever the oldies say. It will soon be the sixties and there's a new set of rules, very different from those of previous generations.'

Winnie giggled, her hand over her mouth in a familiar gesture. 'I don't think Matt's mother would like to be called an oldie!'

'Well, you know what I mean.'

'You mean you still aren't sure about Matt?'

'If it weren't for this baby, I might have changed my mind about marrying him. There's his temper which I find worrying and there's something secretive about him that makes me uneasy.' She hesitated then added, 'There are things I'm not being told. Carol looks shifty when I ask about his life before he met me.'

'Afraid you won't like hearing about his previous girl-friends, no doubt.'

'Maybe that's all it is, but somehow I have the feeling there's more. Anyway, this near-accident and the stay in hospital has given me a second chance. A time to really consider. Lucky for once, don't you think?'

'I never had any doubts about Paul, not for a minute, so perhaps you're right to hesitate. Come on, I'll walk you back home. I expect Matt and Carol are getting anxious.'

Winnie loosened the scarf around her neck, worn against the chill September breeze, took it off and put it around Faith's neck as though she were the mother, then they walked, arm in arm, back to the workshop and house where Faith lived with Matt and Carol.

Faith felt less and less happy as they drew nearer to the house. Carol was waiting for her, looking anxious, and Faith whispered to her friend, 'Winnie, I don't want to stay here tonight.' Matt appeared and she said, 'I'll just collect a few things, I'm going to stay a day or so with Mrs Porter.'

'Why? You can't do that, you'll make me look a fool!'

'Just for a few days, Matt. How can that make you look stupid?'

Matt pleaded, became a little angry, but Faith was adamant. 'No, Matt. I need my old room for a few days, maybe more. All my things needed for school are here. I need to sort them out, then I'll go. Winnie will call every day, and you and Carol aren't far away if I need anything. Just for a while.' She glanced at Winnie, aware she was being stubborn, but something inside her was warning her not to fully accept Matt into her life, nor to cut herself off from everything until she was sure. When that would be she couldn't guess.

Mrs Porter welcomed her with delight but she was curious. With difficulty she refrained from asking questions, filling the first few minutes by making sure Faith's room contained all she might need.

Faith didn't sleep well even though the room with its familiar furnishings felt like home. She was filled with the urge to run away from Matt and the over-anxious Carol and her undefined doubts. But with a baby due in a few months that was no longer possible. What is wrong with me, that I get myself into situations I can't manage and from which there is no escape except to run away, she asked herself over and over again during the dark, silent night hours. Bad judgement? Over-concern with the opinion of others? A ridiculous need to please people, have them like her? Had her lonely childhood distorted her natural good sense? Did the obsessional need to belong at all costs colour every action and thought?

She stayed a few weeks until local gossip was embarrassing Matt so much that she couldn't stay away any longer. She had left her job and Carol called daily and went practically everywhere with her. Everyone told her how lucky she was, what a blessing it was to have such care during her pregnancy, but it made her want to hide like a naughty child. Once she went back to Matt, with him working only yards away, she would never be alone.

With tearful goodbyes to Mrs Porter she went back. Walking in was so depressing that she felt a surge of longing to go straight out again. In spite of Carol's and Matt's protests she insisted on going for a daily walk on her own. Sometimes, like today, she met Winnie for a chat and, while waiting for her friend, she stood at the school gate watching the children enjoying the freedom of playtime. A teacher stood watching them, a whistle on a chain around her neck in case of trouble. Games of tag, hide and seek and hopscotch engrossed many of them but several, gathered in chatty groups, glanced up and described a swollen belly with their arms and grinned saucily before small hands covered their mouths. With her pregnancy now obvious, Faith was aware that she was an excuse for merriment.

Amid all the noise and movement, a timid-looking girl stood alone near the school entrance. She was also observing the groups of boys and girls and Faith thought she knew how the child was feeling. An outsider herself all through school, she remembered the feeling of isolation, the fear of attracting attention, afraid of the teasing and name-calling, which was all the attention she could expect.

In her own case it had been the ill-fitting and old-fashioned clothes she had been made to wear, together with her thinness, her straight, unwashed hair, the big boots that wouldn't have been worn by any other pupil, except perhaps in a Dickensian play. Having a foster-mother who had unexpectedly given birth to a child of her own had meant she was way down the queue for anything new.

The girl she was watching wore stockings that wrinkled over her skinny legs and her feet seemed too large. As Faith watched, memories swooped back as fierce as a blow. She too had been small and fragile at this child's age — seven or eight. The second-hand clothes she had worn would not have been a problem if they had fitted, most children had new only once or twice a year, but the garments had been handed to her foster-mother as hand-me-downs from other children and fit was a secondary consideration. What she was given, she wore.

She turned away and forced a smile as she saw her friend Winnie approaching.

'There's a rush it is to get out in the mornings,' Winnie puffed as she slowed down, too breathless to speak for a moment or two. 'Seeing the kids into school, then going back to clear up and get the meal on. Lucky I am that Paul is home today or I wouldn't have made it.'

'I'm glad you did, Winnie. Now where shall we go, Dilys Jones's café?'

They settled into a corner where they could see the comings and goings and ordered tea, and lemon-and-honey biscuits. Winnie stared at Faith and said, 'Serious you looked, standing there watching the children. Dreaming about your own baby were you? Or do you miss teaching?'

'Both, I suppose. But today it was mostly because I was watching that sad little girl who always stands alone.' She smiled at Winnie. 'I was like that, a loner. And teased? You'd never believe!'

'Never! What reason did they find to tease you?'

'Because I was dressed like a scarecrow and looked like scrag end of mutton!' She laughed and Winnie joined in. Then, serious again, she said. 'I've got Matt now and soon there'll be the baby. But I'll never forget that loneliness. It's hard to explain the feeling of having no one else in the whole world. Mam and Dad must have died or they'd have found me, but I might still have a sister and my dream is one day to find her. Perhaps she found me once and ran away seeing what a scraggy, miserable thing I was,' she added jocularly.

'Come on, Faith, I can't imagine you being anything but lovely.'

'I look more like the best end of mutton, now, with this lump.'

To change the subject that was obviously upsetting her friend, Winnie asked, 'Have you tried to find your sister lately?'

'I've been trying since I was old enough but it seems hopeless. Everything was in such a muddle. When we were evacuated, believe it or not, there was no rule about keeping families together. We were separated and I was only one year old, and Joy just three; what chance did we have to insist we stayed even near each other? She could be anywhere, and if she married she'd have a different name too. I don't know where to try that I haven't tried before.'

'Is that why you're refusing to marry Matt? Keeping your name in case Joy comes looking for you?'

'Partly.' Faith admitted.

'Was your childhood really unhappy?'

'You know I was fostered? Well, my last foster-parents had a daughter within a year of my arrival and after that I wasn't really wanted. I don't blame them. When I arrived they were childless and she didn't know she was already expecting their daughter, Jane. They could have sent me back to the home, so I think they did what they thought was best for me.'

'But it wasn't much?'

Faith made her friend laugh then, telling her about the deprivation as though it were funny. The time she had been given a new coat only to have it taken from her, as it was 'too good' for her and put in a cupboard until Jane was big enough to wear it. She didn't tell her friend how she used to open the wardrobe door and stare at the coat, stroke it and dream about wearing such a beautiful thing. She didn't tell her about the party dress bought for Jane to go to a party, to which she was not invited. Or how she had stood across the road and stared through the window at the children having fun.

She exaggerated when she told her about the boots, and insisted they would have made a perfect home for dozens of mice. 'They were so big I could turn round without taking them off,' she joked. A woman sitting at the next table and obviously listening, smiled too.

'At least it's over and now you've got Matt and he looks after you, doesn't he?' said Winnie. Lowering her voice, aware of a woman listening to their conversation, she asked, 'Why do you have doubts about marrying Matt? Your lost sister isn't the real reason, is it? And you must feel something for him or you wouldn't be — you know . . .' She gestured toward her swollen figure. 'I mean, you're living with him and his mam, Matt's baby is on the way, so why refuse to become Mrs Matt Hewitt?'

'You're never thinking of marrying that Matt Hewitt are you?' the woman at the next table said loudly. 'Poor dab you, if that's his child you're carrying! He's wicked beyond, that one and should never have been let out of prison.'

Startled, Faith asked what she meant, but the woman stood up and walked away, muttering about Matt's mother, 'That Carol Hewitt hasn't got the sense she was born with.' She stopped and added. 'And neither have you if you marry that evil man! Run while you still can is my advice!'

Faith and Winnie looked around as though expecting someone else to explain, but everyone turned away; some studying their plates, or the contents of their handbags, others turning their chairs around noisily to face the other way.

'Come on, let's go,' Winnie said, helping Faith to rise. 'It wouldn't do any harm to ask Matt's mother what the woman meant, mind, just to set your mind at ease. If there is something wrong you're entitled to know. Although the woman has probably mixed him up with someone else.'

Matt's mother, Carol, assured Faith that she knew nothing about her son that could have warranted such a remark, but Faith was aware of an uneasiness about her for the rest of the day. There was so much she didn't know about Matt. He evaded answering when she asked about his past and Carol always gave Faith the impression that she was afraid of secrets being revealed. There must have been other women, he was thirty-two after all, and that wasn't necessarily a cause for such alarm.

Something illegal was Faith's guess but he always became sharp and irritable when she asked what she thought were reasonable questions to put to a man whose child she carried. Getting to know someone always led to questions and answers, but not with Matt. So how was she to find out what was meant by the outburst from the woman in the café?

Matt called in at lunchtime and again at four o'clock, besides popping his head around the door between jobs, then going back to his workshop having reassured himself that Faith was comfortable. So caring, constantly smiling. Faith waited for Carol to explain the strange comment made by the woman in the café, but she didn't and Faith tried to convince herself that it had been as Winnie had suggested, a misunderstanding and best ignored. It niggled though, and she wondered if there really was something in his past to cause the woman's concern. Another attempt to discuss it with Carol brought no result and she tried to forget it. She was beginning to feel like a traitor.

* * *

On the following day Faith went to Dinas Powys and sat on the wall of the churchyard where a wedding was taking place. She was lost amid the crowd of well-wishers, who were waiting for the appearance of the bride and groom. It seemed the whole village was gathered to enjoy the occasion. The sun shone, warming the ancient stones on which she sat and adding a rosy glow to the scene. But Faith's eyes showed none of the joy of those around her and she wasn't part of the group. Standing lonely and ignored by the rest, she sank into melancholy.

This was how she had always imagined her own wedding day, but Matt had spoilt that by forcing her into a sexual relationship for which she had not been ready, then finding out she was expecting a child. Her dreams of a love match, culminating in a white wedding with friends surrounding them and everyone in the village wishing her well, were gone. The temptation to move away, somewhere where Matt couldn't find her, had been strong. But being on her own for most of her life had left its mark and she was afraid of returning to those lonely years. Matt and his mother, a family of sorts, had been too much to give up, even though she feared for a different kind of loneliness in the years ahead.

If only she could run away as she had done in the past. When she learned she was pregnant, it had seemed as though the last door to freedom had slammed and she was trapped. Winnie was a friend whom she would miss, but she'd have coped if it weren't for the baby. A baby was a strong tie between herself and Matt, 'And', she repeated like a mantra. 'running away is no longer possible.'

She glanced at her watch. It was time she went back. It would take two bus-rides and a walk, she'd be very late and Carol would be ringing Matt and telling him she was missing. After any absence of longer than half an hour Carol worried. Coming back to the place where she had been brought up by foster-parents had taken Faith most of the morning.

She wasn't sure why she had come; hope of perhaps seeing a friendly face and maybe making contact with the neighbours she had once known. A pretence that someone might remember her, and care. So far she had seen no one she recognized. After so many years the place had changed. The house where she had lived with her foster-parents had new tenants. When she went to look, a young woman with two small children skipping around her had been washing the front step. She looked happy and the children were chubby and rosy.

The crowd began to murmur and move towards the church door and Faith eased her awkward body away from the wall and moved with them. She might as well see the couple and add her hope that they had chosen wisely and that a happy future beckoned to them. She smiled grimly. The only choice she had been able to make was to refuse to marry Matt, not to give in to his persuasive arguments or his mother's emotional pleading. She had to have his child but at least she didn't have his name. It was a small victory but a victory nevertheless.

To shouts of admiration the newlyweds stood at the doorway and awaited the instructions of the photographer. The remarks changed to more ribald comments and laughter filled the air around her but Faith felt as though she were behind a screen, looking out but unseen, the sounds distant and nothing to do with her. There were tears in her eyes, blinding her to the people as she pushed her way toward the lychgate. She hurried back to the bus stop for the first stage of the journey back to the house she was supposed to call home.

Carol was looking anxiously out of the window and she opened the door as Faith approached. 'Faith! I wondered where you were. You've been gone this ages.' The soft Welsh lilt didn't manage to hide the disapproval in Carol's voice.

'I can hardly get lost, can I? I went on the bus to Dinas Powys, and stopped to watch a wedding.'

'Why? This is your home now.'

'They were called Jennifer Rees and Julian Brown. Lovely couple,' she said, having overheard.

'And you and our Matt will be following them up the aisle soon, won't you?'

'I don't think so.' Avoiding further reprimands about bringing a child into the world without making Matt its legal father, Faith pulled herself up the stairs to the only privacy she had, her bedroom, at least until Matt came in. The privacy of her own room hadn't lasted even a day.

Christmas came and went and the days dragged by. She felt so lethargic, forcing herself to do the small, boring jobs which were all Carol allowed her to do. Surely pregnancy should be a joyful time, she thought sadly. Shouldn't she be busy preparing for her child? Even her attempts at knitting and sewing were taken over by Carol. She felt stifled by the exaggerated care she was given. She felt like a prisoner and the days were long, the weeks stretched out before her with the promise of even more frustration and boredom as she imagined Carol insisting on taking over the care of the baby when it arrived.

As Matt worked so close to the house he could appear at any time, calling in between the stages of his work. And she became jumpy, startled when he opened the door and called to her as though afraid she had moved; waiting between times made her very tense.

Matt was talented and his work was admired, even by those who couldn't hide their dislike of the man. He made everything from the smallest gnome to the most impressive statues, plant-stands, benches, fences and garden furniture. He worked in several materials, including stone, his favourite, and wood. The inexpensive animals were made from moulded cement, and many of his items were skilfully painted. If life were different she would have been filled with admiration for his ability but, as with everything else, she was too wearied by boredom to take a real interest.

Although she visited the yard on occasions, usually when he had made something with which he was particularly pleased, she found the rest of his life a mystery. He was ten years older than Faith, and about his past she knew nothing. Yet he must have had a past. Not all of it pleasant, if the woman in the café was to be believed. One last attempt to persuade his mother to talk about it failed like the rest, and Faith noticed a frisson of fear cross Carol's face each time she asked a question even though they were questions she thought innocuous. Curiosity didn't fade because of this attitude, it increased.

One cold, bright day in early February, a shout from outside woke her from an afternoon rest and she looked out of the window to see Matt lying under a fallen ladder. His stillness was terrifying and she seemed to stay without moving for an age, but in fact it was only seconds before she rose from the bed and ran out to him. It was obvious from the position of his leg that it was broken. She ran to the phone and called an ambulance, which was arriving as Carol returned from the shops.

The ambulance men came, diagnosed a broken leg and took him to hospital. Carol went with him and Faith, having been told to stay at home, followed by bus. As soon as she arrived she was told to go back home. 'You mustn't risk the baby,' Matt warned and his mother agreed. Nearly at the end of her pregnancy she knew they were talking sense and besides, Carol wanted to stay and there was no need for them both to be there. She caught a bus instead of the taxi which Matt advised and made a cup of tea which she took to her room. In less than fifteen minutes she was asleep.

Carol woke her when she returned and they made lists of the people who needed to know. People expecting finished orders, mainly. 'What about relations?' Faith asked. 'There must be some who would like to visit?'

'Oh, we needn't worry about anyone else. It's only you he'll want to see, and me of course.'

'We could get some of his clothes washed while he's in hospital; you know how difficult it is to persuade him to part with his favourites. And his suit and overcoat could go to the cleaners while we're at it. Perhaps I could take some of his clothes to the cleaners tomorrow?'

'Don't worry yourself dear. We can sort all that once he's home.'

The following day Carol went to the hospital on her own. Matt having insisted that Faith needed her rest. Faith had been given his clothes to bring home, so she picked up his coat and began to empty the pockets ready to take it to the cleaners. Her fingers found a bank statement and she was about to put it with the rest of the contents when she realized it was not Matt's usual bank. Curious, she opened it. What she read was puzzling. It was in Matt's name but it was nothing like their normal account. Money went into this separate account at intervals, each transaction different, the dates and amounts varying each month, but payments were precisely and regularly made to an Ethel Holland on the twenty-eighth day of each month.

She stared at the pages for a long time, then, when she heard a car pulling up outside she looked out of the window to see Carol stepping out of a taxi. She stuffed the papers into her pocket and went down to open the door to her.

'I've put his clothes ready for the cleaners,' she said brightly.

'Give them to me,' Carol said. 'Heavens, girl, haven't you got the kettle on yet? Dozy, you are. More go in a damp firework, as my mam used to say.'

When they sat drinking their tea, Faith asked quietly, 'Who is Ethel Holland?'

Carol turned to stare at her. 'Who? Never heard the name. Where did you get it from? Gossiping in the newsagent's again, I'll bet.'

'Matt was muttering in his sleep the other night and said something that sounded like Ethel Holland.'

'Forget it, and don't bother Matt with dreams, he's ill, remember.'

Faith nodded vaguely but thought the newsagent's was a good place to ask questions. Sounding as though she knew more than she actually did would be a good way to begin.

The newsagent's was quiet when she went in later that day. She paid the weekly bill and casually asked, 'Matt told me about the trouble he was in a few years back. D'you think he was innocent? He insists he was wrongly accused.'

The man stared at her uneasily. 'Told you, did he? There's a surprise. I don't want to discuss it, Faith. Loses his temper too quick, that one. Best you ask him what you want to know.'

'How long ago was it, Mr Foster. Five years? Six?'

He frowned for a moment then said. 'More like ten. It was in June, I remember, a hot, sunny day, and — Oh, Hello, Mrs Cooper!' He looked relieved. 'Called for your *Radio Times* have you?' He shook his head at Faith, dismissing the subject and smiled as he turned to the other customer. Faith went out and she was smiling too. If the newspapers had reported whatever had happened, the library was the place to begin.

She went to see Matt, taking the few things he needed, and was told he would be home in a few days' time. 'Your mother has made up a bed for you near the fire so you won't have to struggle upstairs,' she explained.

'That won't do, tell her to put it away. I'm going upstairs as usual,' he replied.

'But won't it be difficult for you?'

'We share a bed, you and I, and that's how it will always be.'

Leaving him before the rest of the visitors departed she went into town. At the library she asked for the local newspapers, for 1949. She wasn't sure where to start, but she had at least an hour before Carol expected her home.

She was too uncomfortable to sit and turn the large pages in their heavy folders, so she stood, glancing down each page in the hope of her eye catching a headline that was relevant. The January to June papers were almost finished when she saw, not a headline but a photograph of Matt Hewitt. The name that jumped out of the pages, beside his, was Ethel Holland.

The story beneath the photograph of the man she lived with made her feel sick, she was afraid she would faint. The print shimmered in front of her eyes, making it difficult to read, but taking deep breaths and forcing herself to be strong, she read it right through, as well as the follow-up, in the July to December issues. Then she sat, pale-faced and distraught, staring unseeing across the hushed room.

Aware of her distress, the librarian came up and led her to the toilets where she allowed her body to make its protests in violent nausea.

She was taken into the staffroom and encouraged to sip a cup of hot tea. It was twenty minutes before she felt well enough to go home. On the librarian's advice, she took a taxi, although she wished she could walk. After what she had read, she was in no hurry to see either Matt or his mother.

Ignoring Carol's demands to know where she had been, longing for peace to think about what she had learned, believing Matt was still in hospital, she went to the bedroom.

Seeing Matt lying on the bed, smiling at her, she screamed and ran back out.

She had to prepare. Ignoring Carol's demand for an explanation she repacked her suitcase ready for the hospital, adding her bank book and a few small personal items and locked it. Then she went to see Winnie but refused to explain the reason for her distress.

* * *

Under the pretence of seeing doctors and the midwife and keeping appointments at the hospital she saw a solicitor, doctors, social workers and child-care officers. She was constantly tearful but Carol believed it was the emotion of the forthcoming birth and was even more caring.

The labour pains began suddenly one morning when she was visiting Winnie and were intense. Without going back to collect her ready-packed suitcase, she went to the hospital with clothes borrowed from Winnie and what money she had in her purse. Winnie promised to collect her ready-packed suitcase for her and take it to the hospital within the hour.

The birth was painful, mainly because she was in such a distressed state. Sympathy from the kindly nurses changed to firmness in the hope that they would shock her out of her misery, but when her child was born later that night Faith turned away from her, and made it clear she would not be feeding the child.

The nurses were concerned. She had been attempting to delay the birth, trying to prevent the baby from being born, and now there was this complete rejection. Although they coaxed in every way they could, Faith was unwilling even to get a glimpse of her daughter.

She gritted her teeth when Matt came stumping in to see her and leaned over to kiss her. 'Soon have you back where you belong,' he whispered. 'They don't keep you in for long these days, and I need you back home.'

She feigned exhaustion and turned away. He pushed her gently and talked to her but she didn't move. The knowledge of what she had to do was shutting out every other thought. Her mind was made up, but her body craved to hold the child. She couldn't sleep. Cries were heard during the night and she wondered whether her baby was calling for her. Several times she almost relented and began to call the nurse but she couldn't change her mind. What she was doing was for the best for the baby.

After speaking again to the social workers and child-care workers and solicitor over the following day, forcing herself to appear calm, she signed the necessary papers. Her heart raced with misery and despair but her signatures were strong. She had to do what was right.

At the end of the second-day stay, Winnie came with fresh clothes and a few things Faith had asked for. Faith hardly said a word. Over the past week she'd had long, exhausting and difficult discussions with doctors and the relevant legal representatives and requested that her daughter be named Dorothy. She now lay exhausted, in an agony of misery but knowing she had done the right thing. The baby was not with her when Matt and Carol visited and she explained that she was in the night nursery as she had a slight infection and they weren't allowed to see her for a few days.

As the visitors shuffled out, Faith hastily dressed in the toilets and, unnoticed, went out with them, leaving her baby behind. Her daughter must never know her father.

* * *

Matt's fury frightened Carol when they went to the hospital and were told that Faith had walked out leaving no forwarding address. She warned him he would make himself ill if he didn't calm down.

'Calm down? She's gone, left me and my baby! How can I stay calm, you stupid woman. Where is she? You must know. She must have planned it and given a clue where she was going.'

'Something upset her, I know that, but she didn't discuss anything with me. The room is ready for her, I'd put the cot beside your bed, everything new and perfect.' Carol sobbed quietly. 'I was so looking forward to having a baby to love and care for.'

Matt put on his coat.

'Where are you going? You should be resting your leg,' Carol said.

'Winnie James. She must know. Close friends they are, those two. Probably planned it together.'

Winnie was clearly surprised and alarmed when he told her Faith had disappeared and even in his anxiety and anger he could see her shock was genuine. She asked more questions than he and when he left they both promised to inform the other when they had news of Faith. Although Winnie knew it was a promise she wouldn't keep.

Winnie received a letter from Faith the following day, posted in Dinas Powys, but it was very brief, an apology for not telling her what she had planned, and promising to tell her the reason one day. Winnie didn't show it to Matt. Until her friend explained her actions she would avoid telling Matt anything that might help him find her.

Matt searched everywhere. He asked the neighbours, teachers and pupils at the school, the shops, people in the park. Wherever he asked, people promised to let him know if they learned something, although many — like Winnie — quickly decided they would not. There had to be a good reason for Faith to walk away from the baby and without telling anyone. Winnie thought of the remarks made by the woman in the café and wondered if Faith had learned something that had upset her. She didn't mention this to Matt. She would say nothing until she had spoken to her friend. Surely she would get in touch with her?

When Carol and Matt went to the hospital to arrange for the baby to come home, there was worse news than the disappearance of Faith. She had registered the baby but not in Matt's name. The authorities had been told the child was the result of a previous relationship and was nothing to do with him.

There were more enquiries, both at the hospital and at the police station, but to no avail. Confidentiality had been assured, especially when the authorities checked on Matt's background.

* * *

It wasn't long before the disappearance of Faith led to the story from 1949 being revived. Matt and Carol were interviewed by social workers and the police, and they blamed Faith. Anxiety was tinged with anger at the trouble and embarrassment her disappearance had caused. The police explained that if they should find Faith, they had no reason to persuade her to come back.

'We believe she left on a bus, which took her to Dinas Powys, where she posted a letter to her friend Winnie, but which didn't explain her absence. Several people saw her up to the time she boarded the Dinas Powys bus, but we haven't yet learned where she went from there.' He stared at Matt. 'A quarrel, maybe?'

'No, there's nothing.' He patted his plastered leg. 'I was just home from hospital.'

'Perhaps you'll think of something, sir. It's rare for a mother to walk away from her baby without a reason or at least an explanation. But as far as we know, we think it unlikely there was a sinister reason for her disappearance. It was all carefully planned.'

Matt locked himself in his workshop and concentrated on fulfilling his orders. At first his fingers were careless, but then he calmed down and did his best work, trying to lose his frustration and ease the pain.

* * *

Unencumbered by heavy luggage, Faith had walked a little way, then got on a bus. She stopped at Dinas Powys to post cards to Mrs Porter and Winnie, then went on to Cardiff.

She was tired and filled with the desire to cry. Forcing herself to hold back from giving in to her grief she stayed fairly calm until she was on the train back to Barry. Then tears ran down her cheeks and she hid them behind a magazine she had bought. If anyone noticed, no one asked what was the matter and she was grateful for that. She had booked into a hotel on the seafront, a short walk from the station and she went straight to her room.

She planned to stay there for a few days to recuperate, after which she hoped to start working for a Mrs Rebecca Thomas, in the role of housekeeper and companion. She had only spoken to the lady on the telephone, arranging for a week's trial on both sides, but felt hopeful of being accepted once they had met and her qualifications had been examined. For now, all she wanted was to cry until she fell asleep.

Breakfast at the hotel was served in a small dining room where four tables were set with white cloths and gleaming cutlery and glasses. She wasn't hungry but knew she ought to eat something. She was still weak after the birth. Several people came in and greeted each other, obviously regulars or even permanent guests. A man about her own age came in, carrying a large briefcase. Each table was occupied by at least one person and he came across and asked if he could join her.

'If you're sure you don't mind?' he said. She gestured to the chair across from her and he put his briefcase on the window ledge. 'Thanks. You've saved me from working through the meal, a very bad habit. Much nicer to talk.' Faith didn't reply. She didn't want to talk to a stranger, she was too near to tears for that.

He seemed aware of her reluctance without anything being said and, apart from a smile as he accepted bread from the plate she passed, he stared through the window. When he stood to leave, he said, 'If you're a stranger here, you'll find the town a pleasant one. A walk along the front is relaxing, and the town has all you might need.'

Ashamed of her rudeness she smiled and thanked him. Unable to explain, she said, 'I'll enjoy exploring.'

'Good luck,' he said, adding. 'I'm Ian Day.' To which she didn't reply, but just offered the faintest of smiles in return.

He stood searching in his pockets, presumably for car keys, and she was able to study him. He had a boyish look, blue eyes with a disconcertingly curious stare, his fair hair was straight and shorter than most wore it. He was about six feet tall and walked upright, proud of his height. Shoulders back, he strode out of the room with a confident air, waving to a few guests as he passed them. Ex-Army perhaps, she wondered?

He stopped at the entrance and from his over-stuffed briefcase took out two folders. She watched curiously, trying to guess what his occupation might be. Then she pushed thoughts of him aside. This was a hotel and she was staying only two more nights, so it was unlikely she would see him again.

Out of season, Barry was still a busy town. New houses were being built and the population was growing, but she knew that during the summer months the place would be crowded with holidaymakers and day-trippers, all intent on having fun. It was the last place Matt would expect to find her, a perfect place in which to hide, filled with strangers and large enough for her not to be noticed, especially after today, when she planned a visit to a hairdresser to have her long hair cut into a short, face-hugging style.

After having her hair cut she walked along the promenade. It was February but the air was still redolent with the remembered smells of summer. Rows of shops, closed now but promising tasty treats, from fish-and-chip meals to jokey sweets made of seaside rock; others offered gifts and postcards showing views or saucy pictures. But that was all in the future. Today, in February, the area was quiet, her footsteps sounding unnaturally loud in the calm air, punctuated occasionally by the sad wailing calls of the gulls.

The man called Ian Day was there again the following morning. He came and sat down with his head tilted in a silent request. This time she smiled and said, 'Please, join me if you wish.'

'I wish,' he said cheerfully. 'My, you look different. What happened to your long curls?'

'It was time for a change,' she said, and her voice discouraged further comment.

'Have you seen much of the town yet?' he asked as their meal was placed in front of them.

'A little. I spent yesterday walking around the local beaches and later the town.' She didn't tell him that she had lived there for months or that she had bought a surprising amount of clothing. Having left everything behind apart from what she had crammed into her small suitcase she had needed replenishments. She had bought what was necessary to prepare herself for the job that awaited her on the following day.

Ian went home thinking about the brief encounter. She was deeply unhappy, that much was obvious. He had recognized another victim like himself and wondered whether a broken romance was the reason she was sad too. His mother, Vivienne opened the door to allow the delicious smell of cooking to escape.

'What's wrong, dear?' she asked, seeing his serious expression as she placed the plates on the table.

'Nothing really, it's just that I've been feeling sad and today I realized I'm not the only one to have had a disappointment.' He told her about the unhappy woman he had met earlier. 'Another romance gone wrong, I'm sure of it.'

'Oh, you're clever! Mind-reader as well as brilliant salesman!'

'And I bet she doesn't go home to a meal as good as this one!'

* * *

On her last morning at the hotel, Faith didn't wait for breakfast but left by taxi before serving began. It was unlikely that Matt would look for her here but the fewer people she spoke to the better. He would probably expect her to have travelled miles away and found work as a teacher, certainly not as a housekeeper companion, and in the same town, so she felt reasonably safe. But there was no point taking unnecessary risks. Her employer, Mrs Thomas, wasn't expecting her until after lunch but Faith thought she wouldn't mind her arriving a little earlier than planned. She still felt weak and didn't fancy wandering around laden with her baggage for hours.

Mrs Rebecca Thomas was a small, slim person with a constant frown on her face. She suffered from arthritis and Faith guessed she was in considerable pain. She spoke abruptly and at first Faith found it irritating to be treated like an idiot, having to listen to her employer explain the way she wanted things done in minute detail. As days passed she became used to it and waited calmly for the lecture to end, after which she did what was required with very few complaints.

She gathered from Sophie, the woman who came in to clean twice each week, that Mrs Thomas had difficulty keeping the small staff she required.

'Not used to it you see,' Sophie explained in a whisper. 'Not brought up to it, like. Now my other ladies they don't have any trouble, they know what's needed and once they sort out who does what they leave it to the staff to sort between them. Now Mrs Thomas, she's unsure of herself if you ask me, so she overdoes the ordering about and people won't stand for it, see.'

'I'll try to make allowances,' Faith said solemnly. 'You're very understanding, Sophie.'

'You have to be, in this job,' Sophie said, 'I threaten to leave sometimes, when she gets a bit much to cope with, and remind her she's lucky to have me.'

'I'm sure she knows that.' Faith tried not to smile.

The work of running the home and keeping Mrs Thomas company between times was not arduous. She did some shopping, using only the nearby corner shops and became known to the shopkeepers as a quiet person unwilling to stay and chat and satisfy their curiosity. She joined the library, choosing books for her personal enjoyment as well as others which she read to Mrs Thomas.

Outwardly she was relaxed and content. She hid her grief well. Walking away from Matt and Carol, and Winnie, seemed to belong to a previous life or a half-remembered dream, except for the moment when she had signed away all rights to her child. The worst time was last thing at night when she waited for sleep to claim her. That was when visions of a baby came to torment her. She saw a child who was sometimes upset and crying as she leaned over her little girl's cot. The worst times were half-waking dreams when she saw Matt looking down at the baby, grief distorting his dark eyes. Those dreams brought guilt as well as tears.

Surely he wouldn't have been allowed to keep the child? She knew she had been cruel by not registering the child in Matt's name. She had lied, and had explained that she had only been a lodger there until she could find a place for herself and her child, that talk of marriage was no more than Matt's optimistic hope. Her decision not to keep the child had made circumstances change and the child would now go to foster-parents until an adoption could be arranged.

She felt waves of guilt that cut into her heart like knives as she thought of her own experiences but hoped and believed that today things would be more carefully monitored and the little girl who was her daughter would be placed with a loving family. She had to believe that or she would lose her mind.

If only she weren't so alone. She thought of her sister, building up an imaginary picture of her, smiling, words of sympathy issuing from a face almost identical to her own. Her life had been separated into stages, but the birth and her latest cowardly escape was definitely the worst. The time with Matt and all that had happened before, was over. This was a lull before what would happen next. Would the new stage be the one in which she found her sister, Joy?

If by some miracle they found each other, what would she think of her, abandoning her daughter after the miseries of her own childhood? Perhaps she would turn and walk away again. That thought, together with imaginary pictures of her baby, meant another sleepless night.

CHAPTER THREE

Mrs Thomas had help around the house for many of the routine duties and Faith found that she was expected mainly to make sure their work was satisfactory. Apart from this there were the evenings when she and Mrs Thomas listened to music or watched the television and the afternoons when she read to her for an hour.

Faith dealt with the shopping and chose the menus for the meals, which she often cooked when the woman employed for that pleasant task was unable to come in. Gradually, as the weeks passed, the cooking became one of her regular tasks as the cook became less and less reliable and eventually gave up altogether. Faith didn't mind this but secretly hoped that she wouldn't be given more work if the cleaners left!

The one potential problem was Mrs Thomas's, so far unseen, son, Samuel. He phoned often and each time the call left her employer subdued and clearly upset. Faith dreaded meeting him. From the little Mrs Thomas had told her about her son, she gathered that Samuel did not approve of her caring for his mother, even though they hadn't met. He wanted Mrs Thomas to move into a retirement home, something his mother refused to consider. 'While I have you to look after me,' she told Faith on one occasion, 'I can continue to live in this house which has been my home for more than fifty years.'

There weren't many callers and Faith spoke to few people. She was afraid to go out, apart from the necessary shopping trips, for fear of meeting someone who would tell Matt where to find her. She longed to talk to Winnie, but as Winnie lived close to Matt and his mother, that wasn't possible.

As spring opened up the countryside with flowers and leaves began to clothe the trees she spent much of her spare time walking, staying far away from the houses, through the fields to Dinas Powys, where she avoided looking at the house where she had lived out part of her sad childhood, or across the fields through Cadoxton to Coldbrook and Merthyr Dyfan.

Fickle spring gave way to summer and more and more people were out enjoying the strengthening sun. Faith's arms ached to hold her child when she watched with painful regret as families piled on to the buses heading for the beach, loaded with buckets and spades and baskets covered with white cloths that obviously held picnic food. The regret was for the thought that she would never belong to one of such lively and excited groups.

The loss of her daughter had been necessary but it was a loss nevertheless and a continuing sadness. She'd had no choice. What might the little girl have inherited? Being brought up without the presence of Matt must reduce the chances of her inheriting his evil ways. She frequently wondered whether her decision had been the right one, but the thought of what the child might have inherited and which, if she'd been allowed to grow up in that house, might have displayed itself, soon reassured her that, agonizing as it was for her to live with, day after day, there had been no alternative but to walk away.

The beautiful sandy beach attracted huge crowds, even now, when holidays abroad were tempting more and more people away from the traditional vacations. She would have loved to wander along the promenade and watch others having fun, but too many people came to Whitmore Bay and the risk of being seen and having to face Matt again made that an impossible dream. So her lonely travels continued to take her through the quiet countryside.

Tempted once or twice, she went to the beach at the end of the day and watched tired families gathering their belongings and mothers coaxing the weary children towards the bus and railway stations. A child was crying, that grizzly cry of a tired child, and she longed to pick her up and carry her. She turned away and walked to the next bay which was already empty of its day's visitors and looked as forlorn as she felt. She sat on a rock, arms hugging her knees, and stared as the tide crept in, obliterating every sign of the day's activities.

The long walks were an attempt to tire herself and make sleep come more easily, but every night she relived the agonizing memories of losing her child. She saw a baby in a cot, or a pram, often crying, although she never saw the face clearly. In her imagination the tiny child always lay with her back to her, the face impossible to imagine, and the distress was heart-breaking.

* * *

Vivienne Day was in the garden of her son's house one day, pulling up a few weeds, when she saw Tessa approaching. She watched as the young woman walked past, then stood looking up at the house, windows shining, curtains blowing gently in a breeze, and at the newly painted front door and neat garden. Vivienne could see the pangs of regret on her face. She had heard rumours that Tessa and Nick were far from happy.

She didn't speak, hoping the girl would walk away before seeing her. She dreaded her son giving their broken romance another try. Tessa could no longer be trusted, having left Ian once Vivienne would always be afraid the disaster would be repeated. Besides, even in this changing world ending a marriage wasn't that simple. Better Ian found someone else.

'Hello, Mrs Day,' Tessa called, a smile masking her previous sad expression.

'Oh, hello, Tessa. I didn't see you there.' She made a pretence of going in but Tessa called her back.

'How are you? How is Ian?'

'I'm fine and Ian is more than happy, thank you.'

'The house looks lovely. I do regret what happened,' Tessa said, stepping closer.

'I'm sure you do.' Vivienne was determined not to invite her in.

'Nick isn't as caring as Ian. He's been seeing someone else,' Tessa went on.

'I'm sorry about that, Tessa, but we make our bed and have to lie on it.'

'What a daft expression. If the bed was uncomfortable I'd get up and remake it!'

'Not always possible, is it?'

'I'm so bored with Nick's parents and with Nick's ego.'

'You made your choice and . . .' To her dismay a car turned the corner. Seeing her son, Vivienne said firmly. 'Goodbye. I have to go, Ian will want some lunch.' She stared until the girl turned and walked away.

'What did she want?' Ian asked as he took off his jacket.

'Just nosing, seeing what you've done on the house. It seems Nick and she aren't happy. I heard rumours about a barmaid,' she said as she bustled about the kitchen.

'Yes, I heard that too. Poor Tessa. She's very unhappy.' She could see he was affected by her distress. 'I still feel something for her, you know.'

'I know, dear, but stay away. You can never trust her again.'

'We were together practically all our lives.'

'What you're feeling is sympathy for someone in trouble, that's very different from love. No more than the sympathy you felt for the woman at the hotel.'

'I wonder whether her problem was a broken heart, too?'

'Yours was bruised, dear, but not broken.'

* * *

With summer in its full glory, the town was bursting at the seams with visitors and day-trippers. Gaining confidence, Faith decided to risk getting in touch with Winnie. Phoning was risky as Winnie's husband, Paul, worked shifts in a local factory but she picked up the phone at a quarter past nine, when Winnie would be back from taking the three children to school, and was lucky first time.

'Faith! There's lovely to hear from you at last! Where are you? Near enough to meet, are you?' Winnie shouted in delight at hearing Faith's voice.

'If I tell you, will you promise not to tell anyone?'

'Of course. I wouldn't want to be the one to lead Matt to you.'

'I have a day off on Friday as my employer is visiting a cousin for the day. Can you meet me in Cardiff?'

It was quickly arranged and Winnie was so excited she was afraid Paul would guess something had happened and wheedle it out of her. She and Paul didn't have secrets but she would say nothing until after she'd spoken to Faith.

Their three children, Jack, Bill and Polly, all came home for lunch. Fortunately Paul would be there on the following Friday and it would be simple to leave a meal ready for them all. She planned the journey and rehearsed a conversation, filling her mind with lists of questions and hoping to be given answers to at least some of them.

She also talked among the other mothers at the school gate to find out what she could about Matt and his mother. Carol was constantly tearful, complaining about Matt's 'wife' and her inexplicable action. Winnie also tried, without any success, to learn something about Faith's daughter. Even leaving the little girl as she had, Faith would surely ask if there was news of her. For the people at the school gate and in the local shops, that was the biggest question of all: why hadn't she taken the child? If she was leaving Matt, how could she have walked away from her child?

Everyone had plenty to say but nothing was known, except that the child had been christened Dorothy. The comments were criticisms of Faith, to which Winnie listened without adding to the conjectures or speaking in her friend's defence. One day the story would come out and until then it was better to say nothing. Specially as she knew so little herself.

They met in the popular café at Cardiff bus station and spent a pleasant few hours together, talking about their lives, exchanging confidences, Winnie cautiously avoiding anything that might remotely be considered prying. She was painfully curious about why Faith had abandoned her child but dared not ask.

Faith asked about the children and their schooling and avoided anything to do with her past. Accepting this, knowing she had to wait until Faith was ready to confide in her, Winnie told amusing stories about the children and about people Faith would remember from the weeks she had taught in the school.

They walked through Sophia Gardens, following the river, and Faith teased her about how slowly she walked.

'I've become quite fit since I moved to Mrs Thomas's,' Faith told her. 'I walk miles every week and spend a lot of time working in her garden.'

'Paul deals with the garden but perhaps I ought to help if I'm going to keep up with you,' Winnie said with a laugh.

When she was back preparing Mrs Thomas's meal, Faith hoped that now they had met once and managed not to be confronted by someone who knew Matt, they could meet whenever she had a day free.

* * *

Faith didn't meet Mrs Thomas's son until August, and when he arrived on that Friday morning she was immediately glad he didn't live nearby. He had called to take his mother to lunch and for a drive in the country. Faith helped her get ready. She herself intended to catch the bus into Cardiff to meet Winnie, as Samuel had graciously agreed she might.

Samuel Thomas was a stern-faced, rather ill-mannered man. He spoke to Faith slowly, articulating with care, as though she were an idiot. She guessed he was in his late forties and his attempts to look younger were ludicrous. He wore glasses over washed-out blue eyes in a pale face. His hair looked unnaturally and suspiciously black. His dark clothes were casual, unlike his speech. He glanced in the hall mirror as he waited for his mother to put on her coat and hat and Faith wondered what he believed he saw there: young and handsome? Suave and debonair? From his slight smile of approval, he clearly didn't see what she recognized as an arrogant, middle-aged man who didn't deserve a lovely mother like Mrs Thomas.

'Make sure you lock up before you go off, won't you, dear?' Mrs Thomas said with a smile.

After getting her settled into the car, Samuel came back and said, 'Remember you are responsible, so make sure everything is secure.' No please or thank you, so Faith responded with as much rudeness as she dared by not replying at all. She waved Mrs Thomas off, then closed the door. If he were around too often life wouldn't be so pleasant.

On the train to Cardiff she began thinking about her future plans. Once she was sure Matt was no longer looking for her she might try to return to teaching. It was something she enjoyed and knew she did well. Her feeling for the underdog, her observant eye for any child being less than happy, was invaluable and something for which she could thank her foster-mother, she thought with sadness.

A man got in at Cogan. 'Hello, aren't you the young lady from the hotel?' He put down his briefcase and offered his hand. 'Ian. Ian Day. Faith, isn't it?'

'Hello! I thought you'd have a car, being a rep.'

'You remembered,' he said, holding her hand in both of his, and smiling delightedly.

She was pleased to see him. Thoughts of her foster-parents were taking her back to her lost child and his pleasant company was just in time to stop the melancholy clouding her mind.

'The car is in disgrace,' he told her, laughing. 'Its clutch is slipping, or whatever clutches do. I have to use trains and buses until Monday. Going shopping?'

'Meeting a friend for lunch.'

'I'm catching the five o'clock train back, see you at the station?' he suggested.

'I have to leave earlier than that. I'm getting a train about four.'

'Four, that's what I meant to say.' He laughed and said, 'Meet you at the station about 3.45?'

'I can't promise,' she said. She had intended to set off nearer three o'clock, but it was tempting. She didn't have to be cautious with a stranger, and he did have the nicest smile.

Ian was smiling too. Going back to Barry at four o'clock was the wrong direction for him, but he found the thought of seeing her again irresistible.

* * *

Winnie was standing on the corner near the theatre where they had arranged to meet. She looked anxious, walking up and down and lifting herself up on to tiptoe looking for her. Faith waved and they ran to greet each other with a hug.

'I'm so glad to see you again, Faith, and you're looking marvellous. Sort of glowing.'

The pleasure of talking to Ian might be the reason for that, Faith thought, but she said, 'I don't work very hard. And you're looking good yourself. Children and Paul all right?' They chatted about ordinary things as they made their way to a café.

Once they were settled Winnie once more evaded asking the questions she wanted to ask and instead, said, 'You say you don't work very hard; what do you do, then?'

'As I told you, I'm a housekeeper companion to a lady in her seventies.'

'That sounds like hard work to me. Don't they keep you running around like a demented terrier?'

'She's a very sweet lady. Most of the time I simply keep her company, listening to the radio or records and discussing what we hear. I read to her, which I enjoy, and I do the cooking and I rather enjoy that, too. I pretend I have a house of my own and imagine I'm preparing a lavish meal for friends.'

'Matt refers to you as "the runaway". Do you regret, you know, running away like you did?'

'Specially today.'

'Of course. It's the fourteenth of August. She will be six months old.'

'It was cowardly and of course I regret it. Specially today. But Matt . . .' She paused, then said, 'There was no way I could have stayed. My regret at walking away is a continuous ache. I long to hold a baby in my arms, but leaving her was something I had to do, I can't regret walking away. And I know leaving Matt was the only choice. There was no way I could stay with him. But my regret at having to leave the baby doesn't get any easier. I try to tell myself I would never have loved her.'

'Of course you would! Whatever the problem was, you'd have put it right. You must have felt something for Matt. You married him.'

Faith couldn't tell her friend the marriage hadn't taken place. She turned away to hide the sudden flood of tears.

'What happened, Faith? Do you want to tell me?'

'One day perhaps. When I feel safe from him.' She waited for the tears to subside then asked, 'What are people saying about me?'

'No one understands. How could they unless you tell them why? The runaway, that's what they all call you.'

'Have you heard anything about the baby?'

'She was named Dorothy and is being fostered, with a view to adoption. Why don't you come and explain things? Matt is entitled to an explanation, surely?'

'Matt wasn't the father.' She looked away from her friend as she lied.

'If Matt wasn't the father, was she Nick's child?'

'No, not Nick. Ironic wasn't it, her being born on St Valentine's Day.' she said bitterly. She quickly asked about Winnie's family, anxious to change the subject before tears began. If they did she thought they would never stop. Winnie knew she would learn nothing more until her friend was ready to talk.

They parted at 2.30 p.m. as her friend needed to be home before the children were out of school. Faith went towards the station but didn't get on a train. She needed something to distract her, stop her thinking about the helpless child, the tiny baby called Dorothy from whom she had coldly walked away. It wouldn't hurt to wait another hour or so before catching a train back to Barry. *The runaway*, the nickname tortured her, repeating time and again in her head until she thought she would scream.

Forcing herself to concentrate on something else, she went to Cardiff's famous market where she bought a few items from the tempting displays of fruit and vegetables. At other stalls she looked at cushions and curtain material and dreamed of one day having a place of her own.

Wandering through Howells's department store, and David Morgan's she went through the various departments, furnishing rooms in her imagination. Living rooms, kitchen, bedrooms, the dreams continued and it was almost 3.30 when she looked at her watch. Time she was leaving.

She was startled to see Ian standing looking around at the approaching faces. She had forgotten him in her morbid mood. He smiled widely when he saw her and she responded with a feeling of relief. She knew the mood would have continued if she'd been sitting in a carriage on her own; he was at least a break from her guilty thoughts. The shoppers were beginning to leave and the train quickly filled up. Friends were chattering, others were meeting by chance and comparing their purchases, laughing, making plans for another trip. If she hadn't met Ian, Faith knew their cheerfulness would have exacerbated her loneliness. They found seats facing each other next to the window and sat with slight uneasiness. They were still strangers and an arranged meeting was at odds with how little they knew about each other.

At first she didn't know what to say. He might be alarmed if she explained about her daydreams of having a home of her own; he might think she was man-hunting! And if he knew about the conversation with Winnie, of how she had given birth to a healthy daughter, then walked away from her, he would surely think she was inhuman.

She did tell him about her job, explaining it was temporary while she considered where she wanted to live and what she wanted to do. 'I'm a teacher,' she told him, 'but I needed a change and some time away to think about what I want to do, so I left the place where I was living, and—'

'You ran away? How daring!'

She stared at him. 'That's the second time today I've been called a runaway. It wasn't like that,' she lied. 'I knew I wasn't happy, so I decided to move right away, consider what I wanted, make a few changes, that's all.'

'Still brave.'

'Maybe.'

They were approaching Cogan and he said, 'Meet me for dinner one evening and we can discuss bravery.'

She shook her head. 'I'm a paid companion and that means I'm needed to spend time with my employer.'

'All the time?'

'Not all the time but I don't have much free time during the day. I cook the meals, besides the companion side of my job.'

'No day off?'

'Sometimes, like today when she went to spend a day with her son.'

'Next time, then? Please?' He took out a notebook and scribbled furiously as the train squealed huffily to a stop. 'My address,' he said as he handed it to her. 'Please write or telephone and let me know when you're free. I'd very much like to see you again.'

She took it and avoided a reply as the train stopped and started then stopped again, making everyone stagger and laugh. She waved until he was out of sight and wondered if they would ever meet again. The thought of confessing how she had abandoned her child, run away without explanation, was like a dark cloud. How could she tell him? And, if they became friends, how could she not tell him?

Slowly she tore up the paper bearing his name and address and dropped it into a litter bin as she walked from the station.

The day out had confused her. She had been happy to see Winnie and flattered by Ian's interest, but for the following few nights sleep evaded her. Memories of how she had felt as she had walked away from Matt and his mother, and the baby, tormented her. Yet there had been no alternative once she had read those newspaper reports.

She went over the conversation with Winnie. She had a six-month-old daughter called Dorothy. Dorothy Pryor. Her wishes had been followed. The child she had refused to accept had been given her mother's name, a mother she had never known. History was cruelly repeating itself in a way she would never have believed she would even contemplate. Abandoning a child to a fate as heartless as her own. How could she have done such a thing?

Dorothy, born on St Valentine's Day, 1960 and fostered with a family who wanted to adopt her. That hurt more than she had expected. Adoption was so final, and there was still a part of her who saw the tiny baby as simply that, an innocent baby, not a tainted human being who might grow into someone as evil as her father.

Over the following weeks she met Winnie several times but didn't ask for news of Matt or his mother. She had to close that part of her life away in a dark corner of her mind, hoping it would become less and less real. She always searched the faces of the crowd hoping for a glimpse of Ian, but his car would have been mended long ago and there was little chance of meeting him again on the train.

* * *

As summer drifted by on a cloud of warm days filled with gardening and long walks, she began to relax and accept the tragedy of her lost child. Mrs Thomas was undemanding and she was as content with life as she could expect. The only irritations were the occasional visits of Mrs Thomas's son, Samuel. He usually came for lunch and quickly made it clear that she was not expected to eat with them, but simply wait at table. She ate her meal in the kitchen like a disgraced child and listened to his list of complaints with stoicism. He was clearly suspicious of her friendliness toward his mother, almost, but not quite, pointing out he was aware of the danger of his weak mother changing her will. After his departure, she and Mrs Thomas would joke a little about his over-fussiness, although Faith avoided mentioning his fears about his inheritance.

* * *

In late September, while the town was still overflowing with holidaymakers, Faith became aware that Mrs Thomas was less active. They always spent afternoons in the garden when the weather was sunny. Sometimes Faith would read to her and when necessary she would weed flower-beds and dig up plants that were past their prime. They went together to the growers and chose their future displays and while Mrs Thomas sat in the shade and advised, Faith did the planting.

Of late, Faith had gone on chatting to her before realizing she had fallen asleep. Then she would go in and prepare a tea tray before gently waking her.

One afternoon when they had planned to dead-head roses, Mrs Thomas said she would stay indoors.

'But it's so lovely now with the fuchsias and annuals still giving such a wonderful display. And besides, I need you to tell me where and how to dead-head your roses,' Faith coaxed.

'Not today, dear. I'll just sit in my armchair.'

'What if I took your armchair outside? The air is so still, I'm sure you'll enjoy it. Just a half-hour or so?'

'My mother says she wants to stay inside. You are bullying her, Miss Pryor.' The voice of her employer's son startled her. She hadn't heard his approach.

'Bullying? What do you mean? She loves sitting in her garden!'

'Not today. She's made that clear, to anyone who's capable of listening.'

Ignoring him she leaned down and asked, 'Was I too persistent? I'm sorry, Mrs Thomas, I didn't mean to bully you. If you're sure you don't want to go outside, then I'll bring our tea in here.'

'Our tea! Mine and my mother's. You can take yours in the kitchen. I need to talk to my mother in private.'

'Of course, Mr Thomas.'

Red-faced with humiliation she went into the kitchen and turned on the radio so he wouldn't accuse her of eavesdropping. She carried in the tea tray and began to pour but she was told to leave. As she walked past, Mrs Thomas held her back and said. 'Thank you, dear. We'd better leave those roses till tomorrow.'

A few minutes later, hearing her name, and angry at the man's treatment of her, her good intentions forgotten, Faith stood near the door and brazenly listened to the conversation. If he were planning to dismiss her then the sooner she knew the better. The voices weren't loud but both spoke clearly and it was soon apparent that she was correct in her suspicions and he was trying to persuade his mother to ask her to leave.

'But you don't need her, Mother,' he was saying. 'I'll get you a daily woman, someone who will know her place.'

'No. Samuel, dear. Faith is like a breath of fresh air about the place. A joy to have around.'

'A servant who takes advantage! She's too friendly. She *works* for you, Mother, and she talks to you as though she is your friend.'

'That's what a companion is, dear,' Mrs Thomas protested.

A chair creaked as Samuel stood up and Faith darted back to the sink and buried her hands in washing-up suds. She pretended not to hear him enter and he called her name sharply as though demanding the attention of a dog, 'Miss Pryor. I've been discussing your employment with my mother and—'

He was interrupted by the appearance of Mrs Thomas, who said, 'And his mother doesn't know what she'd do without you, Faith dear. So Samuel and I hope you're happy here and will stay for as long as I need you.' Samuel turned and left without another word.

'Sorry about that, he's got a lot of worries at the moment and he feels he'd be happier if I went to live with him. Or disappeared into one of the care homes.'

'I do enjoy working for you, you know that, but I am only an employee. When you want to make changes I know I'll have to go, but when that happens, I'll help in any way I can to make sure you're settled and comfortable.'

'Thank you, dear.'

'Now, what about another cup of tea, then I'll start preparing dinner. I have some fresh hake this evening.'

When she went back with the freshly made tea, Mrs Thomas was asleep.

Mrs Thomas had a small appetite but enjoyed her food, so it was alarming to see several meals just moved around on her plate. After a week of partially eaten meals, and a listlessness when Faith suggested any of the activities that they had previously enjoyed, she telephoned the doctor. As a precaution against being accused of not keeping him informed, she also rang Samuel.

'I'll come straight away,' he said.

'No! I mean, that is, please don't alarm her. She's tired and her appetite isn't what it was, but I don't want her frightened into thinking she's seriously ill.'

'Thank you, Miss Pryor, but I do know how to treat my own mother.' He slammed down the phone and Faith went back to tell Mrs Thomas that her son was planning a visit.

A softly murmured. 'Oh dear,' escaped the old lady's lips, which made Faith smile but which she pretended not to hear.

Fortunately the doctor arrived before Samuel and he was reassuring. After an examination and a brief conversation, he told Faith that Mrs Thomas was rather tired and that was normal for a lady of her age. After discussing the meals Faith offered, he said, 'Continue to offer the same meals but in smaller quantities, that way she will be encouraged to finish them and not worry about leaving any. Make sure she has variety — as I'm sure you do, Miss Pryor. I don't think she needs anything more at present, but I'll call again in a day or so to see how things are.'

Samuel was irritated to learn that the doctor had been. 'He should have waited to talk to me,' he complained. After Faith had told him encouragingly what the doctor had said, he wasn't appeased. 'So you brought me here for nothing?'

'No,' Faith said defiantly, unable to put up with any more of his rudeness. 'The decision to come was yours. Perhaps in future you'll trust me to tell you when your presence is urgently needed.'

'I'll stay the night,' he said. 'I've brought an overnight bag.'

'I'll go and put towels and soap in your room,' she replied. She stopped at the doorway and added, 'Perhaps, as you're staying, I can go out this evening? There's a film I would like to see.' She didn't fancy spending an evening with him in the house.

'What about dinner?' he demanded.

'I'll serve that before I go.'

She didn't go to the cinema but instead caught a bus into Cardiff and just walked around the streets, hoping her anger would dissipate before it was time to go back. Samuel was a very unpleasant man and she wondered how someone as sweet and gentle as Mrs Thomas could have produced an aggressive, ill-tempered son like him. Thoughts went from there to her own daughter. If there was such a contrast between

Mrs Thomas and her son, then could it have been the same between Matt and his daughter? Perhaps there was no certainty that her own child would have been a replica of Matt.

Had she been hasty? No, she decided firmly. To have stayed would have meant Matt's involvement in her baby's upbringing and maybe that was where the likeness would have developed, by example; the cruel indifference to people weaker than himself. The urge to force vulnerable people to do his bidding needn't have shown itself in the same way but it could still have been a part of the child's character.

She tried not to use the baby's name, not even in her thoughts. That would make her seem more real, even though the face was still a blank, empty oval, surrounded by that dark, spiky hair which was all she remembered.

It was evening. Most of the cafés were closed and she wasn't brave enough to go into a public house on her own. Even in this new decade, the exciting sixties, she couldn't do that. She would go back to the station and look up the time of the next train. The tempting smell of fish and chips was on the air, reminding her she hadn't eaten dinner, she'd been in too much of a hurry to get away from Samuel. She ignored it, promising herself a sandwich when she got back, and hurried on.

As she passed the Catholic church she heard someone call her name and she turned to see two people running towards her.

'Faith! It's me, Ian. We saw you passing and it took a while to park the car. Whew, I haven't run so fast in years,' he said, as he reached her, trying to catch his breath. 'This is Mam and, fair play, she kept up with me. Good on her, eh?'

Laughing, her sad mood forgotten, Faith held out her hand. 'Well done indeed, Mrs Day. You seem fitter than your son.'

'I go to Keep Fit and he drives everywhere,' Mrs Day replied.

'We were just going for fish and chips, will you come with us?' Ian asked.

'Well, I was just about to go home,' she said doubtfully.

Ian tilted his head on one side, a pleading expression on his face which was replicated on his mother's. Again Faith laughed, 'But there's no hurry. Mrs Thomas's son is there, so yes. I'd love to.'

'And we'll drive you home afterwards,' he promised, taking both their arms and striding off back towards the source of the appetizing smell.

The time they spent together was pleasant. Ian and his mother, Vivienne, had a similar sense of humour and remarks bounced from one to the other at speed — they frequently came out with a remark at the same time.

At first Faith was a little subdued by them but, as she relaxed in their company, she began to add her own comments to theirs, flattered by their genuine laughter.

Vivienne explained that she had lost her husband in the war and was now working in a school as a dinner lady, cooking food for the children and staff each day. Having the school experience in common and with Ian asking questions the conversation buzzed and the time went fast. They had met as strangers but were parting as friends.

Ian insisted on driving her home. When she stopped at the gate she was surprised to see the lights on the porch and in the hall were out. 'Dear considerate Samuel has obviously gone to bed without leaving a light to help me find my way,' she muttered.

Ian turned the car until the headlights shone up the drive to the front porch. The keyhole wasn't where she expected it to be, and she had to feel around with her fingers, but once the key had slipped into the lock she stepped inside after a final wave and a hoarsely called, 'Thank you.' He tooted the horn in response.

She went in quietly and headed for the kitchen where she made herself a cup of tea. As she poured the boiling water into the pot, Mrs Thomas came in and whispered. 'Where did you go, dear? Was it a good film? And who gave you a lift home? Tell me all about it.'

Faith explained about the previous times she had met Ian Day, and how she had joined him and his mother for the unexpected supper.

'So you've met the mother, that's serious,' Mrs Thomas said, and they were giggling like children, partly with the effort of whispering, when Samuel came down.

'I can't believe this, Miss Pryor! Coming in late and disturbing my mother with horns blaring, lights flashing and now giving her tea at this hour of the night.'

'Would you like a cup, dear?' Mrs Thomas asked with a smile. 'It's very weak and milky, mind, but Faith won't allow strong tea after six p.m.'

After settling Mrs Thomas back in bed, Faith washed the dishes and went to her room, where she stared at the night beyond the window and relived the unexpectedly enjoyable evening. It had been an exciting end to a day that had included coping with Samuel.

* * *

Two days later, a letter arrived thanking her for a pleasant interlude and hoping they would meet again soon. It was signed by Ian and his mother, Vivienne Day. She showed it to Mrs Thomas, who said. 'My dear, I enjoyed it too, sharing it with you, I mean. It was such an exciting end to a rather tedious day with Samuel. Poor boy, he can't help it, he's like his father, taking everything so seriously and being afraid of enjoying himself.'

Thoughtfully, Faith asked, 'Do you believe children inherit attitudes, and likes and dislikes from their parents? Does environment play its part too?'

'Such a serious question, dear. But yes, I suppose we all carry something of our parents in us.' She saw an odd expression cross Faith's face and quickly added, 'Yours must have been gentle and loving, so don't start imagining things,' she added, afraid Faith was brooding on her lack of knowledge about her family.

‘What about criminal behaviour? Would that make a child more likely to follow the same course?’

‘Ah, I doubt that very much. That must be most frequently down to deprivation, don’t you think? Apart from those who have everything and can’t find contentment. But that kind of wrongdoing is less common.’

Faith thought about her words but they didn’t give her any peace. If Mrs Thomas was right, then she had left her daughter for no good reason.

As autumn took the last of the gaudy colours of summer and gave its display of still beautiful but more subdued tones, Mrs Thomas went out in the garden less and less. Sometimes she was persuaded to dress warmly and sit on the porch for a while as Faith and she sipped a hot drink but as Christmas approached she rarely left her chair. Faith would help her dress in the mornings and guide her downstairs, and in the evening prepared her for a bedtime that came earlier and earlier.

The doctor came and offered medicine and advice, but Mrs Thomas refused to allow Faith to tell her son. Faith mentioned this in front of the doctor but he smiled and agreed with his patient. ‘We don’t want Samuel bothered unnecessarily, do we, Mrs Thomas,’ he said, and Faith saw him wink.

When Samuel did call, his visits were brief and seemed to consist of a search for reasons to complain about Faith. He seemed unaware of the changes in his mother, as she sat at the table and poured tea, chatting brightly and pretending everything was as it should be. It wasn’t until he had gone that she showed the weariness the effort had caused her. But still she refused permission for him to be told. On one occasion in November he stayed and kept her talking long beyond her usual bedtime, persistently asking the same questions about when she intended to leave her home and find a place where she would be properly cared for. Faith heard them arguing and she waited in frustrated concern for Samuel to leave. Mrs Thomas was overtired when he left, slamming out of the house, like a spoilt child unable to get his own way.

On the following day she was tired and unable to rest. Faith rang the doctor to discuss her employer's condition. She suggested the reason for it and he called, gave Mrs Thomas a sedative and made her promise to stay in bed for the day. She refused her meals, insisting she was too weary to eat, and stayed in bed all the following day too.

'I have a visitor coming this afternoon,' Faith was told two days later. 'Would you mind leaving us alone, dear?'

'Of course not. I might try and take the bean sticks down and I really must move the dahlias before the frost ruins them.'

In fact there were several visitors. The first two were a young man whom she didn't know, with an elderly man who she thought looked like a bank manager or a solicitor. The next to arrive was the doctor who waved as he stepped inside. She prepared a tray of tea for them and then went into the garden. It wasn't her business and Mrs Thomas would call when she was needed.

An hour later she heard the door open and conversation floated on the air. She looked towards the door and saw the group all leaving at once. Again the doctor waved, then he called, 'You can go in now, Miss Pryor, Mrs Thomas would enjoy another cup of tea, I think.'

Faith went in, talking before reaching the living room about what she had achieved in the garden, not wanting there to be a silence that could be construed as her expecting to be told what had gone on. It was probably something to do with a will, she guessed, and Mrs Thomas's private business was not in her domain.

Days passed. Then Samuel arrived one Saturday and explained that he would be staying for the night. 'You can go out if you wish,' he said, 'but don't make a noise when you get back like last time.'

She prepared his room and thought about Ian. There was no time for a letter to reach him but she wondered whether a phone call to his home would be appropriate. Best not, she decided. She didn't want to be too presumptuous and besides, she wasn't free to develop friendships; there were too many skeletons in her proverbial cupboard! And even after all these months Matt could appear at any time; she hadn't hidden her tracks that carefully and had foolishly stayed in the same town. One day she would have to tell Ian and his mother the truth.

Having rejected the option of calling, she heard the house phone ring and Samuel came in to tell her there was a call for her, reminding her not to make a habit of it, and that he was well aware that she was taking advantage of his mother's kindness. Panic stiffened every joint in her body and she couldn't move. Matt. It had to be Matt. Superstitiously she knew it was him because he had been in her thoughts. Only Winnie knew her phone number and she was unlikely to call her here. Matt had found her.

'Are you coming? They'll ring off if you stand there much longer.'

Stiff and filled with panic she followed him down the stairs and picked up the phone.

'It's Paul. Sorry. I know I shouldn't worry you, but I'm desperate. Winnie is in hospital and Mam and Dad are away. Is there any way you can come and look after the children so I can visit her? Just for today and tomorrow? Her parents will be here then. Please, Faith, is there any chance of you getting a couple of days off?'

The relief of hearing Paul's voice when she was expecting to hear Matt made her shake. Samuel asked if there was something wrong. 'One minute,' she said to Paul, then turned to Samuel. In a voice that still shook, she explained, 'It's a friend. She's in hospital and her husband wonders if I could go there and help with the children for the weekend.'

'I'll take mother back with me,' Samuel said at once.

'No, it's all right, I'll tell her I can't go. If she goes with you the journey will tire her, I mean, perhaps she doesn't want to go.'

'Of course she'll want to come with me. It's a while since she came on a visit. Tell your friend you can stay until midday on Monday.'

Faith stared at the phone and he said, 'Come on, you need to get my mother ready.'

Into the phone, she said. 'Paul? Yes, it's all right I can stay until Monday. Give Winnie my love and I'll see you very soon.' She cut off his thanks and hurried to attend to Mrs Thomas's packing.

She hated causing disruption for Mrs Thomas and wished Samuel hadn't been there when Paul had telephoned. Much as she wanted to help her friend, her first thought was for Mrs Thomas and how she would hate being a visitor in her son's home for several long days.

It wasn't until she had seen Mrs Thomas and her son off that the panic she had felt when she phone call came returned, at double strength. She was going to stay with Winnie, just around the corner from Matt and his mother. She was certain to be seen. She set off on her journey feeling like a woman walking towards her death. All the confidence she had built up had vanished and she was that other person, the woman who was afraid to tell Matt she was leaving; afraid he would make her tell him why. She caught the local bus and all the time she kept her head down, convinced that if she raised it he would be there. She reached the house and the welcome she had from Jack, Bill and Polly made it worth the anxieties. Of course she was right to come. Winnie and Paul were friends and she had been wrong to think, even for a moment, of letting them down.

She stayed in the house and hoped for a miracle. They had made the children promise not to tell anyone she was there, explaining it was a secret, a game, but Faith had little confidence in their self-control. A secret is a wonderful thing to share.

Winnie was much improved by Monday and her parents were on their way, prepared to deal with everything. While the three children waited impatiently for Paul to bring Winnie home by taxi Faith busied herself in the kitchen, preparing a meal and filling the tins with home-made cakes, helped sporadically by Polly.

Miraculously, when it was time for her to leave there had been no sign of Matt or Carol and she went to the bus stop, huddled within a large winter coat, hoping her luck would hold just that little bit longer. Waiting for the bus to come was a very long ten minutes and she scuttled aboard, feeling an idiot as she crouched in the back seat, still hiding within the coat's hood.

When she got off the bus she breathed a sigh of relief. It was only twelve o'clock; there was time to do a little shopping and get food ready for Mrs Thomas's return.

Changing the heavy suitcase from one hand to the other she opened the gate and only then looked at the house. There were lights on in every room even though the day wasn't particularly dark. Samuel and his mother were already home, she thought with a sigh. She heard the murmur of voices as she opened the door. Hoping it wasn't the doctor, she called, 'I'm back. Mrs Thomas? Did you have a good time?'

The doctor came out of the kitchen, followed by Samuel. 'I'm so sorry, Faith,' the doctor said. 'Mrs Thomas died just an hour ago.'

CHAPTER FOUR

The shock of the unexpected death of Mrs Thomas kept Faith awake all night. Several times she went down and stared at the night sky and once she made a hot drink, hoping that it would relax her, but thoughts of the time she had spent looking after the lady, memories of the happy times they'd had, made her sad. It was more than losing a job. She had lost a friend and the loss was leaving her with an emptiness far greater than she had felt before. She had moved away and left people behind, but this time it was she who had been left and it was hard to take.

She thought back over the past months and wondered whether she could have done more. Would Mrs Thomas still be alive if she hadn't sent her off to stay with Samuel? Was there some neglect in the way she had persuaded her to sit outside as the weather became cooler? Could she have provided better food?

Sleep came eventually and the alarm she had set for 6.30 startled her into wakefulness. She lay and grieved anew as the memory flooded back. She didn't expect to see Samuel up so early but he was sitting in an armchair, disapproval in his eyes. 'You slept well?' he asked sarcastically. She didn't reply.

Faith had never dealt with funeral arrangements before but she was determined to do her best for Mrs Thomas.

While Samuel was on the phone telling people the news, she began making lists of what she needed to do. Once the date and time had been decided she would plan the food. Mrs Thomas, who, she was surprised to learn, had been seventy-nine, had few friends able to attend. She hoped Samuel would bring people with him, a very small group saying farewell to the lady would make a sad occasion worse.

'Would you like me to write to anyone on your behalf?' she asked when Samuel came to find her.

'What has it to do with you? You'll be leaving now your work here is done.'

'But don't you need my help with the arrangements?'

'You were her companion and as she's no longer here your work is finished, surely you can understand that?'

'You want me to go now?'

'You have no job, so of course I want you to go. Now, if you'll excuse me,' he said with his usual unpleasant tone, 'I need to get on to the funeral directors.'

He sounded so cold she felt sickened. She was still shocked by the sudden loss of her employer and Samuel was talking as though he were booking a meal or a visit to the theatre rather than her funeral. 'I can stay until I find somewhere to live, surely?'

'I'd prefer it if you found alternative accommodation immediately, but perhaps, as long as you don't try to interfere, you can use the room until the weekend. You can pack up her clothes, that will keep you busy,' he added.

The 'Thank you,' stuck in her throat and she walked away after handing him the lists she had prepared.

People came and went throughout the day and she sat in her room, convinced that at some point Samuel would realize he needed help and would call her. But the people, whom she didn't meet, or even see, were presumably given the various tasks to do. To take her mind off thoughts of where she would go and what she would do, she wrote out a shopping list and planned the spread, guessing that there would be no more than a dozen people. On Wednesday she showed him the list and suggested she might go and buy what he would need.

He handed her some money, counting it carefully into her hand as though she were an untrustworthy child. 'Don't forget the receipts,' he said, 'and before you leave I would like to see your accounts.'

'They are all in Mrs Thomas's bureau,' she replied sharply.

On Wednesday, aware that time was running out, she walked around the shops looking for anything that would offer employment and somewhere to live. A few shops had notices in the window asking for assistants. The choice was surprisingly varied but none strongly appealed. There were the fishmongers, where she had been a regular customer, an ironmongery, a corner shop selling the usual assortment of foodstuff and a place selling children's toys. What she really wanted to do was return to teaching but she was afraid that would make it too easy for Matt to find her. Later, perhaps, but how much later? Matt wasn't the kind to give up.

She knew she had to face him sometime but the further away that day was, the better she'd be able to cope with his questions, his hurt and the anger, aware that she had so little time made her face up to making a decision, and she made her first enquiry at the corner shop. To her dismay she was told quite rudely that they needed an assistant with experience. At the toy shop she learned that the place had been filled but, interested in her, they took her name in case the new person didn't suit. At the ironmongers she was laughingly told they needed a man who knew something about tools and how they were used. She felt like a beggar, asking for something to which she wasn't entitled, a scrounger, expecting more than she should.

There was only the fresh-fish shop and she turned away from that. No. Handling the cold, wet fish was not something she could contemplate. Perhaps the best thing was to first find a room. She didn't want to end up sleeping on a park bench! Having a base and enough money to last a few weeks would give her a chance to look around, go to the employment exchange and hopefully find something she would enjoy.

The columns in the local newspaper offered several rooms to let. When she knocked on the door of the first, in a neat road behind the hospital, it was answered by a woman about her own age. She was shown the room, which was at the back overlooking a rather unkempt garden. She took it and paid a week's rent in advance. The landlady, Jean Painter, explained that she needed some extra money as her husband Roland was still a student, studying psychology.

After a friendly chat Faith stood to leave, smilingly convinced that she had found herself a safe haven. 'Now all I have to do is get a job,' she said, having briefly explained her situation.

'Could you cope with looking after three children? I know someone who needs a nanny for three months while the parents set up their business.' So there it was, a home and a job.

After meeting the parents of the three children, and agreeing to start on the following Monday, Faith returned to the house, where subdued voices and the sombre, darkened rooms reminded her of the friend she had lost. Despite her sadness she found great pleasure in telling Samuel that she would leave straight after the funeral.

'But you won't be attending,' he said. 'This is a private affair, family only.'

'But your mother was my friend as well as my employer!' she gasped. 'How can I not say goodbye to her?'

'You'll be here, setting out the food.'

'You told me I must leave, without giving me time to find a suitable place, tell me I'm not to go to the funeral, then expect me to deal with the food?'

'The shopping is done, there will be no more than fifteen people coming back. Hardly an arduous task, is it?'

'Can you see to it that my wages are made up,' she said. 'I expect it later today. All the details of my employment are in the bureau. Before tomorrow, Mr Thomas. And I expect to be paid till the end of the month!' She went to her room, sobs threatening to burst from her. What was it about her that made people behave so badly? The shopkeepers spoke to her as though she were an idiot. Samuel treated her with mistrust. Matt's mother had treated her like a subservient fool. Matt had lied, or at least, hadn't told her the truth which was much the same thing. Did she look like a doormat for everyone to use without a thought?

She walked to the corner and telephoned a shop near Winnie. Being careful not to give her name, she asked the man if he would go and fetch her friend to the phone, which he did, grumbling all the way. Holding back tears she told Winnie what had happened.

'Come now, and stay with us for a couple of nights before you start your new job,' Winnie said at once. 'We can stay indoors to make sure you don't see — you know who.' She said this to prevent the children overhearing Matt's name. 'The children would love it.'

'No, Winnie, I daren't. Now I've found a new job — albeit a temporary one — and a new home, I can't risk his finding me and having to move on.'

'Then can we meet in Cardiff?'

'That would be lovely. As soon as my hours are sorted and I have a regular day off, I'll write and we can arrange it.'

'Until then, I hope everything works out for you. Oh, have you seen Ian lately?'

'No, and he won't know about Mrs Thomas and once I move—'

'He'll turn up again, I'm sure of it.'

'I'm not.' Faith said sadly. 'My luck is not that good.'

* * *

Ian was trying to find her but he had failed. On telephoning the house he had been told by someone who didn't give a name that there was no Faith Pryor at the address. He guessed the voice was Samuel's but had no way of being sure. He called at the house but there was no reply and when he enquired at a neighbours' he was told that they knew nothing except that Mrs Thomas had died. He made another call to the house and this time a man he didn't know told him Faith was far too busy to see him and not to telephone the house again.

Faith was certain to be at the funeral and once he learned the date and time he planned to be there too.

Knowing she was doing it for Mrs Thomas and not Samuel, Faith got up early on the day of the funeral and began cooking. By 10.30 the plates were filled with appetizing bite-size savouries, assorted cakes and sandwiches.

Samuel looked and nodded, but that was the only acknowledgement she had of her work. She held out her hand. 'My money?' she asked.

'You'll be here later, to help serve, won't you? I can give it to you then.'

She disappeared into her room, where boxes and a suitcase were packed with her few possessions. As soon as the guests left, piling into the private cars and the funeral cars, she waited for the cortège to slowly move off towards the church, then she went out, wearing her best black coat and hat, and cut across the fields. When all the mourners were inside the building she slipped in and sat at the back. She wasn't going to allow Samuel to stop her showing her respects for her employer.

As the service came to an end she nipped out, scuttled around the church, and bumped into Ian Day.

'Faith, I'm so glad to see you. I've called at the house but I was told you weren't there or were too busy.'

'Ian. I don't understand. I wasn't told about anyone calling.'

'I telephoned too, and it was only by luck that I heard about the death of your employer.'

'Look, I have to go. I was told not to attend the funeral and I need to get back before the others arrive.'

'I'll come with you, then we'll arrange to meet. I'm anxious to know what you plan to do next.'

They talked as they hurried back over the fields. When they got back to the house Faith went into the kitchen to fill kettles and start making tea. Ian saw the bottles of red wine on the side and opened two of them, took white wine from the fridge and then with a wink, darted out of the back door as the front door opened to a group of chattering women.

The mourners hardly spoke to her as she handed around food and drink. They were strangers and must presume that she had been hired for the occasion. She wasn't upset, her mind was on Ian and his surprising appearance.

* * *

When the last guest had gone Faith stood in the kitchen and looked at the used china and cutlery stacked ready for washing. She went into the living room to find Samuel and asked again for her money. He handed it to her, correct to the last shilling and she put it in her pocket. Then she gathered her luggage and without a backward glance walked out to where a taxi waited. She hoped he'd enjoy dealing with the dishes. Her grief was for the loss of her friend, but seeing the last of Samuel was nothing but a relief and that thought helped to hold back tears.

She walked into her new, temporary home and determinedly concentrated on her future. As usual at such times she wished she had a family, or even a distant relation, someone to talk to. She felt like a pea popping about in a colander, dreadfully, sadly, alone.

She was still making enquiries about her lost sister, Joy, even though her optimism was fading. So she wrote to the various organizations and gave them her new address, just in case something turned up. Then she began the delightful task of getting to know her new charges, Menna Gardener's three boys.

She arrived at their house each morning at eight o'clock and left at four after setting out their tea. She enjoyed looking after them and knowing it was temporary made her more determined to enjoy the pleasant interlude. They were happy boys, easy to entertain and she began to get more and more involved with cooking for the family when she had the opportunity.

Menna was delighted with the extra help. Getting close to the children was something that Faith tried to avoid, aware that the appointment was temporary, but they charmed their way into her heart.

Two weeks after the funeral she received a letter from Mrs Thomas's solicitor asking her to phone and make an appointment to see him. She went the following day at 4.30 and was surprised to see Samuel there.

'My client, Mrs Rebecca Thomas, mentioned you in her will,' Faith was surprised and alarmed to hear. From the expression on Samuel's face it was not something that pleased him. He was staring at her with obvious dislike and suspicion.

'Oh? That surprises me. I didn't know her for very long,' she said, aware of the rising colour in her cheeks uneasy under Samuel's continuing glare. 'How very kind. A small memento perhaps?'

'I am instructed to give you a payment of one hundred pounds, Miss Pryor.'

'But — that's too much. Why would she be so generous?' she muttered.

'That's what I want to know,' Samuel said. 'She said nothing of this to me and I wonder how she had been persuaded.'

'Slander, Mr Thomas,' the solicitor warned in a whisper.

'I had no idea she was going to do this. She certainly didn't mention anything.' Faith looked from the benign face of the solicitor to the now angry face of Samuel. 'Are you suggesting I put pressure on her?' she demanded, rising to her feet. 'I can assure you I did not.' The solicitor shook his head, wearing a half-smile as he looked at Samuel, warning him to say nothing more.

She remembered the visit of the solicitor, the doctor and others whom she presumed to be witnesses to a will shortly before the old lady's death. Turning to the solicitor she asked,

'Did this happen recently? Was that why you came to see her in the week before her death?'

'No, it was added to her will several weeks before, on Monday 28 March to be precise. She told me she was delighted to have found you, said you were a dear friend. More recently, Mrs Thomas arranged a meeting with a doctor and others to be reassured that her wishes would not be overturned.' It was his turn to glare at Samuel. 'Now, if there is nothing further, Mr Thomas?' Rising, clearly dismissing them, he added, 'It will be a few weeks before everything is settled, Mr Thomas. My secretary will be in touch to arrange another appointment.' Then he smiled as he handed Faith a cheque. 'Thank you for coming. I wish you joy of it, Miss Pryor. Whatever you chose to do with it, I hope it will give you great pleasure.' He walked behind them to the door and after closing it he muttered, 'I wish it had been more!'

Faith went out holding the cheque in her hand, glancing down at it as she walked to the bank. It offered many opportunities, but her thoughts were too jumbled to think of how it would be used. She was still angry at Samuel's suspicions and only the rather satisfied smile on the face of the solicitor had calmed her anger sufficiently to walk out with dignity.

The money went into her bank account and she walked away from the counter with realization dawning. There was now no urgency to find work once the three months of childminding were over. She could move right away from here, put as much distance between it and herself as she needed to be sure she'd never see Matt again. Or she could retrain for a new career, buy a second-hand car, take time out and travel, she could perhaps rent a house of her own. The opportunities opened out. Firstly she would talk to Winnie, who was thankfully recovered from her illness. Perhaps this time she'd decide to stay, not take the usual option of running away.

'Wonderful news!' Winnie exclaimed when Faith once again phoned the corner shop. 'Come on, let's meet in Cardiff and celebrate.'

'That will be a second celebration. I'm going back to invite Jean Painter, my new landlady, for her favourite treat: egg and chips at a café. No, better than that, *double* egg and chips,' she joked.

On the following day she thought seriously about how the money would be used. The day was cold, with a cruel wind whipping around every corner. She didn't take the boys to the park as she usually did and instead took out paper, scissors, pencils and crayons. She entertained them by encouraging them to draw pictures and make simple models which they then coloured.

Using their handiwork she talked about shape and colour and later they proudly discussed with their parents what they had learned. For Faith the day was sheer enjoyment and she knew what she wanted to do with her life. It was an idea that had entered her thoughts from time to time, but which she had abandoned as an impossibility. With the generous gift from Mrs Thomas, she would start a saving plan which one day would be used to open a day nursery for pre-school children.

She felt warmed by having made the decision, aware that it would be far into the future, but knowing that it was undoubtedly the right one. But first she had to earn money and add to her savings. Buying equipment and renting accommodation would take a lot more than one hundred pounds but it was a very encouraging start. She silently thanked her employer who had also been her friend.

She had heard nothing more from Ian and she assumed that he had grown tired of her evasive attitude. She hesitated to call him. Until Matt was somehow completely out of the picture she wasn't able to cope with any close friends, specially one who might become something more. Then she met his mother.

'Faith. Faith, dear, wait for me or I'll soon be out of puff!'

Faith heard the call and was filled with dread. The voice sounded like Matt's mother's and the instinct to run was strong. Forcing herself to turn around it was with relief that she recognized Ian's mother, who had dropped her baskets and was standing gasping for breath. 'Heavens, dear, I haven't run as fast as that for years!'

'I'm sorry, Mrs Day. I didn't realize you were calling me.' She picked up the shopping and said, 'Come on, there's a café across the road. I'll buy you a cup of tea to apologize.'

She brought Mrs Day up to date with what had happened since Mrs Thomas had died and was scolded for not letting Ian know where she had gone. 'He likes you, dear, and hopes you consider him a friend.'

'I do, but life is so complicated. So many changes. I don't know what I want, and everything is so up in the air, I wake sometimes and wonder where I am and what I'm doing.'

'Your accommodation, is it comfortable?'

'Yes, and Jean Painter provides me with meals as well as the room so I'm very lucky. And looking after Menna Gardener's three boys has given me an idea for the future.' She discussed her idea of opening a nursery and as she talked the idea began to grow.

As they stood to leave Mrs Day said, 'Come and have lunch with us one day. What about Sunday?' she added quickly as she saw Faith begin to frown. 'Ian will come for you and he'll take you back. Lovely it'll be, just the three of us.'

'Thank you. That would be very nice.' Trying to hide her anxiety Faith asked, 'Where do you live?' If it was anywhere near Matt she would find an excuse not to go.

'Up by Victoria Park, and please, call me Vivienne,' she was told, and she sighed inwardly with relief.

Ian came for her at twelve and took her to a house that was warm and welcoming. There were flowers everywhere, some fresh and some dried and many made of paper. The table was set perfectly and fires in the dining room and living room were blazing brightly. It was a new and wonderful feeling to have someone take so much trouble for her.

The house was quite large, with two bay-windowed rooms at the front and two more rooms downstairs. Behind the house was a long, level garden and beyond lay fields just perfect for taking children on nature walks. She imagined such a place as accommodation for her nursery and dreamed of where each activity would take place.

She met Ian and Vivienne several times during the following days, which took them up to Christmas 1960. Sometimes Ian and his mother were together, sometimes he was alone and they walked and talked, but always she had that tight feeling in her heart, knowing she was keeping from him the most important story of all. Her daughter was ten months old, crawling, standing maybe, and beginning to develop her unique personality. She had left it too long and now it seemed impossible to explain.

She did tell him something about her sad childhood and the years before Matt came into her life and ruined it completely.

'It was the evacuation of children during the war that separated me from my family,' she told him. 'My sister Joy and I were promised a place where we could stay together but we were separated at once and I didn't hear from either Joy or my parents again.'

'Weren't there organizations to deal with reunions after the war?' he asked.

'I tried them all, but my father was dead and nothing was known of my mother. I went from the evacuee accommodation to a children's home. I went from one authority to another which would have made it difficult for them to find me. Then I was fostered several times.'

'Was that better?'

'It might have been, some places were better than others.' She smiled. 'I ran away several times and once I got on a train convinced that at the other end of the journey I'd find my family. I was labelled as a troublesome child and that meant yet another new foster-family, then another and another. I eventually settled with a childless couple but they almost immediately learned that they were expecting a child of their own. I had been chosen as a substitute long after they had given up hoping, but with the birth of Jane everything changed. I was no longer wanted, but I think they tried to do what was right; keeping me instead of sending me back to the home was what they thought was best for me.'

'And there you stayed until you decided to move on?'

'I left when it was decided I was old enough to manage on my own. They did their best, I was fed and clothed and looked after but never loved, specially after Jane was born. I was very difficult, I have to admit that, and I definitely made things worse. They went on holidays to which I wasn't invited. I had to go into the home each time, until they got back.'

'But you managed to train as a teacher. That must have taken determination.'

'As sometimes happens with children like me, difficult, argumentative but with something they recognize as possibilities, a teacher took an interest and talked to my foster-parents. She explained that my difficult behaviour was partly frustration, that I was bright and offered to coax me through my exams.

'Fortunately and thanks to that dedicated teacher, I won a scholarship. I had no friends, so no distractions and I concentrated on my work. I sailed through the exams and qualified as a teacher in 1958 and . . .'

She shrugged and turned away as though that was the end of the story. She couldn't tell him the rest. How could she explain clinging to Nick in desperation when it was fear of loneliness and not love that made her dream of marrying him? Or why she had moved in with Matt when she was far from sure it was what she wanted? Or how she had given in to Matt's persuasions when he decided she was ready for love, and had even booked a wedding that she didn't want. And worst of all, how could she look at Ian's kind and loving face and tell him she had given birth to a child then walked away from her? They went into a café and Ian asked no more questions, sensing her reluctance to say more.

His own story was simple. He was twenty-five, had completed his two years' National Service, which he served in the RAF, and was now a salesman driving from town to town on a series of regular routes, selling office equipment. 'And I still live at home with my mam,' he said with a smile. 'I know I should have moved on, but she's alone and we get on so well that staying seems the sensible thing to do.'

'You've never been married?' she asked.

'I came close,' he said. 'The house where we live was bought with the intention of living there with my then fiancée. She left. It was terrible at first although perhaps the embarrassment of explaining to friends was a large part of that.' He reached out and held her hands, staring into her eyes, his own crinkled with his smile. 'Now I feel nothing but relief.'

'I thought Nick and I might marry, but I don't think we'd have been happy.'

'Nick?' he queried. 'My fiancée Tessa went off with someone called Nick.'

Comparing notes they unravelled the coincidence. 'No wonder we get on so well,' Ian said with a chuckle. 'We're both happy rejects!'

* * *

It had been arranged with Menna Gardener for Faith to have one day a week completely free from the boys and on one of these days she went to Cardiff to meet Winnie. They met in a café where Faith sat in a corner facing the door, warily watching people as they entered, unable to completely relax, afraid of seeing Matt or Carol or someone who knew them. She also continued with the fanciful idea that one day she would see her sister and recognize her, even though they hadn't met since she was one year old and Joy was three.

Their day was spent walking around the shops, stopping twice more to sit in a café and talk, amusing each other by relating stories about the children. They didn't see the man who ran the news agency a few doors away from Matt and Carol. He stopped and watched them for a few moments then hurried off. *This will be something to tell Matt.* He couldn't wait to get home.

* * *

Winnie was getting the children to bed, Paul was watching the television when there was an impatient banging on the door. Paul answered it and Matt burst in calling for Winnie.

'Hey! Get out of here!' Paul shouted, grabbing the man and trying to push him back out through the door.

'Where's your wife? She knows where Faith is and I demand that she tells me.'

Winnie came slowly down the stairs three little heads watching from the banisters.

'Leave now, Matt and I'll come and talk to you later. Otherwise,' she added as he struggled to reach her, 'Paul will phone the police.'

'Just tell me where she is.'

'Later, Matt.'

Matt relaxed, his shoulders bowed, but as he left he straightened up, raised a fist and said. 'You'd better come or I'll come looking for you, right?'

'That's it. My wife isn't coming anywhere near you,' Paul warned and as the man began to struggle again, using aggressive language, Winnie said, 'Look at yourself, Matt! Do you really need me to explain why she left you?'

'I never harmed Faith. What's she been telling you?'

After a few more attempts to persuade Winnie to talk, Matt left. 'I know she's in Cardiff, that's where you were seen,' he shouted, as Paul closed the door behind him. Winnie and Paul discussed things for a while then Winnie wrote to Faith explaining what had happened.

Faith read the letter and sighed. Cardiff was a forbidden area for a while, and meeting Winnie was too risky. What a mistake she had made by running away. If she'd been strong enough to face up to it things would have been sorted out by now and she would be free of him. But thinking of the baby she couldn't really have any regrets. The baby could not have been given to him, and that was the reason why she acted the way she had. This was her burden to bear, she had brought it upon herself with her weakness in not standing up to Matt. Walk away from him, that's what she should have done, not let things go on until she'd had to walk away from her tiny, helpless baby.

* * *

It was February 1961, the month in which her daughter would be celebrating her first birthday, when she looked after Menna's boys for the final week, although she promised to help on occasional Saturday mornings. Jake and Keith would be starting school and nursery respectively after the Easter holiday and the youngest, Patrick, would be able to fit in with his parents' activities as they worked on the new business they were setting up, selling gifts by post. Faith knew she would miss them but thankful that Saturday mornings would continue for a while.

Fortunately, having decided to return to teaching, she was offered a vacancy in the school that Jake would attend, and at the beginning of the summer term she began teaching the fascinating class of first-timers.

She didn't meet the pupils' mothers immediately, although some stopped by and introduced themselves. Most of the mothers had met the teacher at the beginning of the school year in September and the change of teacher didn't warrant much involvement. The children were settled and would soon become accustomed to the new face. She took a long time calling and marking the register on those first few days, looking at each child and beginning to memorize their names.

The school wasn't far from Jean and Roland's house and she walked both ways each day. On Friday when her first week was completed she was surprised to see Ian waiting for her among the chattering mothers. He led her to the car and drove her to a café, where he ordered tea and toasted teacakes and found them a table near the window.

'Mam tells me you're thinking of setting up a nursery for three-and four-year-olds,' he said. 'Don't forget, I can supply all the paper, pencils and the rest.'

'Special price?' she asked teasingly.

'Special price for a special lady.'

'It won't be for some time. The money Mrs Thomas left was a wonderful start, though. Building up a few shillings at a time seemed impossible but with a bank balance like that I feel encouraged.'

'Meanwhile you're happy at school?'

'Very much so. The experience will help too. My job will be partly to prepare them for lessons, to widen their knowledge in an interesting way and open their minds to new things.'

'What else?'

'Social development.'

'It sounds fascinating.' He covered her hand with his own. 'What a wonderful mother you'll make one day.'

The words so innocently spoken ruined her mood and she quickly left, refusing his offer of a lift, insisting she preferred to walk. Ian let her go, remembering that her bags and books were in his car which gave him an excuse to call on her later, when she had calmed down from whatever had so suddenly upset her.

Motherhood? Was that the reason for her sudden distress? Being brought up without a family of her own might still be a painful memory. He tried to imagine a world without his family, nothing to anchor him where he belonged. Affection for Faith grew and he wanted to be her anchor, someone on whom she could completely rely. Then her nickname came into his mind and his dream shattered. He looked at the corner for a last glimpse, hope and happiness flowing out of him, disappearing with the last of her shadow. The runaway. She would leave him too; it was clearly what she did whenever she met trouble. She would leave him just as Tessa had.

* * *

Faith walked for a long time, upset, aware of the mess she had made of her life. She considered the usual solution. Should she walk away now, before she was so deeply involved that the pain would be intolerable?

Approaching the house on Saturday morning, where Menna stood looking curiously up and down the street, she shook away the tempting thought. Standing her ground was the only way she would ever find happiness — but did she have the strength?

She increased her pace and waved cheerily to Menna. Then she saw the van. Matt had found her. He was the reason Menna was looking for her. Just in time she realized that Menna's gestures were not a greeting but an urgent signal for her to go round the back.

'I didn't know who he was,' Menna explained later, 'but there was something I didn't like about his questions. And he seemed to be simmering with anger. I don't want to pry but Roland and I guessed there was something you were afraid of, so I phoned Winnie and she warned me not to tell him where to find you.'

Faith thanked her and promised that one day she would explain. One day, if she really intended to stay, the whole sordid story would have to be told.

CHAPTER FIVE

Faith couldn't sleep. She had to tell her friends the truth, painful as it would be. When Jean came down breakfast was laid and the kettle humming ready to make the tea. When they had eaten, Jean asked her what was wrong, 'Do you want to leave? I'll quite understand if you have found somewhere more convenient.'

Faith looked at her sadly. 'No, I'm very happy here but after I tell you my story you might prefer to find someone more deserving of your kindness. I had a child, you see and for reasons I can't explain, I had her adopted.' Jean listened in silence until Faith had finished.

'Can you tell me why?'

Faith shook her head. 'I've told no one. Perhaps one day I'll be ready to explain, but sufficient for you to know that I'm a woman who abandoned her daughter and after living a childhood like mine, not belonging anywhere, it's impossible to justify without telling the full story and that's something I can't do. I'm sorry.'

Jean said little but she hugged the tearful Faith and said, 'Please stay with us. Knowing you, I feel sure your reasons were good ones. Now, what about another cup of tea? This one's gone cold.'

Faith had arranged to look after Menna's and Geoff's children for the day and after talking to Winnie and explaining that she intended to tell them about Matt, they went together.

'I'm sorry,' she began, when they had been invited in and Geoff had joined them, 'but I don't think I can look after your children again. I don't want to be the cause of bringing that man into your house and I don't think he'll give up now he's found me.'

'What are you afraid of?' Geoff asked. 'We don't want to pry, your life is your own, but surely we can find a way round this?'

'We don't want you to stop being our friend,' Menna added. 'We all love having you here. We trusted you with our children, surely that shows we're your friends?'

'My ex-fiancé has found me and he's an angry man. I can't risk him coming here and causing trouble so I'm moving away. The runaway,' she added tearfully. 'That's what they call me and that's what I am. Any trouble and instead of facing it I move on.'

Geoff quietly but firmly asked for a full explanation. 'We're your friends and so are Winnie and Paul. We can sort this out if you can trust us.'

Faith hesitated. Could she risk telling them? Maybe the story would spread, become distorted, making her into the villain and Matt the cruelly treated victim. But surely it was better that they should have her version first. They waited in silence, waiting for her to speak and after prolonged soul-searching she handed them the notes she had copied from the old newspapers. She watched for their reaction, her heart racing with the fear of their telling her they were no longer her friends. They were the first people she had told.

Matt Hewitt had appeared in court charged with the rape of a fourteen-year-old girl, Ethel Holland, who gave birth to a child nine months after the attack. The charge of rape was dropped under pressure from Matt's defence despite the girl's distress and injuries but he had spent a term in prison for sexual misconduct with a minor.

'The dates are all there, you can see the papers in the library. When I read them I knew I had to leave him. Some say people can change, but do they? He could deny it, claim he was innocent, that the attack was made by someone else, but a fourteen-year-old girl? Giving birth? How could she not have been believed?'

Geoff asked if she'd agree to him talking to the police. 'There are ways of preventing him from bothering you,' he said.

'No. Please. I don't want the police involved.' They were certain to find out about her own shame. She couldn't tell them about the baby she had abandoned. She needed their sympathy and she would surely lose it if they learned of that. Once the police were involved everyone would know. The story would be exaggerated and slanted by different tellers depending on their opinion of her and of Matt. She would be criticized for abandoning her child. For most that would be far worse than an ancient story about a girl who was probably partly to blame anyway — dropping the charge of rape and the sentencing showed that to be the opinion of the court. Rape was still a difficult charge to bring, even with a child as young as Ethel Holland.

Winnie had been silent but she cried as she read the story of the fourteen-year-old suffering such distress.

'So this is why you walked away from your daughter?' she said as they walked home.

'I believed she stood a better chance of growing up without a temper if she lived with a family far away from Matt.'

'Because she was Matt's child?'

'No, I told you. Matt wasn't her father.' Faith lied.

'The part of this that saddens me most is that you couldn't tell me,' Winnie said quietly.

'You're my friend and after this you might not have been.'

'Why ever not? You aren't to blame in any of this. I know how hard it must have been to walk away from your daughter and I know the reason was love for the little scrap.'

For several days after Matt's visit Faith was expecting him to appear at any moment. She walked to school with her head down, dreading to hear Matt calling her name. She hurried home each day and didn't feel safe until she was in her room. Jean was always there and she would bring up a tray and stay for a few minutes to ask about her day with the children. The conversations never included Matt or her lost child.

Grief and distress always strengthened the dream of finding her sister. 'If only I could find Joy,' she said one morning during breakfast. 'I can't help wondering whether my mother found Joy and didn't search for me. Perhaps she simply didn't want me.'

'What a lot of old *tosh*! Didn't you tell me you'd moved several times? Things were confused during and after the war. Houses and even whole streets were demolished and people moved on. Evacuees were sent from one family to another, records were destroyed during bombing raids. It's hardly surprising that people were lost amid it all.'

'I was given the surname of my foster-parents at one stage and it was months before the error was found and rectified.'

'Well, there you are then. That incident alone must have caused chaos.'

'But it's still hard to understand why I wasn't found.'

'These confusions could easily explain why your mother didn't find you, it wasn't that she didn't search. After all, mothers don't abandon their babies, do they?'

That hurt. Abandoning her child was exactly what she had done, so how could she complain if her mother had done the same?

'Oh, Faith, I'm sorry! I understand why you made that difficult decision, really I do.'

Swallowing her guilt, Faith murmured, 'Thanks Jean. I know you're trying to help.'

* * *

Matt kicked patterns in the sawdust on the floor of his workshop and listened without real interest as a customer considered the purchase of a garden ornament. She eventually settled for a heron, one of Matt's own favourites and, because he didn't like the customer's superior manner he added two pounds to the price. The woman paid without demure and he promised delivery later that day.

When she had gone he abandoned work for the day and spent the time getting in touch with the various organizations that had promised to help him. The child was not registered as his and Faith had been thorough in her arrangements regarding adoption. Angry and frustrated, he told several people how she had lied and deprived him of his child before abandoning her. The story of Faith walking away from her newly born child spread fast. The facts were embroidered and weighted against her with every telling and soon everyone knew. Disliked though he was, most felt sympathy for Matt and a few began to treat him with a hesitant friendliness.

* * *

Jean and Roland heard the rumours and said little apart from initial sympathy but Faith could see they were embarrassed. Winnie tried to offer her full support but, not knowing the child was Matt's, even she found her friend's behaviour hard to understand.

Faith apologized to the Painters for not telling the truth and gave them the same explanation as she had given Winnie for wanting her child to live without Matt in her life. Even to herself the story sounded weak. Abandoning a child when she could have walked away from Matt and taken her daughter with her? Without giving them the full story how could they understand? Paul was the only one to agree with her action.

'You were right to keep your little girl away from him,' he said. 'I believe we are what we are born with but influences in our environment decided what we do with what we inherit. She would have learned only bad things from Matt.'

Faith thanked him for his words of comfort.

Every day was a nightmare for Faith. Child protection officers and social workers appeared with polite but determined questions and they were followed by the police who came in answer to Matt's accusations that she had stolen his baby. Many concerned people wanted to know the truth and more and more disbelieved her story, insisting that she was a heartless woman who didn't want the trouble of bringing up her child. Faith gave them all an edited version to which she rigidly adhered throughout every attempt to persuade her to admit the child was Matt's.

Matt's mother came and pleaded tearfully for her to let Matt have his baby but Faith was adamant. 'She was nothing to do with Matt. The baby's father went away and Matt must have known that,' she insisted. She had to continue her lies.

Thank goodness she had refused to marry Matt and thank goodness too that she had delayed moving into his home and his bed. It was those two facts that saved her. The baby, whom she tried not to think of as Dorothy but as 'the child' was born fairly soon after she went to live with Matt and his mother. Her insistence that the child was the result of a previous affair had to be accepted.

The local paper carried the story, making a headline of how local teacher, Miss Faith Pryor walked away from her newly born, illegitimate child and this was seen by enough people who knew her for it to reach the desk of her headmistress. Faith was summoned to the headmistress's office where the woman sat at her desk over which was spread copies of the local newspapers.

The stern-faced headmistress waved a hand over the various accounts and asked, 'Is this true?'

'More or less.' Faith tried to keep her voice from quavering.

The interview that followed was distressing and resulted in her being asked to leave.

'To have a child out of wedlock, then to abandon her is not a suitable background for a woman who teaches small children,' she was told. The Easter Parade in 1961 would be the end of her teaching career.

As always, her instinct was to move, start again somewhere far away from the scene of her disgrace, reviving her nickname of *the runaway*. Winnie and Paul persuaded her to stay.

'You can't outrun stories like yours,' Paul said wisely, 'but you can outlive them. Next week there'll be someone else's story to talk about and although yours will be revived from time to time, the immediacy will be gone. You'll be old news.'

'Give it a chance,' Winnie pleaded. 'Stay with Jean or here, with us. You won't find it difficult to get work even though it won't be what you'd choose to do. Give yourself time to decide what you really want to do with your life.'

They didn't ask any more questions about the baby but listened sympathetically when Faith needed to talk about the distress of parting with her and Faith was grateful for their friendship.

Ian arrived one day and she knew the time had come to trust her friends with the truth. 'I need to talk to you about this stuff in the papers,' she said.

'Good,' was his almost casual response. 'We can walk in Porthkerry Park, it's quiet there. Was it Nick's child?' he encouraged when the silence stretched out. 'Did he leave you once he was told about the baby?'

'The child was Matt's. But please,' she begged, 'please don't tell anyone. I've told no one else that particular truth. Not even Winnie and Paul.'

'Winnie's your friend. You should have trusted her.'

'After lying to the authorities including the police? I dare not.'

He nodded but then a frown creased his forehead and she had to tell him more. 'Matt was forceful, difficult to refuse,' she said. 'I know that makes me sound weak but I was desperate to belong to a family and the temptation was too much, I ignored the warning signs. Carol, Matt's mother, was kind and gentle and very persuasive and although I wasn't ready for more than friendship and the occasional kiss, I was persuaded, encouraged into . . .' she glanced at him and changed what she had been about to say. 'When I told them I was expecting a child they were overjoyed. I felt important for the first time in my life, I was wanted, and cherished. I didn't love Matt, in fact I was a little afraid of him, but the need for a family was strong. I'd almost given up on finding my sister. That hope comes and goes. I delayed sharing his home for as long as I could. I knew it wasn't the right thing to do but I ignored the doubts and, well, I moved in. After being alone all my life, with not a single person who belonged to me, I was looking at a bleak future if I walked away from what might have been my last chance of marriage and children.'

'Is that why you were with Nick? The fear of being alone.'

'I'm not proud of it, but yes. I clung to him as an escape from continually running from one place to another, always alone.'

'I think I understand that. You didn't settle because all the time you hoped to be reunited with your family.'

She stared at him. 'You're the first person to understand. I don't think I understood it myself, not until you put it into words.'

'And leaving the baby?' he coaxed.

'I longed to hold my daughter in my arms and I accepted that Matt would have to be a part of my life. Then, by chance I found this newspaper story and fear, for my baby, and myself, completely engulfed me.' She took the notes from her handbag and waited while he read them. 'I knew I had to escape but where would I go? The birth was imminent and I had very little money. So I invented the story I would tell and made all the arrangements. I gave birth then ran away. The Runaway, that's what they call me,' she added tearfully.

Ian said nothing. They walked back to the car in silence and when he drove her home he kissed her gently as he left. She had the heart-breaking belief that the kiss meant goodbye.

Winnie deserved to be told the truth and she went round and told her and Paul everything. 'Winnie, I'm sorry I lied to you,' she apologized.

‘So it really was Matt’s child?’

‘Yes, she was Matt’s child. There has never been anyone else. I didn’t want her brought up in that house with its threat of violence.’

‘But why didn’t you take the baby when you left?’ was Paul’s question.

‘I believed that if I denied that Matt was the father the baby would grow up free of him, that being brought up in a home far from any influence he might have, would be the best chance for her.’ She looked at them and knew that they weren’t convinced.

* * *

A week later Faith made her decision. It had been a week of watching the local children enjoying their spring holiday, groups of them in the park, noisily playing on the swings and roundabouts, some picnicking on the grass among the early flowers. Being a part of all this was what she had imagined. She heard the laughter she was unable to share and felt that her life was over.

She had a small amount of money, enough to rent and furnish a house and, if she could take a paying guest it would give her a chance to consider what to do next.

She had seen nothing of Ian since she had told him of her sordid past and didn’t expect to. Although he hadn’t shown it, he must have been shocked and disappointed to learn that she was capable of walking away from her child. Even with the explanation she had given he would no longer be able to trust her. After a glimpse of real happiness she was alone, as she had always been. She could not have known that he had waited outside the school each afternoon for several days before presuming she had seen him and chosen to avoid him. She was alone and it was better she faced it. That way life couldn’t throw up any more disappointments.

She chose a house in a lane not far from the railway station in the older part of the town. Cadoxton had once been a separate village with its school and beautiful old church but now it was a part of the expanding town of Barry. The house was small but double-fronted with bay windows and although it was neglected she knew it had once been an attractive property and might be again. The main rooms were a reasonable size and a once beautiful wooden-framed sun room was at the back where it would catch the early-morning sun.

The whole place was in dire need of attention. The paintwork was scuffed and in places what had been good-quality paper was hanging from the walls. The ceilings were dark with neglect. But the rent was low and she planned gradual improvement, looking forward to wielding a paintbrush — something she had never before attempted.

She said a regretful goodbye to her pleasant room and promised to keep in touch with Jean and Roland, although she thought that unlikely; she was going to be kept busy. She gathered her few belongings and went to No 3 Railway Cottages. Had she at last found the place where she would make her home, she wondered?

A shop in the main street provided her with the tools and paint needed for the first stage, painting the front windows and door. As she was arranging for its delivery later that day a voice called her name. She turned with dread, and was so relieved when she saw Ian and his mother in the doorway that she smiled and ran towards them. Then she stopped. They wouldn't want to show any sign of pleasure at seeing her, not after being told the truth. Sadly she stopped and asked, 'How are you?'

She was surprised when Ian said, 'Better for seeing you.'

'We were sorry about the newspaper story, dear,' Vivienne said. 'But you shouldn't have avoided seeing us, we're your friends, aren't we?'

'I thought you wouldn't want to see me now the truth is out. When you didn't call or write I presumed . . .'

'Presuming, now that's dangerous,' Ian said. 'I don't recommend it.' And to her relief his smile widened.

Her items were put in a box and he pointed to it. 'It's all right, I'll take this for the lady.' He lifted it off the counter and said, 'Lead on, the car is outside. Open the boot, Mam, and I'll put these instruments of torture in. Sandpaper, paint, brushes, a garden spade and fork, seems like a lot of work, where on earth are you living, a building site?' Suddenly the project was imbued with an air of fun.

Vivienne looked round the house with Faith as Ian unpacked the supplies. Then they all went round together as Faith explained what she intended to do. 'A lodger or even two might be possible,' she explained. 'I have the permission of the landlord, especially as I've promised to do the necessary repairs and decoration.'

No further reference was made to the newspaper story as they stacked the paint tins and the rest. Ian looked at the woodwork and the loose wallpaper and made a few suggestions about the necessary treatment. 'I have a quiet week next week so, if you like I'll come and help.'

'I'm told that the preparation is the most tedious part, so yes please, if you're sure you want to. Specially as I don't really know what I have to do apart from what the man in the shop explained.'

The first thing Faith did when she moved in was to write to all the people who might be able to help find her sister, giving them her new address. Even though so many years had passed and the possibility of finding Joy was only a dream, she would never completely give up hope.

During the following week Ian came whenever he was free, sometimes with Vivienne, sometimes alone, and he helped prepare and paint the front of the sad-looking house. When he wasn't there Faith cleaned and tidied the inside and began preparing two bedrooms for prospective lodgers. She slept downstairs on a couch that had been left by a previous tenant, planning to prepare a room for herself once the arrangements for paying guests were complete. Second-hand shops provided the minimum amount of furniture she needed and even curtains, and cleaning and adjusting her finds kept her up long into the night.

She concentrated on the house to the exclusion of everything else, although she knew the need to work and earn money could not be ignored for much longer. Apart from Ian and his mother and a few shop assistants, she saw no one. That too mustn't continue. Changing from the Runaway to being the Hermit, was not a step in the right direction, she warned herself.

The advertisement for a paying guest had appeared in the local paper in July and at first Faith fussed over the house as though its cleanliness was an important exam. She watched the lane for the sign of a caller but the only person she saw, apart from Ian and Vivienne, was Winnie.

'Have you thought about a job, yet?' Winnie asked, when they were settled in the shade of an apple tree in the overgrown garden.

'Not really. I've been concentrating on getting the house clean and tidy. Working with children is what I do best but that's no longer possible and I can't decide what to do next. Any ideas? I've prepared a couple of rooms with the help of Ian and his mother and, I've advertised for a lodger.'

'Any replies?'

'Not yet. I suppose people are still talking about that newspaper article and are afraid to take a chance on me.'

'Pity you left the school.'

'Pity I left? I was told to go when all this came out!'

'Their loss!' Winnie replied crisply. 'Come on, we can walk around and look at the advertisements in shop windows and buy the local paper, reply to a few enquiries. There must be plenty of people looking for a decent place to live.'

'Decent place?' Faith laughed. 'You haven't seen the rest of the house! I've cleaned a couple of rooms plus the kitchen and the small sun room but the rest is still a mess.'

'Can I see?'

It was wonderful to discuss it with someone. Apart from Ian and Vivienne no one had seen it since she had moved in. Despite all the stories and rumours, Winnie was still her friend and she was grateful.

'We've got a few things you might be able to use,' Winnie said as she explored the remaining rooms. 'A chest of drawers and a couple of chairs. Paul can bring them if you'd like them.' For a reply. Faith moved towards her and gave her a hug.

Ian arrived as Winnie was about to leave and she stayed a while longer, going into the kitchen where paint tins and the rest of the paraphernalia of decorating filled a rickety table, and making tea. She chatted to Ian about her childhood memories, making him laugh and add stories of his own.

Faith sat a little apart from them and it was as though she were a stranger there. She wanted Winnie to leave. Frightened and inexplicably apprehensive, she felt like an outsider looking in. Was it a reminder for her not to take anything for granted? To remind her that friendships were transitory and Ian was just a naturally friendly and helpful man?

He had called to deliver a pair of curtains his mother had found and when Winnie left, he walked to the gate with her. They stood talking and laughing for a few moments, then Ian obviously offered her a lift and, with a wave, they set off together.

A few days later, the two rooms she had managed to prepare for lodgers, or paying guests, as Vivienne called them, were completed, although only one was fully furnished. Faith had received several enquiries and had set up interviews with two of them.

Winnie and Paul and their family arrived in a van with furniture, a few ornaments and cushions and pictures. Jack, Bill and Polly ran from room to room like frantic puppies, shouting at each discovery. Ian and Vivienne arrived and, seeing Winnie breathless as she and Faith tried to move a chair into the chosen position, Ian went to help, laughing, teasing Winnie and calling her Olive Oil, Popeye's skinny girlfriend. The two men sat and discussed the garden, drawing plans of what could be done and the evening ended with them all in the garden, sipping some home-made lemonade brought by Vivienne.

When she went to bed on the now familiar couch that night, Faith felt hope and rising excitement. Perhaps this really was the place where she would finally make her home. Ian might not be a transient friend just helping out someone in trouble, but might stay and become a permanent part of her life. Her life was certainly beginning to open out in the most unexpected way. All I have to do now, she reminded herself, is get a job, and fill these empty rooms.

Then as sleepiness began to make her thoughts hazy, the usual sorrowful picture that always ended her day raced back and she imagined the tiny form of her child. Seeing only her black hair, her head turned away from her, so her face was unimaginable.

CHAPTER SIX

Several people called to look at the larger of the rooms Faith planned to let, and she eventually took two single women, nurses, who were working at the local hospital. Both said they wanted the accommodation for three months only and Faith decided that that was a good plan. The alternative was to advertise the rooms as holiday accommodation, and that would mean more work, dealing with changed occupation every Saturday. Three months would give her a chance to try the idea of sharing her very first home with strangers. She could change her mind if she wasn't completely happy about it.

Ian's mother, Vivienne, continued to offer support and called often with a few additions to the furnishings. She brought flowers, as well as some small items similar to those Winnie had considered necessary, such as ornaments and cushions, the things that made a house into a home. Ian was away from home, travelling around the towns and villages of Somerset on his monthly visits.

It was as she was putting the finishing touches to the third bedroom, which would be her own, that Mrs Monk called. Olive Monk was in her late forties and her two sons came with her. She introduced them as Colin and Graham, aged twenty and twenty-one. 'They're in the Navy, see,' Mrs Monk explained, 'and they want me to find a safe little room where I can wait for them to finish their time. Then we'll get a house together.'

Something about the story seemed odd. Young men would be looking for a place of their own, wouldn't they? When she suggested this, Mrs Monk nodded agreement.

'I keep hoping they'll find a nice wife and settle down but they insist they want me settled first. Lovely boys they are.'

Doubtfully, Faith showed them into the house where she explained about her own intention to deal with the breakfast and, if required, an evening meal. 'I won't allow the tenants to cook,' she said apologetically. 'My rooms and the kitchen are out of bounds apart from breakfast which, I hope, we'll eat together.'

'I understand,' Mrs Monk agreed. 'Can we see the room?'

Faith had given the largest room to the nurses. Later, if the nurses didn't stay, she would use it for summer visitors. Having chosen the middle room for herself, she showed the small back room to Mrs Monk and her sons.

'Oh dear,' the woman remarked as the door was opened. 'This'll never do. Never fit in here I won't, will I boys?'

'It's quite a good size, twelve feet by twelve. Plenty of room with just a bed, a chair and a wardrobe.'

'Where would I put me stuff?'

'If you would like another cupboard I can probably find one.'

'Not another cupboard. I need somewhere to sit and stretch me legs. Haven't you got something larger?'

'Sorry Mrs Monk, but this is all I have.' Faith felt a surge of relief, thinking the woman would walk away. There was something about the woman that made her distrustful, although she would have found it impossible to explain exactly what that something was. She didn't like the careless way the two young men were dressed. Their clothes were shabby and in need of an iron. On their feet they wore what the locals called daps — plimsoll's — that had once been white. Although she had no experience with Navy personnel, she didn't think these two looked the part. They weren't smart enough. The Senior Service, wasn't that what they were called? Neat and tidy was how she imagined sailors to be; surely, with the limited space on a ship, they had to be? And one of them had a moustache, small and a bit uneven and she half-remembered being told that a sailor had either the full set, full beard and moustache or had to be clean-shaven. Although, she conceded, that might no longer be true.

The two young men were standing at the window, looking out. One of them touched his mother on the shoulder and said, 'Mam, I think you should take it. Come and look at the garden. It's such a nice place to sit and look out at the flowers.'

'Not many flowers yet,' Faith said, 'but that will be my next project, to get some colour in the borders and improve the lawn.'

'We can help when we have our next leave,' the one called Colin offered.

'You'll enjoy watching the birds from here,' the other son said.

'All right, my sons know best, I'll take it.'

Faith nodded but with a feeling of regret. 'A month's trial on both sides?' she suggested on impulse and the woman stared at her but agreed. Then Mrs Monk spent several minutes trying to persuade her to reduce the price. Faith remained firm, still half-hoping the woman would change her mind. But eventually everything was agreed and two days later Mrs Monk moved in, with her sons helping. Again, seeing the odd collection of boxes and packages that went into the small room, Faith had misgivings, but she decided to give it a try. Thank goodness she'd added the month's trial proviso.

To her relief, Mrs Monk was a quiet tenant and caused her no concerns. Her sons, Colin and Graham visited and after three more days, shook Faith's hand and told her they were returning to their ship and wouldn't be back until October.

'Look after our mam, will you?' Colin asked. 'She gets very lonely while we're away.'

'Yes, there's no one else, see, only Mam and us boys.'

The nurses Catrin and Debbie moved into the front bedroom and the house settled into a pleasant routine. The rather ancient lean-to at the back, beyond the kitchen, was in need of attention, but it was sturdy and after a thorough cleaning it became the breakfast room. It was built of wood which, after sanding, staining and varnishing was discovered to be beautifully carved. Two cracked panes were replaced, the windows given some curtains and the slate floor a cheerful rug and it had an air of elegance that Faith had not expected.

With everything gleaming it was a pleasant place to sit. Ian had climbed up and removed the dead leaves which had fallen there from a nearby tree and washed the glass, letting in a surprising amount of extra light.

The first evening meal, a welcome to her guests, was a pleasant affair with each of her new lodgers adding to the friendly conversation and a little banter. It all augured well. Perhaps, Faith thought, crossing her fingers with hope, this new phase of my life will be a happy one.

At the end of the first week, Faith suddenly realized that her fear of seeing Matt arriving, forcing his way in, had subsided to little more than a memory. Thoughts of her daughter though were as powerfully painful as ever.

She was sitting in the breakfast-room one morning after clearing the breakfast dishes when there was a knock at the door. She went to answer it, a smile on her lips as she wondered whether it was Vivienne calling on her way to the shops. It was Mrs Monk. 'Sorry I am but I've lost my key. Silly of me. Do you have a spare?'

'No, I don't, but I'll get one cut when I go to the shops. I'd prefer you to find it though. Can you remember when you last had it?'

'I must have lost it between here and the main road. I'll ask in a few shops.'

‘I wish you would, Mrs Monk. I’ve already handed out three and I do want to keep track of where they are.’

‘I’ll go back now this minute.’ With a wave she trotted back down the path and through the gate. Twenty minutes later she was back, calling Faith, letting herself in with her key. She held it up and waggled it. ‘There, found by a young man it was. He was just about to hand it in to the butcher’s.’

Faith didn’t have a good look at the key but she thought it looked different, more shiny. Could she have had an extra one cut without telling me? Now I am getting paranoid, she thought with a grim smile. ‘Will you leave your door open on Friday,’ she asked. ‘I need to get in and clean.’

‘No need, Miss Pryor. I’ll do it myself. Oh, I’ve ordered a wireless, that all right? Love the wireless I do.’

Although most of her time was spent at the house Faith saw little of her neighbours. Apart from a smile and a polite wave, she hurried past their houses without any attempt at friendship. Using work as an excuse, she told herself that one day, when everything was settled she would talk to them and behave as a good neighbour should. Until then, she felt happier avoiding chatting with strangers.

The story in the newspapers, and the fact she had been asked to leave the school on the grounds she was unsuitable to work with children caused her shame and constant anxiety. Everyone must know about her troublesome past and she had the choice of explaining to practically everyone she met, or staying out of everybody’s way. She preferred the latter. Shopping, a walk through the fields to Dinas Powys or a brief visit to the park where she sat and watched children at play, these were her only escapes from the house and all the work it entailed.

She had explained to Vivienne her reluctance to go to Cardiff, but she was persuaded to change her mind and make arrangements to meet Winnie. ‘I’ll come with you and be your guard dog if you like, but I don’t think you’ll need me. Best for you to go on your own, face up to your fear. If you go during the week he’ll be working, won’t he?’

Arrangements were made by letter and, to reassure Faith, Winnie suggested they should travel separately, Winnie by bus, Faith on the train. Stepping off the train and seeing Winnie waving, smiling as she approached, was as exciting as some dates had been she told her friend with a smile. 'I feel like a prisoner let out of prison. Although the house doesn't really feel like a prison,' she added swiftly. 'I love it and working on it has been fun. My paying guests are very little trouble, more like friends.'

It was good to sit and exchange news. Faith made Winnie laugh as she listed her suspicions regarding Olive Monk, making them sound ridiculous. Although, she still had doubts about the woman and decided she would watch her with extra care.

Before they parted, Faith hesitantly asked if there was any news about the baby.

'Nothing. There isn't any way I *can* hear news of her,' Winnie reminded her gently. 'It's April 1961, she'll be fourteen months old and settled with her new family. I expect the authorities will be keeping a watch over her for some time so she'll be safe.'

'And Matt? Has he given up trying to prove he's the father?'

'According to his mother he is still demanding to have the child, but I presume the adoption has gone through and there's nothing he can do.'

'I always refer to it as fostering, it seems less final, but yes, she's legally adopted and no longer mine.'

'I'm sorry, Faith.'

'I made the right decision. If I had taken the child there'd be no end to Matt's determination to take control of her life. I couldn't wish him on my precious child. I did the right thing, I'm sure of that, no matter how I ache to see her, hold her, watch her grow. It was the worst thing I ever did in my life but the best for her. Can't you see that?' Tearfully, she kissed her friend goodbye and hurried towards the railway station.

'Yes. Yes, I can,' Winnie called after her.

* * *

Although she tried to hide it from her son, Carol Hewitt was constantly grieving. Life was cruel. She had two granddaughters, neither of whom she could see. The first one had been born after an accusation of rape and the trauma of the prison sentence, the second born to Faith who ran away and left her child, insisting Matt was not the father, denying her a granddaughter for a second time.

After the affair with Faith and the loss of the baby Matt showed no evidence of having a woman friend. He worked alone and was solitary in his spare time.

She had seen him flirting with customers once or twice but nothing came of it. It was as though Faith had destroyed a spark within him and there was no sign of it reigniting.

He was a handsome man with his strong physique, thick, jet-black hair and those deep, dark eyes, but women could see the underlying anger there and wouldn't take a chance. Anger swelled within her towards Faith. *Why hadn't she talked to me? I'd have explained, made her believe the story of the attack and rape of Ethel Holland was a lie.*

She was standing at the window when she saw a young woman come into the yard. She'd seen her before. She had bought a small rabbit statue as a gift for her parents. She crossed her fingers, hoping she had come back to talk to Matt.

She watched as they talked for a while and he showed her round his store and sketches of work he was soon to undertake. Then, to her relief, she saw him follow her to the gate and talk some more. They seemed reluctant to part.

'Who was that?' she asked casually when he came in later.

'Her name is Sue and I'm taking her out Saturday night,' he said.

'Good. She looked rather pleasant.'

On Friday, while Matt was at the bank, Sue knocked on the door and handed Carol a note. 'I'm sorry, but I can't manage Saturday. Will you give this to your son, please?'

'Another day?' Carol said amiably.

'I don't think so.' The girl looked anxious to leave.

'Heard some gossip I suppose. It isn't true, you know. It's lies, all of it. My son has been treated unfairly and—'

'I'm sorry.' The girl pushed the note into Carol's hand and hurried away.

When she told Matt he just shrugged. 'She knows Winnie, so I expect it was she who told her not to trust me.'

As soon as Matt left the house, Carol went to Winnie's door. When Paul opened it she demanded to talk to his wife.

Paul shook his head. 'No, I'm sorry but my wife is unwell,' he explained.

'Just tell her to stop interfering in my son's life!' Carol shouted. Paul apologized for his rudeness and firmly closed the door.

'She must have come to complain about Sue,' Paul said with a shrug. He sat near Winnie, who lay on the couch, her breathing laboured as they waited for the doctor to arrive.

* * *

Ian came home at the weekend and on Saturday afternoon he called to see Faith. She didn't hear the knock at the door and he found her in the garden. Brambles had torn her apron and brought chaos to her hair, her cheeks were rosy with the strenuous effort of clearing the overgrown hedge, there was mud on her cheeks and he thought she was beautiful. He stood for a long time just watching her, enjoying the sight of her.

The sound of the wireless came from the window of Mrs Monk's room and Ian nodded towards the sound. 'Your new lodger, I presume. Behaving, is she?'

'Ian! I didn't see you there. Yes, Olive spends a lot of time in her room and when she does go out she locks her door. She pays her rent on time and apart from the music being a bit loud at times, I have no complaints, although I've no way of knowing whether she keeps the place clean.'

'No smells of rotten cabbage or smelly socks?' he joked.

'No and I've no right to be curious,' she said as she threw down a pile of branches and walked towards him. 'She rents the room and everything behind the door is her private domain. It's strange just how little I see of her, though. I suspect she buys food and eats it in her room. She comes down for breakfast, that's included in the price of the room. And if there's any toast left she picks it up and takes it with her, says it's for the birds.' She laughed. 'Perhaps I don't have enough to do, eh? If I were working all day I wouldn't have time to worry about mysteries that don't exist.'

'Does she have any post? I presume her sons write from time to time.'

'That's another puzzle. She tells me news of them but I haven't seen any letters.'

'I thought I saw them the other day. They were pelting along the lane at the back of the houses not far from the town centre. I had the impression they were being chased.'

'It couldn't have been them, could it? If they were on leave they'd have come to see their mother.'

'Maybe.' Ian looked doubtful.

'I wish she'd let me go in and clean the room.'

'Don't worry. She's obviously happy to do it. Just waiting for her sons to come home must be very boring.'

'I can't help thinking there's something not quite straight about her.'

'What about the nurses?'

'They're pleasant, always stop for a chat and sometimes a cup of tea when they get in after their shift. I have to ask Mrs Monk to keep her wireless low when one of them is on nights and she willingly agrees.'

'So, not much trouble.'

'Everything is fine. I do want a job though, but what can I do? I'm trained to teach and with that denied me I'm at a loss.'

'A shop? Office work? What about your idea of opening a nursery for four-year-olds?'

She forced a smile and said, 'A nursery will probably be impossible, the education authorities will feel the same about nursery children as they do about schools. I'm unsuitable.' The smile slipped a little and she turned away.

'You could try,' he coaxed.

How could she tell him she couldn't face another rejection? Meeting Matt and being attracted to him had ruined more than she had realized. She felt tainted and wondered why Ian didn't feel that same distrust.

'Why have you remained my friend through all of this, Ian?' she asked softly.

He shrugged. 'Some people you warm towards, others you instinctively know you don't want in your life. And there are others who float past like motes in sunbeams, pleasant but unimportant. I don't want you to float past, I want you to stay.'

'Thank you,' she whispered. 'You have no idea how much it means to me to have you and your mother in my life.'

He grinned shyly. 'I might have hugged you, but you have dirt on your face.'

Her hand went to her cheeks and she looked down at her grubby apron, at her feet in muddy wellington boots. 'What must I look like?'

'A mucky cherub,' he replied. He put an arm on her shoulders and guided her to face the house. 'You go and tidy up and I'll finish piling this lot ready for a bonfire.'

'A bonfire? That sounds like fun.'

He sorted out the tangled branches and dead foliage, then built a fire, tucking newspapers and small twigs into the heart of it. 'It's a pity you haven't met your neighbours, we could have had a party.' He turned to look at her. She had changed now into a summer dress, her hair brushed back, sandals on her feet instead of the wellingtons. 'Now might be a good time. You're dressed for a special evening, what d'you think?'

Later that evening, as twilight invaded the garden and lights came on in the few nearby houses, they lit the bonfire. Ian carried out some potatoes and tucked them in the red-glowing edge. 'Add a few more,' Faith said. 'I'll see whether the neighbours will come and join us for an alfresco supper.'

Two hours later there was a party atmosphere in the garden of No 3, Railway Cottages. People she hardly knew came, and several brought flagons of beer and lemonade. It was the best introduction to the neighbourhood she could wish for. The nurses were there and they knocked on the door and invited Mrs Monk to come down.

'I'm in my dressing-gown,' she called back through the closed door.

'Then get dressed!' was the response, and she did.

One of the nurses brought her purse and said. 'I'm going to knock up Mrs Ellis, she won't mind.' Mrs Ellis ran the corner shop which sold everything from food to firewood and after a few moans about the inconsideration of people these days, she handed over bread and sandwich fillings and some crisps, together with a couple of flagons from her husband's supply. 'Pay me tomorrow,' the nurses were told. 'Closed I am and I don't want to open the till for you.'

'Come over and join the party, why don't you?'

'Right then. I'll bring a bit of cake.'

There was great activity in the small kitchen as food was prepared to add to the potatoes cooking in the garden fire. Everyone tried to help but it was impossible and eventually Faith and Olive Monk dealt with it.

The smoky smell from the fire and the crackle of wood burning reminded many of other such evenings, memories were revived and stories told. Nostalgia added its magic, giving an added charm to the tales of a dozen childhoods. The talk didn't stop people eating and the food disappeared swiftly. Mrs Monk found a loaf and some corned beef and cheese and Faith ignored the evidence that she was disobeying the rule about no food in the room, smiled knowingly and thanked her. The two women made more sandwiches to feed their unexpected guests.

The night grew dark, yet no one seemed to want to leave and when the moon climbed in the sky and gave its romantic light to the scene, the mood became sentimental. Songs were included in memories and the low singing was as beautiful as many a professional chorus, the lower voices harmonizing perfectly with the rest.

For Faith this was increasingly hard to take. Her own childhood had included no happy occasions like this with friends standing, or sitting on their coats, talking and laughing and singing sentimental songs. With her own child growing up in another family she wasn't making her own memories either. Her life was a mess.

The thanks, the affectionate remarks as the neighbours eventually departed, the promises to 'do this again,' were like arrows piercing her heart.

Ian and Mrs Monk stacked the dishes and Faith insisted on them leaving the rest for her to deal with in the morning. 'It's late,' she said. 'I'm always up early. Thank you both for helping. I don't know how we managed to have an impromptu party, but I know it wouldn't have been as successful without you, Mrs Monk, and you, Ian.'

'Friends we are, dear,' Mrs Monk said as she climbed the stairs. 'Call me Olive.'

'Call me soon,' Ian joked as he too departed.

Faith made herself one last cup of tea and prepared for bed. She was tired, but the bitter-sweet party had unsettled her. She no longer felt sad. There had been something uplifting about the unexpected friendliness of the people who lived nearby. She realized she had been foolish to lock herself away wrapped in guilt. She had made serious mistakes, but she was young enough to outgrow the gossip. As Winnie's husband Paul had said, news was immediate and as soon as another new story appeared, the old one was forgotten. As long as she didn't revive it by attempting to work with children, she was old news and could get on with her life.

Money was dripping away; it was time to find a job. She was no longer able to teach, so what could she do? Olive Monk gave her the answer to that. At breakfast the following morning the conversation was all about the party. Later, when the nurses were gone, Faith mentioned her need to work. 'I'm a teacher,' she said, hoping she wouldn't have to explain. 'But I want something different.'

'Mrs Palmer, her at the baker's, she's looking for an assistant. Good with people you are, you'd suit her perfectly.'

'In the shop you mean? I've never worked in a shop.'

'Yes, a shop. Why not? It can't be hard to learn.'

'I need to be here for breakfasts.'

'You do the cooking and I'll do the clearing up,' Olive told her firmly. 'I'm not looking for a reduction in my rent, either. I'm very happy here with you, and I'll help willingly.'

'But I've never worked behind a counter.'

'Time you did, then. I believe we ought to try everything, that way we find the right place instead of struggling to make our way along a road that doesn't suit us.'

'Wise words,' Ian said when he was told.

Faith went to see Mrs Palmer, a small, neatly dressed lady, whom Faith warmed to at once. There was a brief conversation during which Mrs Palmer told her she knew all about the newspaper story, and considered it an irrelevance to selling bread and cakes. The job was hers.

It took a bit of arranging but after working for Mrs Palmer for a week, things settled into place. The nurses were given permission to use the kitchen for cups of tea and snacks and her more relaxed attitude gave Faith the feeling that the house was filled with friends.

The customers at the shop accepted her and apart from a few gossips who went into a huddle outside the shop, glancing at her occasionally and presumably passing on any snippets they had gleaned from others, the days were pleasant enough.

The neighbours who had shared the bonfire party came in as customers and greeted her with obvious pleasure. Ian's mother called to buy pasties and a few cakes. Jean called, as did Menna and her three children. Winnie came and shared the occasional lunch break. Life, she decided happily, was good.

* * *

Ian was driving home one day when he saw a figure he knew. Tessa, the woman he had once hoped to marry, was walking past the house that would have been hers. He stopped the car and waited until she reached him.

'Tessa? What brings you here? Were you coming to see me?'

'No, just out for a walk,' she replied, staring at him intently. 'The house looks nice, although I don't like your mother's choice of curtains,' she added with a smile. 'And I'd have painted the front door red.'

'What d'you mean, *you'd* have painted it? If you had it would have been the first time you'd picked up a paintbrush!'

'No. I didn't help very much, did I? That's just one of my many regrets.'

'Aren't you happy with Nick?'

'I suppose I am, but he isn't as reliable as you.'

'Reliable? Isn't that a synonym for boring?'

'No, you were never boring, Ian.' She started to move away. 'Leaving you was the biggest mistake.' She hurried off and was around the corner before he could think of a response.

'Was that Tessa you were talking to?' Vivienne asked when he went into the house. 'I hope she isn't trying to come back into your life.'

'She said she regretted leaving.'

'And you? How do you feel?' she asked.

'I'm not sure,' he replied. 'I still feel a bit guilty living here in what was to have been her home as well as mine.'

'Make sure you know what you want before walking away from Faith and back to Tessa,' Vivienne said quietly, aware she was interfering but afraid to ignore what had happened.

'Faith and I are friends,' he said. 'Just friends.'

He felt uneasy after the brief encounter with Tessa. They had been together for several years and had made great plans. Could he go back and make it work? Visions of Faith invaded his thoughts and she represented greater happiness, didn't she? Or was his attitude coloured by the way he and Tessa had parted? He wondered whether he should tell Faith that things seemed less than happy between Tessa and Nick. Would she too have second thoughts and consider going back and trying again with Nick? The thought made him anxious and he tried to tell himself his concerns were for Faith and the risk of her making a decision she would regret.

* * *

Going home to No 3 every day gave Faith a real sense of belonging. She would open the gate and walk towards the front door with a beating heart, knowing it was a special place, filled with friends, a place where she was being healed of her unhappiness. Sometimes Olive Monk would be in the kitchen with the kettle humming its promise of tea. She didn't deserve such happiness, she told herself, but it was impossible for guilt to invade her sense of well-being for more than a brief moment. A flash of shameful memory, a picture of the tiny child and of Matt's distraught face were quickly dispersed by Olive calling.

'Hello, dear. The kettle's bursting its boiler wanting to make you a cup of tea. Shall I make it while you take off your coat?'

Faith ran up the stairs smiling. How could I have felt suspicious about Olive, she wondered. First impressions aren't always right.

Ian called that evening and she told him about her week, describing some of her customers, 'including the gaggle of gossips', as she called the groups gathered outside the shop to exchange comments. Then she talked about Olive.

'When she first came to see the room I was doubtful. In fact I hoped she would find it too small and look elsewhere.'

'D'you remember why you were unhappy about her?'

'It sounds silly now, but her sons were untidily dressed and I couldn't imagine them as sailors or any other occupation where standards are so high. They were probably dressed for work, putting their mother's furniture in store or something. She must have some. Although, that was something else that puzzled me. Where was her home? If they were going to buy a house they must have furniture and household goods. She came here with an odd assortment of boxes, she won't let me into her room, and . . .' She caught Ian's amused expression and laughed with him. 'Oh dear, it seems I'm still not happy about her. Yet there isn't anything I can put a finger on, just a vague uncertainty. She obviously cooks while I'm out of the house, I come in to the smell of food hovering around the cooker, and — oh, I'm being silly.'

'I think she's a kind person but a private one. Perhaps they've hit bad times and she and her sons are dealing with it without everyone knowing about it. I can understand that, can't you?'

'Better than having your shame spread over pages of the local paper,' she agreed with a sigh. 'I wonder if they lost their home for non-payment of rent? That can happen, even in the sixties. Perhaps she's really short of money. I'll be more sympathetic towards her and pretend I don't know she's using the kitchen for more than the occasional snack and eating meals in her room.'

Olive was cooking a steak-and-kidney pie, anxiously watching the clock when someone came to the door. Faith was looking after Menna's and Geoff's children for them while they went to a meeting and she was alone in the house. She grabbed a tea towel to wipe her floury fingers and opened the door to see Matt standing there.

'What d'you want?' she demanded, adding, 'Not selling, are you? I never buy at the door, mind.'

'I want to talk to Faith and I'm not leaving till I do.' He spoke softly, but glared at her, determined not to be refused.

'You'll have a long wait then, dearie. No one with that name living in my house.'

'Your house?'

'Of course it's mine. No one called Faith, Hope nor Charity that I've ever heard of round here.'

He stared in a threatening manner and she outglared him boldly until he turned and walked away.

She told Faith what had happened when she reached home and Faith wondered how long it would take before Matt realized he had been lied to and tried again. She had begun to relax, believing she was safe from Matt. Although he had been put off by Olive, it was clear he hadn't given up trying to find her. She'd been foolish to stay in the same town, but it was a warm, friendly town and it had seemed a small risk.

* * *

The nurses decided to stay another month. 'At least it means I won't have the effort of finding summer visitors and all that that would entail,' Faith told Winnie when she met her friend with Jack, Bill and Polly.

Winnie had suffered a severe chest infection and felt the need for some fresh sea air, so they were taking the children to Barry Island beach. At eleven o'clock Faith had met them at the railway station and with the three excited children they waited for the Barry Island train, surrounded by bags packed with food and all the paraphernalia needed for a few hours on the sands.

'I need the toilet,' Polly began to wail leaving Winnie with the others, Faith ran back with her to the house.

'It's only me, Olive,' Faith called as she hustled the little girl into the bathroom. No reply. Olive must be out. Then she saw that Mrs Monk's door was open. Unable to resist, she peeped in and was amazed at the muddle. Piles of bedding, clothes, some of them men's clothes, were strewn across the chest of drawers. Used and clean dishes were piled near the bed and the bed itself was hidden by large boxes.

Polly called to say she was ready and Faith hurried to the bathroom and out of the house, afraid Mrs Monk would return and guess she had seen the chaotic room. Faith needed time to decide what to say before she met her.

'I've never seen so much stuff in one room,' she said to Winnie, when she caught up with her at the railway station. 'I told Ian I was curious to know where her home is and I think most of it is in her room!'

'What will you do?'

'Nothing, I suppose. She might be in real trouble and I don't want to add to it. She pays her rent and if she wants to live in such a muddle I can't really interfere. For one thing I'd have to explain I'd been snooping.'

'It is your house. There might be reason to complain because of the fire risk. You need to think seriously about this,' her friend warned.

'Let's forget Olive Monk and her muddles and enjoy the beach with the children.'

The weather wasn't perfect. Summer was almost spent, but the sun shone and for anyone living in the town that meant fun at the beach. There were quite a number of families enjoying the afternoon and the relaxing activities on the warm sand. Boys played football, girls dared to paddle in the cold water's edge and ran back screaming as though it had been painful — which it probably had. Women built sand tables, covered them with cloths and set out food. A few brave souls went in for a swim.

When they were on their way home, Winnie was quiet and Faith suspected she was still unwell. Risking being seen by Matt, Faith went home with her, only leaving her at the gate when Paul came out to greet them.

Walking so close to Matt's workshop gave her a cold sensation between her shoulder blades, she felt vulnerable, imagining Matt's gaze upon her. She went home by a devious route in case he was following and only when she was sure he wasn't there did she hurry along to No 3 Railway Cottages.

There was no sign of the nurses or Olive. Olive's door was again firmly locked and Faith pushed the problem from her mind and made a cup of tea. The cooker was greasy, someone had been frying. She knew she had washed the cooker thoroughly after preparing breakfast. Should she remind Olive of her rules? If one was allowed to cook then the others ought to be too, she mused. She decided to do nothing, afraid to upset the pleasant atmosphere in her home.

Ian and his mother called that evening and she told them what she had discovered.

‘I should at least question her but, coward that I am, I’m avoiding it,’ she admitted. ‘Should I ignore it for the short time she’ll be staying? Her sons will be out of the Navy at the end of the year, and if I tell her to leave she will have to face another upheaval.’

‘Just wait. An opportunity will come,’ Ian advised. ‘And in the meantime, I have another mystery for you.’ He led them into the garden and pointed to the roof of the sun-room-cum-breakfast room. In the fading light, two clear footprints showed on the wood at the edge of the glass roof. To the left of the glass roof was Olive’s room.

‘Good heavens! We might have been burgled! I haven’t noticed anything missing. In fact, there isn’t anything of value in the house, unless the nurses have lost something. D’you think I should call the police?’

‘Shush.’ Ian warned. He pulled himself up into the tree and holding on to a branch, stepped onto the roof. He crawled up and with his face to Mrs Monk’s window he looked inside. He almost fell with shock when another face peered out at him. The face gave a yell, then disappeared.

‘Her sons are in there!’ Ian shouted. ‘Go and stop them!’ He slithered down the sloping roof and jumped to the ground as Faith disappeared into the house.

Faith ran inside just in time to grab one of them as they ran down the stairs.

CHAPTER SEVEN

It was a silent, unmoving tableau that remained frozen for a long time, or so it seemed to Faith when she thought about it later. Ian held an arm of both young men and they all just stood there, unable to decide what to do next. Disbelief showed on Faith's and Ian's faces, fear on those of the two young men. Then Olive Monk appeared at the top of the stairs and she moved, painfully slowly, down to join them.

'I'm so sorry, Faith. We were in such difficulties you see. My husband died and we were in debt and had to leave our flat. I thought that a few months living here and paying such a small rent we'd have a chance to recover, get enough money to rent again.'

Faith felt sympathy for the woman, but Ian said, 'You were prepared to lie to Faith after she had befriended you? That isn't the way to sort out your problems. Faith knew you cooked meals and ate them in your room, she chose to ignore that. She was kind and considerate and all the time you were hiding your sons, cheating on her.'

The boys had remained silent but now one of them said, 'We were doing our best to pay off our father's debts. Saving on rent was making that happen faster. We're very sorry.'

Faith was tempted to allow them to stay. 'Perhaps they could stay; the boys could use the front room as a bedroom, if—'

'What were you doing running from a house in Kitchener Street late at night?' Ian interrupted. 'Exactly how are you working to pay off these supposed debts? Legal, is it?' His voice became louder and louder as he asked, 'Or burglary? Would the police know your names? Shall we ask them?'

Without another word they left, the boys dragging a suitcase and an over-filled box, Olive carrying clothes in untidy bundles over her arms.

Faith stood in the doorway of the back bedroom staring in disbelief at the mess. Mrs Monk had been allowing her two sons to live there and it showed in the overfilled rubbish bin in a corner and the pile of dirty bedding on the floor. She remembered when the woman had arrived to inspect the room, how she had considered it too small but had been persuaded by her son to take it after he had looked out and saw the convenient tree outside that would make access easy.

With a sigh she began sorting out the chaos, gathering the rubbish into a box and piling the dirty bedding on top of it ready for the ashmen to take the following day. Stale food accounted for the unpleasant smell and she wondered why she hadn't been aware of it before, while her unsuspected visitors were there.

Two hours later she had finished scrubbing the linoleum and skirting boards. The windows were wide open, and outside two mats were drying, swinging gently on the clothes line. She had to decide whether to relet, or cope on the small wage she earned working for Mrs Palmer in the baker's shop. She knew she needed the rent of the rooms to make life bearable. The nurses were leaving soon and they had agreed to make it known at the hospital that there were rooms to let. The nurses were perfect tenants. In case there were no nurses, she decided to advertise the vacant back room in the local shop windows, where notices were displayed for a few pence per week; she couldn't be unlucky a second time.

A neighbour called as she was pulling the now dry rugs from the line and Faith told her what had happened.

'She seemed very nice, but I found her evasive, you know, cautious of giving away more than she meant to.'

'I must be a fool to be so easily deceived.'

'It's not a bad thing to trust people. Life can be miserable if you're looking for trouble with everyone you meet.'

'I'll have to look for new tenants now, the nurses are leaving soon.'

'I know of a couple needing a room for a few weeks. It's while their house is being repaired, or they're moving house, I'm not sure. It will give you a chance to find someone more permanent.'

Mr and Mrs Gretorex arrived later that day and took the small room. They were neatly dressed and brought very little luggage. They said very little apart from asking the usual questions and offered no explanation for their needing a room when they were obviously able to afford better. Stiff smiles were the only attempts at friendliness and Faith accepted that they were very quiet people who would be model tenants but not willing to become anything more. Having been told light-heartedly about the previous tenant, they formally told Faith they would keep their possessions to a minimum.

The nurses came home after their late shift bringing a nervous young woman whom they introduced as Gwenllian Hughes.

'Call me Gwennie,' the young woman said, after apologizing for her late call. 'I could move in the day these two move out, if you agree.'

After a few questions during which Faith learned that Gwennie was also at the hospital, but as a cleaner, it was agreed she would move in. Faith went to bed that night still sad about Olive Monk but relieved that the financial situation was secure, for a while at least.

The following morning she wrote to Winnie to tell her about the changes and invited her and the children down for another day at the seaside on the following Sunday. She also wrote to Ian and his mother to tell them about her new lodgers. Then she studied her list of things to do, to decide what her next project on the house would be.

She had heard nothing from Matt since Olive had sent him away and began to hope he had given up trying to talk to her. She could say nothing except repeat her lie that the child had not been his. She could do nothing except listen while he ranted and raged about what she had done. He must have given up.

Everything was beginning to settle. She had Ian — at least as a good friend, she had a job, and a house that earned her extra income. Life was promising good. Then the letter came.

It was not news she was expecting. None of the things she dreaded most: further threats from Matt or Ian bidding her goodbye; it was from her landlord and he wanted her to vacate the house by the end of September.

Her first impulse was to phone Ian. Being in business he had a telephone at home, but she had rarely used it. She was still hesitant about taking his friendship for granted, but this was an emergency.

His mother answered the phone. 'Faith, dear, how nice to hear from you.'

'I'm sorry, but I've had a shock and I wondered if I could talk to Ian?'

'He isn't here, but can I help?'

'No one can, really. I just want an excuse to talk about it. I've been given notice to leave the house by the end of September and it was such a shock I had to tell someone. I really believed I was settled. I've done so much to the place and I thought I was being a model tenant.'

'People are beginning to buy their homes, I suppose the temptation to sell it and raise some money was too much for him. I'll tell Ian you called and if you give me the number of the phone at the end of the road, he'll ring you. Shall we say eight o'clock?' Long before eight o'clock Faith had decided there was nothing Ian could do apart from listen to her complaining.

The nurses were moving out the following day and the new tenant, Gwennie Hughes was not on the telephone so there wasn't much she could do to stop her moving in. Tonight when they got home she would tell the nurses and ask them to tell Gwennie. She would have preferred to explain to the young woman herself but the important thing was to try to stop her leaving her present place, although, she thought sadly, she was probably too late for that anyway. It seemed likely she would have to allow Gwennie to move in, even though the room was available for less than a month.

Just before eight o'clock she was sipping a cup of tea before walking to the phone box, mulling over what she would do, when Ian arrived.

'Mam told me about the notice to quit,' he said, as he took another cup from the dresser and began pouring himself some tea. 'Damned nerve of the man. He charges you rent and waits until you've made the house habitable and in good order, then tells you to leave. Nice little profit he'll make out of you!'

'I was just beginning to feel that my life was getting straight after — after all that had happened — then this. Lady luck certainly has it in for me.'

'Have you thought of buying the place?'

'Buy a house? How can I afford it, and how could I afford to run it?'

'Didn't you say you have some money left to you by Mrs Thomas?'

'Not enough. With what I'd put aside I've less than one hundred and fifty pounds. If I were a man I could get a mortgage for the balance but as a woman, who works in a bakery shop and takes a few tenants, I'd be laughed out of the office.'

'Could one of your friends help?'

'How can I ask?' She shook her head. 'Whatever I do it will be without embarrassing people I care about. If I could somehow borrow the money, and find the confidence to buy this place, I'll start off in serious debt. It isn't possible, Ian.'

'What about a bank loan?'

‘The bank? They’d laugh!’

‘But you will try?’ he coaxed.

‘All right, I’ll see the bank manager tomorrow.’

‘Great!’

‘The first thing is to tell my new tenants they might have to find somewhere else to live. Mrs Gretorex is calling in the morning to bring some of her things and I can tell her then. And if I’m not mistaken, here are the nurses now.’

The door opened and the two nurses came in, laughing, chattering about their day. They always stopped for a cup of tea and a chat and Faith knew she would miss them. When her news was announced they both thought their friend Gwennie would still come.

‘Too late to stay where she is,’ one of them said.

‘Glad to get away from her landlord with his lecherous ways,’ the other agreed.

‘But it will only be until the end of the month,’ Faith warned. ‘The first of October and I’m out of here.’

‘Plenty of time for her to find somewhere else. Don’t worry, Faith. Things have a habit of working out for the best.’

Not for me they don’t, Faith thought, but then, she reminded herself, I don’t deserve it. Tomorrow she would talk to her landlord and find out his intentions, then, it would do no harm to go and see the bank manager. She closed her eyes and sent up a thankful prayer for Mrs Thomas and her generous and unexpected gift.

Gwennie was quite untroubled by Faith’s news about the unexpected move. ‘I’ll stay until you have to move out,’ she said cheerfully. ‘Plenty of time to find a place then. It’s always easier once the holiday season is over. Plenty of landladies looking to fill empty rooms then there’ll be.’ She brought very few things with her and settled into the routine of the house with ease.

Gwennie worked early mornings and was gone from the house before Faith rose from bed. She made herself some breakfast as Faith had agreed but left the kitchen tidy, much to Faith’s relief. Mrs Gretorex had eaten breakfast with her and had seen her off to work like a mother, which amused Faith, and she left for the shop in a light-hearted mood. An appointment had been made to see the bank manager during her lunchtime and this threatened to be a more sobering affair.

The shop was very busy and the morning passed without allowing her any time to worry about the important meeting. The bakery was behind the shop and the smell of the freshly baked bread made her very hungry. She had explained to Mrs Palmer about her appointment and fifteen minutes before the shop closed for lunch she was told to take something to eat and get ready. 'It isn't the sort of thing to do in a rush,' Mrs Palmer said kindly.

Faith's first call was to her landlord, who brushed aside her remarks about her disappointment, then, when she asked about purchasing No 3, he looked thoughtful. He gave her a price, and said, 'Go and see if you can arrange finance then come and see me again. Ten days should be enough.' She thanked him and tried to do sums in her head to work out whether the idea was feasible. Then she went to the bank.

There is something formidable about a large office in which a man sits behind a heavy desk and smiles a stiff, practised smile. Faith wanted to run away. How could she ask this man to lend her some money?

Unfortunately she had not added regularly to her bank account, having used most of the incoming money to improve the house. Asked how she was going to pay back a loan if there was no surplus from her incomings, she nervously explained this, adding that the house was now clean and orderly. She gave a full account of her finances including the rent she could expect from the three rooms she had available. The extra room was because she had decided to continue to sleep downstairs, making her living room into a bedsit, to show a better prospective weekly income.

'If this loan can be agreed, you will need a guarantor,' he told her. 'Is there someone who will cover the loss if you fail to find your agreed monthly payment?'

Who could she ask? Life had improved for her immeasurably, but when it came to situations like this she was still on her own. 'I need to think about that, and make sure there is full agreement before I give a name.'

'Of course. Do that before you get back to me, say one week from today?'

She almost ran from the office, her heart was racing with the thought that he had not dismissed her application, there was a chance, small, but shining like the evening star.

Two days passed and she still had no answer to the bank manager's question. To Ian she said nothing. How could she involve him in her difficulty? All she said in answer to his questions, was that things were moving.

When Ian found an abandoned letter on the Thursday following her appointment at the bank he learned the truth. Hiding the letter, pretending he hadn't see it, he said, 'Faith, Mam and I have been talking and we realize you might need a guarantor for the loan. Please give my name. Knowing you, my cover will be quite safe. I trust you completely.'

'Ian, that's so kind, but I couldn't.'

'I doubt whether the loan will be agreed without such a signature, even with the house being such a good buy. I wish you'd agree; for one thing it will prevent further delays which could cause the owner to sell to someone else. You don't want to risk losing it, do you?'

On Sunday evening, when she faced the fact there was no one else to whom she could turn, his persuasions won and she agreed. She promised herself that she would do anything, anything at all, to prevent dropping behind in her payments for even a day.

Still filled with trepidation she saw the owner, got in touch with a solicitor, then met the bank manager again and the sale was agreed. Three weeks later, on Monday the second of October, she was the surprised owner of No 3 Railway Cottages.

* * *

She hadn't seen much of her newest lodger. Gwennie sat with her and Mr and Mrs Gretorex at breakfast on her days off, when she didn't have to leave so early, but apart from that Faith saw nothing of her. One morning, when Faith was leaving the shop at lunchtime she decided to take a snack and eat it in the park. As she found herself a seat in the shade of a tree Gwennie walked past. She stopped and they shared their lunch hour.

'Split shifts today,' Gwennie sighed. 'Two of the cleaners are off sick and we have to cover the work between us.'

An old man came and sat beside them, and within a very short time, squirrels appeared and moved closer, obviously used to being fed. One at a time they came close to the bench and accepted treats brought by the old man. 'They're so bold, they'll be forming an orderly queue soon,' Gwennie joked. Adding to the nonsense, Faith said, 'I can see them, shopping bags on their arms, collecting food for their families.'

Laughter froze on Faith's face when she saw the newsagent from near Matt's home approaching. She lowered her head hoping he wouldn't see her. A shadow crossed between her and the sun and a voice said, 'Faith Pryor! Happy and laughing as though she hasn't a care in the world. Not a thought for the man you left devastated or the poor little baby you abandoned.'

Faith stood and turned from him, ready to hurry away, unable to bear the pain of his attack. 'Shame on you.' he said as he walked off.

'What did he mean?' Gwennie asked. Suspicions aroused, she unconsciously moved a little away from Faith, sliding along the bench towards the old man as though to avoid contamination.

'I might as well tell you,' Faith said in a low, defeated voice. 'You'd soon hear of it anyway.' Briefly she explained what had happened, explaining about the newspaper story and how it had made her determined the child would grow up without knowing Matt.

'You are *that* Faith? Matt's wife?' Gwennie looked at Faith in disbelief. 'You stole his child, then abandoned her.' Gwennie's voice was quivering.

'If you'd read the report of the trial you'd understand why I couldn't allow him to be a part of my child's life.'

'I not only read the report, I was there, in court for every moment. Matt is my cousin and he was innocent of the charges that wicked girl made.'

'I can understand your reluctance to believe what happened, but the sentence wouldn't have been given if there had been any doubt.'

'The girl was a fine actress. Dressed for the court appearances she looked like a somewhat simple schoolgirl. When she set out to attract men she dressed like an eighteen-year-old tart.'

'I'm not listening to this. The girl was only fourteen. I know what he's like. He was forceful, impatient and there was more than a hint of anger in his determination to get his own way. Doesn't the fact that I instantly believed it tell you something?'

'That you didn't know him and certainly didn't love him.'

'You're right about my not loving him,' Faith replied sadly. 'He persuaded me into — into doing what he wanted and I was too weak to resist.'

'Rubbish. You left him in pieces and even now you can't admit you were wrong.'

'I would like you out of the house by the weekend,' Faith said, her voice sounding as though she were being severely shaken.

'Don't worry, I'm leaving today! I won't stay in your house for a minute more than necessary!' Gwennie called after her.

And she'll go straight to Matt to tell him where I am, Faith thought sadly. This time I can't run away. At least the child is safe from him. That thought gave her strength. And I'll have a bedroom for a while instead of that old couch!

When she got home that evening she could hear banging about in the bedroom occupied by Gwennie. Ian arrived soon after she had taken off her coat and at once she told him what had happened. Before they had finished discussing it, Gwennie came down the stairs, dragging her suitcases. Ian went into the hall. 'Can I help you with those?' he asked politely.

'If you had any sense you'd leave with me. She's evil. Ruined Matt's life, she did, and she won't admit she was wrong, even now.'

They both watched as Gwennie half-carried, half-dragged the cases along the road. At the end a delivery van waited, its engine running. Matt's van, Faith recognized with dismay. The driver jumped down and helped Gwennie with her cases, lifting them with ease and throwing them into the back of the van. He politely helped Gwennie into the passenger seat, then, without looking at Faith and Ian, he drove off.

'So he knows where I am. He'll come back,' Faith said.

'I hope I'm here when he does,' Ian said, smiling encouragingly.

'Could she have been right? Could he have been innocent of the girl's accusations?'

'Could Matt have been the victim? It's possible I suppose,' he conceded.

Faith's heart gave a sickening lurch. 'You believe her?'

'There are such things as predatory females. You know Matt and you saw the reports of the trial. I didn't. All I have to go on is what you told me and the notes you made from the newspaper reports. No one believed him, so it's more than likely he was guilty.'

'What if I was wrong?'

'You went by what you knew at the time and even if something new emerges, that doesn't make what you did wrong. Hindsight is no use to anyone, except a rabbit being chased by a fox, so don't blame yourself.'

'If I made a mistake, you mean? You do believe Matt was wronged.'

'How can I know either way? Perhaps, if I spoke to Matt I'd be able to judge.'

When he left later that evening depression fell about her like a wet shawl, draping her in an icy chill. She didn't think she would ever feel warm again. Her life would never become easy. For some mysterious reason, she didn't deserve it to be. She remembered the times she had been difficult with her various foster-parents, and to some teachers who tried to help; she recalled neighbours who had befriended her to whom she had been ill-mannered and ungrateful. Depression is greedy; it feeds on moments of weakness and builds up into the darkest of clouds, engulfing everyone near.

She awoke the following morning after a restless night and her first thought was of Ian. He believed she had been cruel, taking away Matt's child without fully knowing the facts. She hadn't given Matt a chance to explain, to give her his side of things. She tried to picture a thin little schoolgirl, afraid and vulnerable, but Gwennie's description got in the way and she saw a bold-eyed girl, dressed and made up to look older and she was filled with doubts.

She went to work and forced a smile for the customers. The day was unexpectedly warm and at lunchtime she didn't go home. Instead she went to the beach and stood watching the families having fun. Such ordinary pleasures, but not for me, she thought. She leant on the strong sea wall and listened to the shrieks of children's voices interspersed with mothers shouting, calling them for food, all against the background of the roaring sea, and tried not to think.

During the afternoon two people came into the shop and, slightly embarrassed, cancelled their orders for bread. Mrs Palmer frowned but accepted the cancellations without comment. When a third customer came, this time a small boy bringing a note, she showed the note to Faith.

We don't want any more bread because we won't be served by a woman who abandoned her baby.

'I think I know who is doing this. D'you want me to leave?' Faith whispered.

Mrs Palmer shook her head. 'No point running away from this sort of talk. We'll work our way through it, shall we?'

'But you're losing customers.'

'They'll be back. Ours is the best bread in the area, isn't it? They won't settle for second best for long.'

The house was empty when she reached home at six o'clock, Mr and Mrs Gretorex were out, Gwennie's room was empty and the place sounded hollow. She wasn't hungry, but made a slice of toast and bit into it without tasting it. There were several letters, including one from Vivienne in which she remarked on the surprising end to Olive's tenancy. Faith laughed at her reaction to the stowaways, as she called Olive's sons. It was good to have contact with a friend sharing good news and bad. The present situation had hardly been a cause for laughter, but Vivienne's letter had at least cheered her briefly out of her dismay.

She sat in the kitchen aware of the emptiness of the house. Thank goodness she didn't have to live there alone, the quiet was unnerving. She listened for the sound of the Gretorexes returning. The sound of a van didn't penetrate her brain for a few moments, then the slow hum as the vehicle rumbled over the uneven surface hit her like a blow. She ran to the window and saw Matt's van pull up outside. Without a thought, she dashed through the back door, over a neighbour's garden and up to the park. The thought that she was living up to her nickname didn't stop her.

Matt knocked, then went round to the back door and walked in. There was a half-eaten slice of toast on a plate and, touching the teapot he found it was warm. He ran back out and called her name. 'Damn it, she'll have to come back sooner or later,' he muttered. He sat inside for half an hour, making himself fresh tea and helping himself to biscuits. It was almost 7.30 when he gave up and walked back to the van.

Parking behind him was a Vauxhall car. He walked up to the driver and asked, 'Are you Ian Day?'

'Yes. And I presume you're Matt Hewitt.'

'No prize for guessing as it's written on the van!'

'Is Faith in?'

'No. I've waited ages. She must have darted out of the back door when she saw me. Running away as usual!' He smiled, encouraging Ian to share it.

'Can I give her a message?' Both men were speaking with cautious politeness. 'Or would you like to wait a bit longer?'

'I'd like to talk to you.'

'Fine,' Ian replied hesitantly.

'My cousin told me she was living here, had a boyfriend and was completely happy. She thought the baby — my baby — was forgotten. She told you about the baby, I suppose?' Ian nodded. 'Then you must know she stole my child, denied I was the father and put her up for adoption, then walked away without even an explanation?'

'She read the account of the trial, which you hadn't told her about, and was afraid for the baby being brought up by a . . . forceful man.'

'Forceful? Don't you mean violent?'

'Do I?'

'It wasn't like it said in the papers.'

'It rarely is. But the victim was a child, and rape is an ugly word and not easily forgotten.'

Matt climbed back into the van. 'Just don't believe everything she says. Faith can be as dishonest as that girl I'm supposed to have attacked.'

Ian was confused, although he couldn't deny that Faith had done what she considered to be the right thing, based on what she had learned. But Matt might have been less of a villain than the courts pronounced, and he had lost a child and that was a terrible price to pay.

He didn't go inside although the air was cool and a breeze was rising, he sat on the step in the gathering darkness and waited. Footsteps approached and he looked up to see Faith walking through the gate. She was only wearing a thin dress with strappy sandals on her feet.

'Here I am. The runaway.'

'You must be cold,' he said, 'I'll make us a cup of tea. Have you eaten?'

He spoke as though the day had been an ordinary one, and it was a long time since she'd had one of those. When she had found a jumper and was sipping tea, and tinned spaghetti was warming on the stove, Ian told her Matt had been there.

'I know, I saw him coming and ran,' she admitted, her hands trembling with anxiety. 'What did he want?'

'Your lodger had told him you were here and very happy, having forgotten all about your child. He wanted to tell you how wrong you were, I suppose. He told me instead.'

'Gwennie has been busy spreading gossip. Mrs Palmer lost several customers today, they refused to be served by me.'

'Does she want you to leave?'

'Not yet. But if more people change to another baker, who knows?'

She put toast and spaghetti on two plates and Ian sighed and said, 'Perhaps one day you'll show me some of the skills you practised for Mrs Thomas. Didn't you tell me you could cook?' He was joking and she smiled.

'Come on Sunday, bring your mother and I'll show you what I can do.' Then she frowned. 'If you still want to, of course, now you've spoken to Matt and heard his side of the story?'

'Mam and I will be here at twelve and we'll be starving, so it had better be good!' He hugged her lightly as he left an hour later and she imagined she could still feel the pressure of his arms as she drifted into sleep.

* * *

The following day, Ian went home to find his ex-fiancée, Tessa being entertained by his mother.

For a moment he felt the urge to run as Faith had so recently done, but he removed his coat, put his bag and files in his office and went in to greet her. He kissed his mother and gave Tessa a casual 'Hello.'

'Tessa was walking past and begged a cup of tea,' Vivienne explained. 'She was so cold, weren't you, Tessa?'

'Before I forget, Mum, you and I have been invited to Sunday lunch at Faith's. All right?'

'Lovely, dear. There are a few dahlias left in the garden, I'll take her a bunch, she loves flowers.'

'You do know who Faith is, don't you?' Tessa asked, staring at Ian.

'The woman who had an illegitimate child then abandoned her? Yes, Mum and I know who she is. Now, if you're going straight away I can give you a lift. Mum and I are going to the pictures, so I don't have much time.'

It was the first Vivienne had heard of it but she stood up and handed Tessa her coat.

'Lovely to see you, and thank you for the tea,' Tessa said, as Ian rushed her to the door.

'That was rather rude, dear,' Vivienne said, when he returned a short while later.

'I think Faith and I have sufficient complications to concern us without Tessa trying to be your friend, Mum.'

'I think she had something to tell me but you came before she could say it.'

'She made her choice.'

* * *

Customers at the bakery weren't the only people to show their disapproval of Faith. People who had been friendly seemed unable to know how to treat her when they met. Most simply changed direction and walked away, others glared as she passed and ignored her smiles and greetings. After several unpleasant encounters, she was choosing some fruit when she saw Olive Monk appear. Olive saw her and, for different reasons from the rest, began to back away.

'Hello, Olive. Come and have a cup of tea, the café is open for a while yet.'

'Oh, Faith, dear, I'm so sorry. I wish—'

'Forget sorry, the truth is I can't honestly say I wouldn't have done the same if I'd been clever enough to think of it. It's difficult to criticize when I've never been in your situation.' In moments they were chatting like friends again.

Ian saw them as they stepped out of the café later and offered Olive a lift home but she refused quite firmly.

'I don't think things are very good,' Faith told him. 'She was evasive when I asked where they are living.'

'She probably waits till dark and shins up an apple tree,' he joked.

* * *

Olive walked back to yet another unpleasant room. The most recent one had been infected with bedbugs and the swelling on her skin made her refuse to stay another night. 'I'd rather sleep in the fields than in a filthy place like that,' she had said tearfully. Colin and Graham had promised that the next one was an improvement.

'It isn't perfect. Nothing like what we want for you, Mam, but we've stayed there before and the owner has promised us one of his better rooms once one becomes vacant.'

They were walking past a shabby building with a broken door and boarding over several windows and her spirits fell when they stopped and Colin pointed to the steps leading to a once grand door swinging on one hinge.

'Not here?'

'Afraid so, but it isn't too bad inside.'

The boys showed her to a small, dismal room. Furnished, the advertisement had said, but as Olive looked around at the ancient bed and the scratched wardrobe and the sagging chair, she wondered how it could be so described. 'It's a mess,' she said sadly.

'It's only till we find something better, Mam. You can manage here for a few weeks, can't you? We'll get a decent job soon.'

'A few weeks?' Olive looked around the miserable room and shook her head. Winter would be gloomy enough all alone, but to spend it in this place was unimaginable.

'We're going to ask Granddad for help,' Colin said.

'No! I won't have him knowing just how badly we're managing.'

'He owes you something, Mam,' Graham argued.

'Perhaps you could go and see Faith, see if you can change her mind?' was his brother's suggestion.

'I can't do that either. How can I ask her to help us after what we did?' But the idea was very tempting.

'We'll get a job soon,' Kenneth promised, but again she shook her head.

Why was keeping a job so difficult for her sons? In what way had she failed them? She unpacked her few belongings and bits of shopping and tried to make the place look less like an abandoned building and more like a place fit for human habitation. She had brought very little with her and the velvet cushion and the china ornaments only succeeded in making the room look more shabby than ever.

CHAPTER EIGHT

Faith couldn't concentrate on preparations for Sunday lunch for Ian and his mother. Thoughts of Matt filled her every moment; if Gwennie was right and he was innocent, then she had robbed the man of his child. She knew she had to see him and try to make him tell her the truth.

Saturday was usually an early finish at the shop. Once the cakes and bread had sold out there was no point in keeping the shop open. Mrs Palmer had been correct and after a few days of protest, buying their needs elsewhere, the customers had returned and business was as usual. On that Saturday, an early rush had continued all morning and everything was sold out by mid-afternoon. She began the cleaning at 3.30 and an hour later they closed.

She didn't go home. The bus took her back to where Matt and Carol lived, and with a racing heart she went straight to the workshop, from where she could hear banging. Matt was knocking some dry cement out of a wheelbarrow and he looked up as her shadow fell over him and stared. He stopped what he was doing and walked across.

'I need to talk to you,' she said. She watched him as he walked slowly towards her, his eyes so intense, dark and seeming to penetrate her very soul so she felt again the magnetism of the man. Nervously she lowered her gaze and studied the floor until he spoke. 'A bit late for talking, now you've stolen my child.'

'I had to send her away. I didn't want you in her life. One day she'll have found out what you did and besides, if you could do that once you could do it again. How could I know we'd be safe?'

'That girl didn't tell the truth.'

'That's what your mother said, but the court thought differently and I couldn't take the chance.'

'Why have you come?'

'I want you to tell me the truth. I need to know I wasn't wrong.'

'You want me to ease your conscience?'

'Please, Matt. If I ever meant anything to you you'll tell me the truth now.'

'The girl wasn't the victim. I was.'

'Please, Matt.'

'You were wrong, Faith.'

'Don't do this to me, please.'

'Go away. I won't bother you again, you can forget all about me and my little daughter. There, does that help you feel better?'

She ran off, fighting back tears. She would never be free from what she had done. The memories would never fade. Time will heal? That must be a joke! She knew, exactly to the hour, how old her daughter was at every moment of her days. How could that ever change?

She had to shop on the way home to gather all she needed for the planned Sunday lunch. Roast chicken wasn't exactly adventurous, but with a special selection of vegetables and followed by an extravagant pavlova, she knew they would be impressed. With a base of meringue, she'd add mandarin slices, kiwi, strawberries, grapes and banana, mostly tinned, all covered in thick cream. She consulted her list and went into the greengrocer's where she regularly bought her fruit and vegetables. As she waited in the busy shop to be served she decided that it would be a good idea to invite Mr and Mrs Gretorex to join them. They might welcome the opportunity to get to know her better. The table would just about seat five, if she could borrow a few chairs.

A notice across the road attracted her attention. There was a jumble sale taking place at the church hall. Tempted, she waved to the assistant and told her she would be back, and ran across the road.

No 3 Railway Cottages still lacked many of the basic items and as the place was about to close, she thought she might find a few bargains. Fifteen minutes later she had bought two bentwood chairs, a small table, two saucepans, a couple of cushions, three flower vases, an assortment of cutlery and china and a tablecloth. The organizers willingly agreed to deliver them.

The tablecloth had seen better days; it had been neatly darned a few times and the colour was no longer white, but with the repairs hidden by vases of flowers, the table would look better than with the bare wooden surface.

Having the meal to think about helped take her mind off her brief meeting with Matt, and she was smiling, anticipating the occasion as she went back into the greengrocer's shop. Her smile faded when she was told that, no, they wouldn't deliver. 'In fact,' the woman said quietly, 'we'd prefer that you go somewhere else for your order. We no longer want to serve you.'

'But why? I pay on delivery, the house isn't very far away. In fact, you deliver to my neighbour.'

'We don't want to be seen to support you after — you know. People talk, and they might think we agree with what you did.'

'But it was a long time ago!'

'Never long enough for some things.'

'Has someone spoken to you recently and persuaded you I'm unfit to be a customer?' she asked in disbelief.

'Sorry, but we'd prefer you to leave,' the woman said defiantly.

'Matt Hewitt? Gwenllian?'

'Next please.' The assistant smiled politely at the person behind her. Without another word Faith stumbled from the shop.

It was getting late and soon the shops would be closing. She caught a bus to the main shopping centre of Holton Road and walked into the first greengrocer's she came to.

'It's very late, I know, but can you possibly deliver an order for me?' she asked.

Doubtfully the man looked at the clock. 'All right, missus, so long as you're quick. It's very late but we don't like to discourage anyone who might become a regular customer.'

'I possibly will become a regular customer,' she said, 'but you're right, it is rather late.' She handed him her list and asked them to put everything into a strong box. 'Just for today I'll treat myself to a taxi,' she said. The shop didn't have all she needed, but she knew it would be sufficient to provide a good lunch. The man helpfully rang for a taxi and lifted the heavy box in for her.

She felt angry rather than tearful over the other greengrocer's spurning of her custom, but this time the temptation was not to pack up and leave, to try once more to make a fresh start somewhere where she wasn't known. No. This time she'd stay and face things. Previous fresh starts hadn't achieved a thing except weary her and make her feel even more alone. She wouldn't run away. Not this time.

As she stepped out of the taxi and the driver was carrying the box to the door, another vehicle pulled up, a van this time and glimpsing just part of it, for a moment she thought it was Matt. To her relief it was the delivery of the items she had bought at the jumble sale. They were carried inside for her and placed in the kitchen.

Her next task was to invite her tenants, Mr and Mrs Gretorex, to have lunch with her the following day. They accepted with pleasure. Faith looked into the empty room so recently vacated by Olive and wished she could invite her to join them too. She worked late into the evening cleaning the items she had bought. The cutlery looked much improved after a good rub with Vim powder and everything benefited from a lot of soap and hot water. She was very tired when everything was set out ready for the next day but she was well content. So what if that stupid woman refuses to serve me, there are plenty of others who will, she thought as she yawned her way to bed. She was tingling with tiredness but sleep didn't come as easily as she expected.

As she settled to sleep, the thought that she had been wrong and Matt really had been the innocent party nagged at her. He had seemed so positive, so truthful that doubts flooded in. If only she knew for certain. Then she could really put the tragedy behind her and dream only of her daughter happily settled with a loving family. She slept eventually but her dreams woke her. She saw her daughter in one of the many homes she herself had experienced where she had been ignored, unwanted, and had dreamed only of finding someone who would love her. At six she got up and began preparing the vegetables.

Ian and Vivienne arrived at twelve and Vivienne found a clump of mint in the garden with which she made some mint sauce. 'I know it's only supposed to go with lamb, but I love it with practically everything,' she admitted. 'Daft it is to deprive yourself of something you enjoy because it isn't correct.'

The meal was a success and the guests seemed like old friends. As she went into the kitchen for the dessert Faith stopped to listen to the rise and fall of the conversation and the occasional bursts of laughter. Matt is a part of the unhappy past, she told herself and nothing from the past can be changed. I must look to the future, where things can be as I want them to be.

'How long will you be living here?' Vivienne asked Mrs Gretorex, as they were sipping coffee later.

'Oh, we aren't in a hurry to leave. We're very comfortable here and Faith is a generous landlady,' She patted Faith's hand. 'Despite warnings.'

Faith felt her insides lurch. 'You were warned not to stay?' She tried to keep her voice light and forced a smile.

'We were told to leave, that you were not as kind as you appear, you know, gossipy, troublemaking sort of things.'

'Matt! I saw him yesterday and tried to make him admit he was guilty of attacking that girl but he refused. He said he wouldn't bother me anymore, but he's already done as much damage as he can, telling everyone he meets his side of the story; the untruthful side.' She began telling them about the greengrocer who refused to serve her but Mrs Gretorex interrupted.

'Oh no, dear, it wasn't a man. It was a woman who tried to persuade us to leave.'

'A woman? But who could it be? Oh, it wasn't my ex-lodger, Gwenllian, was it?'

'No, dear, it wasn't Gwenllian.'

Surely not Olive Monk? She dared not ask. She hadn't driven Olive and her sons from the house; having been found out they just gathered their things and had left. No anger and certainly no force had been applied. They had left without paying the rent that was due and somehow Faith didn't resent Olive for that. She wondered where she was living and hoped she had found somewhere comfortable. Olive had been considered a friend — another disappointment.

Faith tried to put the mystery out of her mind and began to clear the dishes. As she carried them into the kitchen, Ian followed. She deliberately changed the subject.

'Fancy your mother finding mint in the garden. I must take a closer look, there might be other herbs, or perhaps I could plant some.'

The meal seemed to have relaxed the new tenants and they discussed the garden for a while as they cleaned and stacked the dishes, then they all walked outside and began making plans. 'Cutting back will be the worst job but will give the biggest improvement,' Mr Gretorex said.

Ian agreed. 'Perhaps I can make a start next weekend.'

'We could have some wonderful bonfires,' Faith said. This was discussed, other ideas were shared and the garden promised to be an enjoyable project.

'I can start clearing the ground but it will be next autumn before I can really set everything out,' Faith said. 'If I'm still here,' she couldn't help adding, and at once Ian went inside.

'Come on, Mum,' he said, reaching for their coats. 'Time we weren't here.'

'Oh, I hoped you'd stay for tea,' Faith said. 'I made some coconut pyramids specially.'

'Sorry, but we have to go,' Ian said, and there was a sharpness in his voice that alarmed her. Had she done something, said something to upset him? They had been talking about the garden and it was he who had suggested helping, so what could it have been?

* * *

As the car turned in the road, watched by an anxious Faith, Ian was tight-lipped and Vivienne sat silently beside him. Like Faith, she wondered what had been said to cause the sudden change of mood. Later that evening she brought the subject up. 'What happened between you and Faith? I thought you and she were getting on well.'

'I thought Tessa and I were in love and intending to spend our lives together, but she ran off, didn't she?'

'Be fair, Ian, you haven't known Faith long enough to know whether she will be the one. Don't be in such a hurry. Spend time with her and see if friendship grows into something better.'

'Tessa and I were friends. Friendship grew stronger, then she found someone she preferred and she walked away.'

'So you think Faith will do the same?'

'Of course she will, you heard her, "If I'm still here". Running away is what she always does.'

'People can change.'

'I want someone who'll stay whatever happens. She ran away and left her child.'

* * *

Faith watched the car disappear around the corner and turned to see Mrs Gretorex watching her. 'I don't know what I said, but I don't think they'll be back.'

'I hope it wasn't my fault, mentioning that stupid woman's attempt to make us leave.'

'No, of course not. I'm just not lovable,' she said, then made light of it adding: 'A pain in the neck, that's what several of my foster-mothers called me. Now, can I persuade you two to sit in the garden and help me eat these cakes?'

Guessing the young woman needed company, Mrs Gretorex agreed. The sun shone weakly in a hazy sky and the three of them sat in the garden for a while, wearing warm coats and wrapped in blankets, enjoying the calm quiet of the winter afternoon, sharing the cake and drinking cups of tea until the sun disappeared from its brave showing. A light breeze and the approach of evening encouraged them back indoors.

When Mr and Mrs Gretorex had gone to their room and everything had been tidied away Faith sat and wondered who the woman could have been. Someone who hated her enough to want to spoil her peace of mind, someone who had taken the trouble to call on her lodgers and tell them they should leave. There was no one, unless Matt had other cousins willing to shout his corner as angrily as Gwenllian had done.

* * *

Olive was attempting to brighten the miserable room with the addition of a few flowers, when her sons called.

'Good news, Mam,' Kenneth called. 'Almost all of Dad's debts are paid.' He handed her a few receipts which she stared at in disbelief.

‘We’ve brought a treat too,’ his brother said offering her a carrier bag issuing tempting smells.

They unpacked the hot food. Olive shared it between three sections of the wrapping paper and they ate. She was afraid to ask how they had managed to find the money to clear the debts left by their father but Colin guessed her thoughts and said, ‘Gambling, that’s how we got the cash. We had a few tips and we were lucky.’

Olive smiled as though she believed them. An hour later two policemen called and from the questions it was clear her sons were suspected of breaking into a house and stealing a cash-box containing seventy-four pounds.

‘Last night?’ Olive queried. ‘They were here with me. Brought food they did, haddock and chips. Lovely it was. Look, the wrapping paper is in the bin, see?’ She showed the recently deposited wrapping paper and hoped they wouldn’t touch it and find it still warm.

‘What time did they leave?’ She shook her head. ‘Talking we were until at least three this morning. They make me laugh, my two boys. Lovely company they are.’

‘So, everything’s lovely, Mrs Monk?’ the constable said sarcastically.

‘Just lovely, officer. Want a cup of tea?’

When the police had left, Olive stood and stared at her sons.

‘All right, Mam, we did steal the money but we promise this is the last time. We had to clear the debts, and this was the only way we could find such a large sum of money.’

‘We’ve both got a job now and we’ll stay on the straight. We promise.’

* * *

No news of Olive Monk came to Faith through customers at the shop, even though she regularly asked. She was concerned. Surely the family wasn’t destitute? No post had come for her so she presumed she must have another address. Faith continued asking people if they had seen her but it seemed that Olive and her two sons had disappeared. So I'm not the only one to run away from trouble, she thought wryly. She hoped they had found a suitable place to live.

The job in the baker's shop and the rent from two remaining lodgers were enough to keep the bills paid and allow for a few small jobs to be done in the house. Advertisements offering a room to rent had failed to attract prospective tenants and she began to accept that the room would remain unoccupied until people's memories had faded. Ian hadn't appeared for almost a week and Faith despaired of seeing him again.

Alone with her thoughts she became convinced that Matt had been telling the truth. She had robbed him of his daughter, deprived herself of a child to love, and it had been her own stupid fault. Why hadn't she questioned Matt? Talked to Carol before making such a momentous decision affecting all their lives? Now it was too late; there was nothing she could do to make amends, the child was legally adopted and out of her reach. She was past crying, but the ache in her heart threatened to destroy her.

She wrote to Ian, explaining how she felt, the doubts over what she had done. She also said she understood that he wouldn't want to see her again after what had happened. Posting it, she wondered whether to go back on her decision and move. She could probably let the house to a family and the rent would provide enough income to pay the loan to the bank. The runaway. Why was running always her solution?

A few days later she was walking along the road heading for No 3 when she saw someone standing at the front door. She touched the gate and the woman turned to face her. She was young, pretty and dressed attractively in a blue suit over which she wore an off-white swagger coat.

'Miss Pryor?'

'Hello?' Faith said questioningly.

'I'm Kitty Robins,' the woman said offering a hand. 'I'm looking for a room for myself and my husband, Gareth. We have references,' she added quickly as she saw the doubt on Faith's face. 'We need it for at least the winter, maybe longer.'

'You'd better come in.' Faith unlocked the door and carried her shopping through to the kitchen. 'The truth is, I'm not certain I want to relet the room,' she said.

'Oh, it would have been perfect. My husband works on the railway and we had to get out of the rooms we were renting last week and Mam's place is so inconvenient and . . . sorry, Miss Pryor. I won't waste your time if your mind is made up.'

Aware that she was wavering, Faith smiled and said, 'Let me unpack my shopping and we'll have a cup of tea.' She had bought a couple of cakes at the shop and she put them out on one of the pretty plates she had found in the jumble sale. As the young woman talked, Faith felt herself warming to her. Perhaps this was a sign that running away was not the right thing to do, but she already knew that. Coward that she was.

'We're going to have a baby,' the woman confided, and the impulse to tell her to leave there and then was strong. 'But I'm sure we'll find a permanent place by the time he arrives.'

Faith fought her anxiety, afraid of having to cope with the girl's situation, comforting her in bad times and congratulating her when things were good. In her imagination she saw a future scene in which she was helping to care for a small child, like the dark-haired little one she had abandoned. 'Of course you must stay,' she said, wondering if it really was her voice speaking the words. 'But before you decide, would you like to see the room?'

Before the excited and happy girl left to tell her husband the good news, Faith gave her a brief outline of what had happened to her and how she had abandoned her child. 'Do you still want to live here?' she asked, and she looked at the girl's large blue eyes and pleaded silently for her to agree.

'Please, Miss Pryor. The room will suit us perfectly and I'll make sure we find a permanent place before the baby is born.' She looked at Faith, then away. 'I — we — we did know your sad story,' she admitted. 'But despite being told in a spiteful way, I believe you. You were very brave to do what you did, and I'm sure you were right. You'd have given him the benefit of the doubt if you weren't certain he was capable of such a thing.'

Faith thanked her but her own doubts were still there.

She had to buy a double bed in place of the two singles the nurses had used, and a second-hand shop provided her with a wooden bed plus a matching wardrobe. Mr Gretorex helped the delivery man to move the beds out. The new one was placed against the wall, allowing room for a small table and a couple of easy armchairs she had bought but had left in the shed. Her money was dwindling away but she had a feeling that her new guests would be happy there and she wanted to do all she could to make them welcome.

On the day Kitty and Gareth Robins were due to move in she lit a fire in the small grate in their room and left a vase of flowers on the window sill. She smiled when she heard the squeal of delight when Kitty saw what she had done.

From the first day they were not like lodgers. They treated her like a friend and Kitty frequently popped in and out of her room, knocking respectfully but calling her and opening the door at the same time, with some snippet of news: a sale on at one of the shops, a fresh supply of navel oranges at the greengrocer's, or Christmas trees at a temporary stall, or just something happening that had amused them which they wanted to share. If it weren't for the continuing absence of Ian and his mother, life would be approaching contentment.

Sunday lunch became a regular event. Kitty and Mrs Gretorex taking turns with Faith to provide and cook it. The house had a warmth Faith had never known before. If only Ian and Vivienne could share it. Olive too. They had all been such good friends and the end of it had been such a disappointment.

* * *

Winter deepened its grip and with the shops filling up with the tinsel and treasures of Christmastime, Olive was feeling low. Her sons rarely called and she spent too many hours alone in the miserable room. If only she hadn't agreed to their using her room as a free lodging she might still be with Faith and the others. It had been such a happy time, and her boys had ruined it.

She was putting on her rather ancient but thick, warm coat, having decided to walk around the shops to kill a few hours of her lonely day, when she heard footsteps running up the stairs. The door opened and her sons came in. As usual, it was Colin who did the talking.

'Come on, Mam, we've got something to show you. We've found you a new home.' They hustled her out of the flat and she grabbed her shopping bag and purse, intending to buy a few vegetables on the way back from whatever flight of fancy this was.

To her surprise they went on the bus and stepped off not far from a row of cottages that had been built many years before for farm workers. Could they really be renting one of these? Excitement rose, then fell rapidly as she was led through a gate into a field. There, alongside the hedge, was a caravan. Her son handed her a key and said. 'It's yours, Mam.'

Bemused, she stared at it. 'How can I live in a field?' she asked quietly. 'There's three or four months of winter ahead of us. I couldn't survive in that. I'm better off in that room, awful though it is.'

'The farmer has agreed to your staying and you can use the water tap in the barn. Best of all, Mam,' Graham said, 'he'll give you electricity from his generator. There's electric light, a heater, a cooker and everything. How's that?'

'The electricity goes off at nine, mind,' Colin warned, 'but you can use candles or we can find you an oil lamp, maybe.'

Find an oil lamp, she thought. Not buy. They were still finding the easy way out, although they must have paid money for this caravan. She shivered and tried not to wonder where and how they got the money.

'Honestly earned?' she dared to ask, not expecting a truthful reply.

'Yes, we're paying in instalments and it's taken out of our wages each week.' Colin showed her a small payment book and she saw that half had been paid as a deposit and the monthly amounts were noted beside the dates on which they were due.

'Dad left us in a right mess, Mam, and we got out of it in the only way we could. But from now on it's all legit.'

Reassured, she relaxed. It must be true, they wouldn't offer her a place like this if it belonged to someone else.

After an inspection she was encouraged to try living there. She would have neighbours in the cottages and the farm promised interests to fill her time. Better still, a few days later, Graham came with a mail order catalogue and suggested she might find a few customers to buy from it and earn a little money for herself. 'You'll have to embellish the address a bit,' he warned with a grin. 'The caravan, beside a hedge, in Hunter's Field, Barry, might not be acceptable.'

With Graham's help she gave her address as Rose Villa, Golden Grove Farm and was accepted by the catalogue. Two of the cottages provided her first customers. She felt hopeful of settling at least for the next few months and this time, she was determined the boys wouldn't ruin it for her.

* * *

With the approach of winter Faith's garden was gradually being tamed. Paths had been unearthed and ashes used to improve them. The shrubs and trees had been cut back. Small plots were cleaned and marked out ready for spring planting. The smell of the freshly turned earth excited her and she worked harder than ever, getting it ready.

A clematis had struggled across a wall and had been nurtured back to life and, to her delight, a Chinese wisteria was discovered in a corner, where it had climbed over a neglected arch. Mr Gretorex had repaired the arch and in summer it would be a focal point for the garden. There was even a small pond, made from an abandoned bath found by Kitty and Gareth and dragged home.

One Saturday, Ian unexpectedly called at the shop in time to walk home with her. 'Sorry, but I've been stupid.' he said.

'I presumed you and Tessa were going to try again,' she said. 'I hear all sorts of gossip in the shop and know she and Nick are far from happy.'

'So far as I know they're still together,' he said.

Puzzled, she waited for his explanation of his absence.

'This will make me sound like a petulant child,' he said with a wry grin, 'but you always suggest running away and I'm afraid to become too fond, too dependent on your . . . friendship.'

'I'm not running away. Not anymore.' Nothing more was said and she was left feeling unsatisfied and let down.

He called once or twice but seemed ill at ease and when he left there was no mention of further arrangements. She didn't see Vivienne and wondered whether this was an end to their friendship and he was trying in his hesitant way to let her down lightly.

* * *

One Sunday morning in December, Faith rose early. It was her turn to cook the lunch — now a tradition they all enjoyed. Ian might be fading out of her life but she was happy here with her friends. She had a job that was pleasant enough and a house that she loved. She stretched contentedly, then, reaching for her dressing-gown she leaned on the window sill and looked out at her garden. Then a cry escaped her lips. She stared in disbelief. Everything had been trampled and cut down. All the plants on which she had spent so much time were in ruins. Trees had been chopped and even the pond was filled with stones. When could this have happened without someone seeing?

Ian heard of the damage from one of his neighbours and went straight around. Like Faith he was horrified that someone could do such a cruel thing. After walking through the garden and looking more closely at the destruction he sat on the doorstep, waiting for Faith, who had gone to buy a morning paper, quietly working out the best strategy for persuading her to call the police.

If this was down to Matt Hewitt spite and anger were perhaps understandable, but this was a dangerous step up from spreading gossip. He shuddered, wondering what Faith could expect next. However hurt Matt had been, if this was his handiwork he had to be stopped.

Faith came along the road and turned her head away from the sight of her ruined garden. So she saw Ian before she reached the gate.

'So you've seen the latest reminder of my wickedness?' she said, her voice strained, her face pale and heavy-eyed. 'This can hardly have been done by a woman, so how many enemies do you think I have? Two? Three? Thirty-three?'

'Can I come in?'

She nodded, unable to speak any more and he followed her into the kitchen, where he held her close and spoke soothingly, as though she were a child. Then he moved away and filled the kettle and put it to boil. 'Faith, you have to inform the police,' he said. 'This is malicious damage. A big step up from name-calling, and I'm afraid of what the man will do next.'

'You don't think this was the work of a woman?'

'It's possible, but I think a woman might have been noticed walking along with a bag of tools. A saw was used, and an axe. Heavy stones were carried to fill the pond. No, I can't see a woman doing this. Olive Monk's sons?' he suggested.

'I'll never believe it was Olive's sons. They were in the wrong, staying here without my agreement, but Olive is a good, kind person and her sons weren't difficult or threatening when they left.'

The police came and took statements from Faith, Ian, her lodgers and the neighbours but she didn't hold out much hope of finding the person responsible. She made it clear that she didn't accuse Olive's sons, nor did she suggest Matt as a possible suspect. She didn't want to remind people of her leaving her child.

The newspapers took up the story and connected it with other similar acts of vandalism, for which she was thankful, but they published a large photograph of her looking at her destroyed garden and for a few people there were murmurings of satisfaction at her 'punishment'.

After taking photographs of the ruined garden, Ian, Mr Gretorex and several neighbours made a start on clearing it. Vivienne came to do what she could and she was sometimes joined by some of the neighbours. Gareth and Kitty helped too and despite the chilly weather bonfires were once more an excuse for eating baked potatoes as a pleasant end to an afternoon's work. Many of the plants were past saving, but there were plenty that accepted the harsh, aggressive pruning and struggled to show signs of life. As Christmas approached the garden was left in peace and they waited patiently to see what spring would bring.

Whatever had kept Ian away for those weeks was forgotten, and thankfully Faith prepared for Christmas with friends.

Christmas shopping with Winnie was fun, specially as the children's new bicycles were hidden in Faith's shed to keep them from prying eyes until Christmas Eve. She helped Ian choose a gift for his mother, and Gareth to buy a pretty bracelet for Kitty.

The stall selling trees was visited one lunchtime and they spent too much time choosing the perfect shape. Faith ran back to the bakery as excited as a child at the prospect of filling it with baubles and small gifts.

Winnie was surprised when, on opening her door one morning, she saw Matt standing there. She instinctively tried to close it but he looked subdued and pleaded with her to listen to him. Paul was at work and she was alone, but she agreed and he stepped inside.

'It's Christmas, it makes me feel my loss more than ever,' he said, sitting on the edge of a chair. 'My little girl, Dorothy, is a year and ten months old and I know I'll never, ever see her. I pass toy shops and dream of what I'd buy for her.'

Winnie said nothing; she stared at him, so different from the man who had burst into her home and demanded to see Faith. All uneasiness had gone and she felt deeply sorry for him.

'It's sad for my mother too,' he went on in that same low, defeated voice. 'She has a grandchild she'll never know. She lied, didn't she? The child was mine and she lied and gave her away.' Anger flared in his dark eyes and Winnie stood and opened the door. He left slowly, head bowed, the flash of anger gone. 'Help me,' he said. 'Tell the authorities she was lying. I want my child back.'

'The adoption was legally binding, there's nothing to be done,' Winnie said. She watched him walk away, wishing she could help him, her thoughts on him and his painful loss, her friend Faith a guilty, hovering shadow.

* * *

Faith headed back to the house loaded with parcels and mysterious packages. She had bought gifts for Winnie's three and for Menna's and Geoff's children whom she'd looked after for a few months. She was laughing as she struggled with the gate but immediately sobered when she saw Winnie standing at the door with a solemn expression.

'Is everything all right?' she asked anxiously. 'You aren't ill?'

'I've seen Matt. Faith, I felt so sorry for him. He's desperately unhappy, grieving for his child. Are you sure you didn't make the wrong decision?'

'Do you think I'm not haunted with the terrible fear that I was wrong? That I made a terrible mistake? Awake and in my dreams I continually wonder if Matt was innocent of the charge of attacking that girl.'

'I'm sorry, Faith, I was upset by his visit.'

'I'm not stupid enough to think the man is automatically the one to blame. Women can cheat and lie and twist facts this way and that to save themselves. I know that. I'll never know the truth about Matt and Ethel Holland and those doubts fill my nightmarish dreams night after night.'

'I'm sorry.'

'Don't be sorry. I understand how you feel. I can only tell you that when I read it I believed the newspaper story and I made the only decision possible.'

She went inside and put her parcels on the kitchen table. Suddenly the decorations looked tawdry, the voices of carol singers coming from Mrs Gretorex's radio sounded insincere. Her doubts were distorting everything that was good.

She unpacked her shopping, drank a cup of tea and slowly recovered from the black mood. For the next hour she concentrated on decorating the house with boughs of holly and dried, painted grasses, which were displayed with glittery branches.

The acquisition of a small fridge meant that food could be stored in readiness. Faith had lists of things to do and things to buy and Kitty jokingly said she would soon need lists of her lists.

To her delight she met Olive Monk one day as she walked through the fields. At first she didn't recognize her as she was wearing a riding mac and had wellingtons on her feet. She was clumping along in a most unusual way.

'Olive? Is that you? Are you a farmer now?'

As before, Olive was apprehensive at first, but seeing the friendly smile on Faith's face she ran towards her. 'My dear, it's lovely to see you.'

'What are you doing out here? I didn't imagine you as a country girl.'

'Surprise, surprise. I'm living on a farm, or at least, near one.'

'Tell me more.'

'Better than that, I'll show you. Come on, it isn't far away.'

Olive led her across a field and through a hedge and pointed proudly towards the caravan, its windows shining in the bright sunshine. After explaining about her son's solution to her accommodation problem, she showed Faith proudly around her new home.

'I've settled in really well,' she said as she made a cup of tea for her visitor in her tiny kitchen. 'One of the farm cats visits regularly and neighbours call for a chat and sometimes bring a bit of cake. And you'd never believe how many customers I've got for my catalogue.' Faith looked at the fat catalogue with interest as Olive explained about regular weekly payments.

'Best of all, I've got a bank account. What about that, eh? I send off the weekly cheque like I've been dealing with banks all my life.' She thought of asking Faith to become a customer but doubted that Faith would trust her.

'Are your sons all right?' Faith asked.

'There was a bit of trouble with the police, but it all blew over. They aren't angels, I know that. They've both been in prison for burglary in the past, but they've promised to go straight and I believe them.'

'I'm so glad.' Faith reached out and patted her hand. 'They must be pleased to know you're happily settled here.'

'Got jobs they have, lorry driving. And a room in a boarding house where they're fed well, so I'm happy about them now.'

'Look, why don't you join us for Christmas Day?' Olive looked doubtful. 'Please come,' Faith pleaded. 'I've really missed you.'

After a few refusals Olive agreed and then wanted to know all about the new tenants. So additions were made to the lists and Faith excitedly continued with preparations.

With the approach of Christmas, an occasion she had previously dreaded, Faith welcomed each day with delight. Every spare moment was spent baking. The lodgers were all having Christmas dinner with her and the small dining room was as beautifully decorated as she could manage while still leaving room for six people to eat.

Ian and his mother were invited to join them for an early supper. The bad times were behind her and she knew that despite moments of grieving for her daughter and moments of guilt about Matt, it was going to be the best Christmas she had ever known.

On Saturday the twenty-third of December, when the shops had all closed for the holiday, everything changed.

CHAPTER NINE

Faith had been dealing with the last-minute shopping. Mrs Gretorex had gone with her and when they had succeeded in buying all they could possibly need and the shops were beginning to close for the holiday, they went into a café and ordered tea and cakes. With their bags of food at their feet, they sat and went over their plans for the following day.

'As Christmas Eve is a Sunday, it will have to be a less important meal or Christmas dinner will be a bit of an anti-climax,' Mrs Gretorex said. 'We can't do the usual Sunday roast dinner, can we?'

'It would spoil the effect of the big spread we plan for Christmas Day,' Faith agreed. 'What about bacon and eggs?'

'Tinned spaghetti on toast,' her friend announced with a laugh. 'My husband will hate that but he'll enjoy the big Christmas dinner more because of it.'

The café was full and very noisy, the excitement of the holiday affecting everyone. People were waiting impatiently for a table to be clear and as soon as they stood to go, they knew a couple of women would rush to take their places. It was dark outside and the traffic had eased. Stepping out and shutting the sound of the noisy café behind them was like walking into a different world. Heaving their baskets onto their arms they began to trudge towards the bus stop.

The buses were crammed full and the conductor had difficulty moving around collecting fares. Like the people in the café, everyone was talking and laughing and Faith marvelled at the joy of the season.

As they approached No 3 they saw Kitty and Gareth waiting for them. As they drew nearer, they ran to meet them and it was clear that something was wrong. Neighbours had gathered nearby, standing with arms folded, waiting patiently to find out what had happened. Alarmed, Faith put down her shopping and asked. 'What is it? What's wrong?'

'I'm so sorry, Faith,' Kitty said. 'But someone's broken in and . . .' She broke off, sobbing. Gareth put an arm around his wife's shoulders and led them all to the front door.

The mess was visible without going inside. The decorations had been pulled from the walls and the table holding the small Christmas tree had been overturned. With a gasp of disbelief, Faith stepped over the ruined tree and looked into the living room. There was more of the same, but it was the kitchen that was the worst shock.

The fridge was open and no light showed. The food that had been ready for the celebration was ruined, packages had been opened and stamped underfoot, the debris spread around the floor. Cakes and mince pies were broken into pieces, the iced cake and its colourful decorations a sad echo of its previous splendour. Jars of pickles had been smashed into the sink, cream poured over the vase of dried flowers in the centre of the table.

Gareth's voice seemed to come from a long way off as he said, 'I hope I did right, but I phoned for the police. I think they should see this before we start clearing it up.' On cue, the sound of a car pulling up entered her confused mind and she turned to see two policemen entering, calling her name.

'We were out buying the last of the shopping,' she murmured. 'Now it's all ruined, and it's too late to buy more.'

She answered their questions but later couldn't remember anything that was said. It was Gareth who told her that they took the attack very seriously and promised to investigate but warned that the holiday would make things difficult.

Hours later, after photographs of the devastation had been taken, they began the sad task of clearing up. Kitty brought down some large boxes, having taken out the contents — things they owned but had not intended to unpack. Slowly, with the help of neighbours, the debris was removed and order was restored. The sadness and disbelief remained.

Kitty and Mrs Gretorex had come to a decision between them and, as the last of the mess was stacked outside ready for the next refuse collection, they told her their plans.

'The meat is no use, but I have a tinned chicken you can have,' a neighbour offered.

'I have corned beef, ham and some mysterious luncheon meat with a name I've never heard of,' another offered with a smile.

'Fruit for starters, plenty of vegetables for the main course with a choice of tinned meats.' Mrs Gretorex said brightly. 'How does that sound?'

'There's an apple tart which I left cooling on the bedroom window sill,' Faith said attempting to smile.

Kitty offered to bring it down and found it upturned on the floor. She couldn't tell Faith the intruder had gone this far, so she slipped outside having gathered it back on to its baking tin and brought it as though from the garden. She had stuck some grass and a couple of leaves amid the broken pieces. 'Bad luck!' she said, encouraging laughter. 'It must have fallen out!'

When Faith eventually went to bed she saw the mark on the carpet and guessed what had really happened. As Kitty had known, the thought of someone actually being in her bedroom was even worse than the disaster downstairs. She pulled the blankets off her bed, tiptoed down and, after checking all the locks, slept on the couch once more.

Sunday, Christmas Eve, was a strange day and they were all subdued. The fridge was unharmed, it had simply been unplugged and rescuing some margarine and finding the rest of the required ingredients, Faith made some cakes and a few mince pies. Whoever was doing this, he wouldn't ruin her Christmas. Her friends would make sure of that.

* * *

Matt's mother was staring at her pantry with its generous supply of food. She felt terribly guilty over what she had done. Gwenllian watched her and, seeing the woman was troubled, persuaded her to talk about what she had done.

'Come on, Auntie Carol. I know something's upsetting you. It's Christmas and no one should be unhappy at Christmas time. Except Faith Pryor!' she added bitterly.

'I've ruined her Christmas,' Carol said quietly.

'Good on you! How did you do that?'

Shamefully at first, then, as Gwenllian encouraged her with more malice, Carol told her how she had gone into No 3 and ruined as much food as she could. She looked at her niece, expecting disapproval, but Gwenllian was delighted.

'I wish I'd thought of it. You didn't ruin the garden too, did you?'

'I was so angry I couldn't sleep. Thinking of Faith happy and laughing with friends while Matt is grieving for the daughter she stole from him, I went out and worked for three hours and wrecked it.' She looked at Gwenllian tearfully and whispered, 'Matt must have inherited his temper from me.'

'Nonsense, you don't need a bad temper to relish revenge. That can be coldly and calculatingly carried out.' She hugged Carol. 'I can fully understand how you felt. And I admire your bravery in carrying it out.'

'I don't feel brave. I feel utterly ashamed.'

* * *

On Christmas morning Faith woke early and was instantly aware of the silence that tingled with that special feeling of excitement that the day brings. Memories of other Christmases came to her, most of which echoed with low expectation and disappointment. Despite Saturday's disaster, this one would be different.

Dinner was planned for two o'clock and she prepared the vegetables and part-boiled the potatoes for roasting. At nine o'clock she had everything ready, and the table was set for six. She made a pot of tea and was just about to sit down when there was a knock at the door. It opened and Ian called. He was carrying a spray of holly, ivy and mistletoe arranged in a small vase. 'Mum thought you'd like this,' he said then stared in disbelief when she burst into tears.

When he had been told what happened he promised to talk to the police. 'You have to tell them about Matt,' he told Faith. 'How can they help if they don't have all the facts?'

'No,' she insisted. 'Matt wouldn't have done this. He might be angry, but this was a spiteful act. He'd face me with his anger, not sneak in and do this. More the behaviour of a child in a temper than a grown man.'

'Do you know a child who would do this?' Ian asked doubtfully.

'No, nor an adult. It's just unbelievable that someone could hate me so much.' She shivered, her arms wrapped around herself. 'The worst part for me is knowing that someone must have been watching us, waiting for the opportunity.'

'Don't think that. It was more likely to have been an opportunistic action.'

'More publicity for me I suppose, although I don't know why I worry about more publicity,' she said as he was leaving. 'By this time everyone knows! But I keep hoping it will end and people will be allowed to forget. Whatever happens, I'm considered to be the villain.'

'I'll go and fetch Olive,' he said, 'then I'll see you later in the day.'

Olive came filled with excitement, waving a letter. 'It's from my boys,' she told them. 'In London they are and both with a job. They've got a flat and they want me to visit. What about that, then!'

'I'm so pleased,' Faith said, and wished them luck, with the others adding their good wishes. It was a happy beginning to the celebration.

'You couldn't have asked for a better Christmas present,' Mrs Gretorex added, and there was a sadness in her voice, although, Faith didn't question her. Mrs Gretorex and her husband were very private people and Faith knew no more about them than she had been told on their first day at No 3.

'I know my boys have been difficult but they aren't really bad. Once they find their feet they'll be model citizens, you wait and see,' Olive said happily.

There was a scattering of parcels under the table where the tree had once stood and they took it in turns to open them. Jean and Roland had sent a gift, as had Menna and Geoff and Winnie and Paul. Each of the friends had packed a surprise for the other tenants so the laughter filled the small, overcrowded room. Winnie had been unwell during the days before Christmas but the children had made Faith a calendar for 1962, on which they had stuck an enthusiastic number of stars.

The meal was declared a success, but the praise wasn't exaggerated, no one found it necessary to compensate artificially for the disaster of the previous Saturday. They sat squashed together to listen to the Queen's speech, played a few silly games instigated by a very happy Olive, then they stayed together for the rest of the afternoon talking, listening to the wireless and playing board games, before returning to their own rooms, planning to come back for supper.

The easy way the day had passed showed the strength of their friendship and Faith was grateful, although the cheerful atmosphere was a little forced because of what had happened two days previously. She saw the mess created in her home every time she closed her eyes and Matt's dark, handsome face seemed to be standing looking at it with her, with a frown of satisfaction on his face and amusement in his eyes. Matt or some mysterious stranger: who could hate her enough to do this?

Supper was an easy meal shared by Ian and Vivienne. They had brought a wind-up gramophone and they listened to Russ Conway, Frankie Vaughan and David Whitfield and sang along with the popular tunes. When everyone had gone home, Faith was so tired and happy that for once, sleep came easily.

* * *

For Matt and his mother, Christmas was a quiet affair. Matt spent most of the time working, the sound of hammer on chisel a reminder to Carol of his solitary state. He grew angry with her when she asked him to stop. 'I'm lonely too,' she reminded him.

'Then go out! Visit one of your friends, have fun with their families!' His bitterness was apparent and she grieved for him.

* * *

The next time the police called to see Faith it was simply to tell her they had nothing to report. One of them, Sergeant Meyrick, looked at her in silence for an unnerving minute. 'Are you sure you can't tell us anything more, Miss Pryor? It's unusual for a victim not to have some idea of the perpetrator.'

She hesitated for a moment, then took out copies of the newspaper reports of Matt's imprisonment and the one about her walking away from her child. Under his gentle persuasion she told him her reasons for abandoning her daughter although she still insisted Matt was not the father. She could never go back on that lie. He listened and nodded silently, looking thoughtful but giving away nothing of how he felt. She presumed that, as a man, he would support Matt, believe his story that the girl was the guilty one, that she had been very wrong to deprive Matt of his child.

'I might have been wrong,' she murmured when the silence seemed to go on and on, and her guilt was increasing with every second. 'Perhaps the girl was to blame and exaggerated her side of it to get sympathy for herself and her child.' Still he said nothing, just stared into space perhaps considering her situation at the time — or that of Matt.

He closed his notebook into which he had written very little, and stood to leave.

'Thank you, Miss Pryor. I hope whoever did this is satisfied with ruining your Christmas and won't bother you again.'

'He — or she — didn't ruin it. My friends and I had a very happy time.'

'I'm glad.'

Faith felt depressed after his visit, convinced that her story had made her less of a victim and more the villain. She searched through the newspapers every day, fearing more publicity, but days passed and the papers were filled with world events and information about pounds, shillings and pence one day changing to decimalization, which seemed unlikely. Thanks to the timing of it, there was no mention of what happened to her on 23rd of December.

She was screwing up newspaper to light the fire one day when a headline caught her eye. It was a report on the availability of a birth control pill and she wondered how differently things would have worked out if such a thing had been available when she met Matt. Would she have married him? Marriage and a family of her own were things she had needed so badly after more than twenty years of being alone, and she thought she would have done, eventually.

Perhaps, if the pill had been available she might not have had her daughter, but she could still have tied herself for life to Matt, a man capable of violence against a young girl. Learning about it from that newspaper article would have come too late. That would have been much worse. She began to think of the birth of her daughter in a different light. Her instantaneous protective love for the child she hadn't begun to know, whose face she could not envisage, had given her the strength to walk away.

Ian and his mother called. He went to talk to Faith, hugged her, trying to cheer her out of the sadness that clouded her eyes.

'They seem very fond of each other,' Kitty whispered to Vivienne, smiling to encourage confidences.

'Little chance of romance developing,' Vivienne replied sadly. 'Faith doesn't give the impression that she plans to stay. Ian was badly hurt by a previous love who left him when they were planning their marriage. Now he fears becoming too fond of her, afraid to give more than the friendship they enjoy.'

Faith overheard and depression deepened. She felt unlovable, but it passed and she told herself how fortunate she was to have the friendship of them both.

Christmas was always a time of mixed emotions. Happiness as friends gathered and surprises were revealed, but a time also when other people who had been lost were brought poignantly to mind. Faith thought of her sister and her parents, and wondered if they too were celebrating the occasion among friends. She daydreamed about what they were like, how they had spent their lives and sometimes imagined ordinary people doing ordinary jobs. At other moments she imagined them as successful business people, content and without giving her a thought. They don't even know I'm alive, she thought, and I have no idea whether they survived the bombing all those years ago. My mother must have died, she comforted herself. If she'd lived she would have searched until she found me. She would never have given up.

Shops reopened and gradually things returned to normal. The weather became colder but on her day off and sometimes in the evenings she went for long walks. A fall of snow coaxed her across the fields and she came back cold and hungry, and happy to have a place of her own and friends to share it. It was here she should concentrate her efforts, not the impossible dream of a family suddenly appearing, to enfold her in love. They'd probably dislike me anyway, she believed in her most miserable moments. They'd walk away and I'd still be on my own, only more unhappy than before.

* * *

Olive Monk called one Sunday morning and to their amusement, announced that she was there on important business. Having spent Christmas Day with Faith and being unaware of any distrust, she had decided to brave it.

'I want you to look at my catalogue and chose something you'd really like,' she said. 'And also, if you like, you can join my Christmas Club. Start saving every week and get it all out at Christmas in vouchers to spend in the high street.'

They all asked questions and tried to hide their doubts about the risk of handing over money to a woman who had cheated on Faith.

'The vouchers can be used in several shops,' she reminded them. 'And if you start now you'll have a nice little sum to spend next Christmas.'

Because of, rather in spite of, her doubts, Faith knew she had to agree. She decided on a weekly sum and others did the same. Her tenants were intending to stay in the area so there was no reason not to join.

As in the past, Faith's mind immediately flew to the thought that, unlike her tenants, she herself might not be there, but she calmed the thought away. She owned this house and whatever happened, no matter how many times her past was revived in malicious gossip, she was going to stay.

Olive proudly handed out payment cards and filled the details into her notebook.

As it was a Sunday morning the three woman were getting the vegetables prepared for their lunch. Olive looked longingly at the teapot. 'Any chance of a cuppa? I've been out for two hours already today and I'm sinking for a drink.'

Smiling, Faith began to make tea. Olive made herself comfortable and began telling them about her varied customers. Then she startled Faith by saying, 'I've been to London to visit my cousins. My sons are up there now, both working, that's good news, eh? I stayed with them at their flat. It's small but very smart and only up two flights of stairs. They seem to be settled at last. And talk about coincidence, I heard of someone with the same name as you. Someone called Mary Pryor.'

Faith heard the name and it felt like a blow. 'Mary Pryor? She could be a relation. My family were from London and lived there until the war.' Faith tried to keep her voice calm, hold back on the excitement the name created. This was certain to be another disappointment.

'Green her name is now, but she was a Pryor,' Olive continued. 'I asked, of course, but she said she had no connection with South Wales.'

'My sister and I were from London, we didn't come to Wales until we were evacuated in 1939. Do you have an address? They might know something that would help me find my family.'

Olive shrugged as she reached for a biscuit. 'Unlikely, according to her. She said they haven't any lost relatives.'

'A cousin, maybe,' Faith urged. 'Cousins lose touch after a generation. How many people keep in touch with second cousins?'

'All right, I'll ask my boys to give me the woman's address. And what if I give them yours, so they can offer it to this woman? She might write and tell you about herself. Unlikely, but you might find a connection. Now where's that tea, before I collapse like a pile of desiccated coconut?'

For days Faith watched for the postman like a lovesick girl but there was nothing from London. Weeks passed and at the end of March, having been promised a few days off before the summer visitors began arriving and the shop became extra busy, Faith decided to go to London.

She was checking her minimal wardrobe, trying to decide what to wear, when Olive offered to lend Faith her warm winter coat. As her choice was between an old-fashioned linen swagger coat or the even older black showerproof she wore to work, she agreed. On the morning she left she realized that Olive's coat was too big and slightly more shabby than she'd been aware, but it had once been very smart. She'd have felt better wearing her own but couldn't hurt her friend's feelings, and she was glad of its warmth. As she walked to the station she noticed that a corner of a pocket was torn and on the train a button fell off. There was a faint mark across the front, probably from carrying shopping. She regretted choosing it but it was too late to worry now.

It wasn't the first time she had tried the agencies and election registers, but London was such a huge place and in the past she'd had no idea in which area to begin her search. At least this time she had a starting point. She went first to see Olive's sons, who introduced her to their landlady.

Gaynor was a large woman, slow of speech and sluggish in movement. She was far from helpful.

'The Mrs Pryor you speak of was only visiting,' she said. 'My friend says she's passed on your address but it's up to her whether or not she writes. So there's no point in worrying her.'

'If I could just speak to her,' Faith pleaded. A shake of the head was the only reply.

Fortunately, Olive had given her the name of the person who shared her name and she knocked on doors persistently for the rest of that day and the next.

She lost count of the number of times she had asked if the person opening the door knew the name but then, during the late afternoon of the last day, she had a response.

'Mrs Green, yes, she lives in number fifteen.'

Faith gave a huge sigh of relief when she was told the woman had previously been Miss Pryor. 'But,' the woman went on, 'she might be away from home, she travels around buying fancy stuff to sell in that posh shop of theirs.'

Telling herself not to be too hopeful, that a name didn't mean they were a part of her missing family, Faith had a job to hold herself back from running as she followed the directions and headed for the 'posh' shop.

Two buses and a walk eventually took her to the address. 'Posh' shop was a good description, she thought as she looked in the windows of the place called Beautiful Homes, admiring the expensive wallpapers, glass and china ornaments, and elegant furnishings. Drapes decorated the walls and small areas of the interior were set up to represent rooms. Many of the items on display were from foreign lands and everything looked seriously expensive. Faith took a deep breath and went inside, conscious of her untidy appearance.

The sales assistant, or Design Adviser, as it said on her label, approached. She was smartly dressed and skilfully made up. Faith guessed they were around the same age and she smiled nervously. The young woman looked at her doubtfully. She can tell before I speak that I couldn't afford to buy anything from this place, Faith decided, but she held up her head and in what she called her best 'teachers' voice asked to see the owner, a Mrs Green.

'I'm sorry, miss — er — madam, but Mrs Green doesn't see anyone without an appointment. May I give her a message?' The haughty expression, the accent, the hard look in the young woman's eyes almost made Faith run from the shop, but she took a deep breath and said, 'Not really, there's something I need to discuss with her, a private subject.'

'Sorry, but in that case I really can't help.'

As Faith walked out she saw the young woman brush down her skirt with an impatient hand. As though just talking to me had offended her, she thought. She was disappointed but at least she now had an address and could write again. Her contact, through Olive, mustn't be lost. She would come again and this time she would be better prepared, not allow herself to be scared off by the over-confident young woman. She would speak with more authority and carry all the information she had on herself, her parents and sister.

In Beautiful Homes the assistant stared after her curiously. 'Mother,' she said to the woman sitting in the office, writing in an order book, 'a strange woman with a Welsh accent just called and she was dressed, well, hardly better than a tramp.'

'She didn't come to place an order for refurbishing her town house then?'

'Hardly.' She picked up an invoice and put it back, her movements nervous. Who was the strange woman who had asked to talk to her mother? Best not to take a chance, there were some very odd people about. 'She might have been an eccentric millionaire,' she said with a smile.

With her mother too far away to hear, the young woman instructed the secretary to hold back any letter for her mother with a Welsh postmark. 'It must be handed to me in private,' she explained. 'Someone is bothering my mother and I want to prevent it going any further.' Better safe than sorry.

* * *

Faith sat on the train on her way back to South Wales and allowed her imagination to drift, seeing scenes in which she was reunited with her sister, Joy. Although her vision of her sister was completely imaginary, and she simply pictured someone like herself. If she was like the young woman in Beautiful Homes she didn't hold out much hope of their being instant friends. Had she been wrong to have concentrated on finding her sister rather than her mother? They had all been lost to her for so long it was hard to remember that her mother would still be in her forties and was almost certain to be alive if she had survived the years of bombing. Maybe it wasn't a sister she'd find but a parent. Just so long as there wasn't a connection with that awful Design Adviser!

As the train pulled into Cardiff she began composing the letter she would write to this Mrs Green, who had once been called Pryor. Try as she might to stay calm, excitement was sparkling in her eyes as she hurried to the platform for the Barry train.

* * *

In his workshop Matt stood looking at the statues he had completed. Beautiful, he knew that, but impossible to sell. While business had slumped following the revival of talk about his court case and imprisonment, he had concentrated on the fine work he so loved. There was a mermaid, six feet long and beautifully designed to enhance a garden pond, and a deer, its expression startled, which he envisaged peering out from a shrubbery. These were indulgences, only suitable for large imposing gardens, too expensive to offer for sale, but the more mundane stuff wasn't selling anyway, so he allowed his imagination free rein.

His present obsession was a fairy figure, four feet tall and with a smaller figure holding its hand. The delicate carving was painfully slow and he had been working on it between other projects for two years, but at present, time was something he didn't lack, and his concentration was absolute and gave him a rest from his concerns.

Carol called to tell him his meal was ready but it wasn't until she went into the workshop and touched his arm gently as he stood and stared at his burgeoning masterpiece, that he was aware of her, or his hunger.

'It's perfect,' Carol said softly. 'You have such a wonderful talent and deserve recognition.'

A woman came into the yard as they were walking to the house, Matt stopped to attend to her. She went into the workroom and stood in front of the almost finished work.

'Can I help you?' Matt asked.

'Are you Matt Hewitt?

'Yes. Heard about me have you?' he asked, expecting her to be another reporter or just there for more gossip.

'This fairy statue, it's a commissioned piece?'

'No, it's something I wanted to do.'

'And it's for sale?'

'It might be,' he replied cautiously. 'But it's very expensive.'

An hour later, he had made a sale, received a deposit and had given a promise that it would be completed by the end of April.

'I'm Julie,' she said offering her and. 'Julie Charters.'

'My name is Matt Hewitt and before you go, I have to tell you, I'm the one the papers have been writing about. I've been in prison accused of attacking a young woman. So if you want to change your mind—' He held out the money she had just given him.

She closed his hand over the money with both of hers. 'I know all that,' she said. 'But if you create work as beautiful as this, why should your past disasters stop me from owning it?'

They talked for a while during which he learned that she was a widow and owned one of the large houses near the lake and the pebbly beach. They walked around his store room and she praised him, gasping at some of his creations.

Carol was pleased to see that he was smiling when he came in for his afternoon tea but she said nothing, just crossed her fingers and offered up a prayer.

The young woman came almost every day to watch the progress of her statue and they talked a lot. She also sent several people to buy from him: mostly, his cheaper pieces, but it was pleasing all the same. After a couple of weeks Matt invited her out, and she accepted.

They went to the restaurant at the Ship Hotel, not far from the old harbour and afterwards walked along the road to the beach. Standing against the sturdy sea wall, close together for warmth, they braved the cold wind and exchanged details of their lives and other things, finding that they had many opinions and attitudes in common.

* * *

Faith waited every day in the hope of a reply to her enquiry in London, but after two weeks had passed she gave up. Someone with the same name, that was the closest she had come but it was going to end in disappointment like the rest. Perhaps it was time to forget her dream of finding a family, who would be strangers anyway, people she might not even like. She would be wise to accept the contentment of today; living in the pleasant town of Barry, with some genuine friends, and the hope that one day she and Ian might move their friendship on to something stronger.

* * *

Olive Monk, who in her new role of catalogue agent and Christmas Club collector knew everyone's news as soon as they did, told Faith that Matt was going out with a very charming young lady and it looked serious, even though it was just a few weeks since they had met. 'Wealthy she is, mind. A widow with a big huge house not far from the lake.'

'I hope they stay together and she makes Matt very happy,' Faith said, and she meant it. It would ease her conscience considerably if Matt found someone else.

* * *

The fairy statue was almost complete. Matt had taken Julie out several times and she seemed content with his company. Her kisses had become more passionate and he began to believe they had a future together. They arranged to have dinner together at his house and Carol had excitedly cooked the food, then gone to visit a friend. A proposal was in the air, happiness on both their faces. The food was in the oven and as Carol slipped out of the house she saw the girl arriving.

'Matt?' she heard her call, and she imagined Matt opening the door to her and sweeping her into his arms.

In reality Matt did just that, but after their first few exciting kisses, Julie became alarmed. He sensed a withdrawal from his kisses and stood back.

'Is something wrong?' he asked.

Pulling away from him she said, 'The food, Matt. Shall we eat? Where's your mother, in the kitchen?'

'We can eat later,' he said. 'Forget about my mother, she won't be back for hours.'

'Please. Matt, I'm hungry.'

'Later,' he said and began kissing her again. She pulled away from him with difficulty and after staring at her with a curious expression on his face, his eyes as black as coal, he once again held her close. 'Julie, you must know how I feel about you,' he said, between kisses that she struggled to evade. 'I know we haven't known each other long but I knew straight away we'd make a perfect couple.'

'It's too soon, Matt.'

'Marry me,' he said, staring into her eyes. 'Marry me. I love you and I'll care for you, you'll never want for anything.'

'No Matt!' she exclaimed. 'I'd need to know you a lot better before I could think of marriage.'

'But you feel the same as I do?'

'Of course I do. Very much.'

'Then what else d'you need to know?' He reached to kiss her again, his hands pulling at her clothes, pressing her against the wall then half-carrying her towards the stairs.

His strength alarmed her. She screamed and pushed him away. 'You frighten me. I can't stay here alone with you, I'm scared.'

'That's what you wanted, was it? To see what it would be like to be with a dangerous man?'

'Yes, it was!' She ran from the house across the yard and at the gate she called back. 'Keep the statue. I don't want anything more to do with you. I've heard the stories but I didn't believe them. But they're true. You're an animal, Matt Hewitt.'

He slammed the door, took the food out of the oven and threw it into the sink. Then he grabbed a coat and went out.

Carol heard him coming in at 3 a.m. and went down, expecting to be told of his engagement.

'She was playing with me,' Matt said bitterly, 'playing with danger, thinking I was a dangerous animal. That was what she called me, an animal.'

'This is all down to Faith Pryor. She spread this gossip and she won't let it rest.'

'It isn't Faith, it's me.' His voice rose and she tried to calm him.

‘Matt, there’s nothing wrong with you. Faith lied about the baby and put her where we’ll never see her. How can that be your fault? It’s all Faith’s fault.’

He stood over his mother, glaring down at her. He held her arms tightly and she gasped at the pain. ‘Stop it! Stop it!’ he shouted. ‘Stop pretending. I lose my temper and that’s the truth.’

‘But you never did with Faith. She was the one who let you down.’ Carol went on talking, trying to soothe him, make him stop blaming himself, but he wasn’t listening. ‘Let me go, Matt, dear, you’re hurting me,’ she said softly. He threw her from him and she fell against the table.

‘She’ll have to come back to collect the fairy statue,’ he said after a while, unaware of her distress. ‘Or I’ll have to arrange for its delivery. Perhaps I can put things right.’

‘Leave it for her to arrange.’ Carol tried to keep her voice normal, ignoring the pain of his fierce grip and the fall. ‘The woman’s a fool. She had it at a ridiculously low price anyway. If you count up the hours you worked on it, besides the skill you have to make such a beautiful thing, it’s worth far more than you told her.’

‘You’re right,’ he said after another silence. ‘She’s crazy. I’ll keep it. I doubt that she’ll be back. She didn’t really want it, she just wanted to see what it would be like to be with a man who — who was accused of attacking a young girl.’

‘Accused, but not guilty.’

‘I don’t think I’ll ever sell it. Perhaps I should smash it up.’

Carol looked thoughtful, then suggested, ‘Why not put it on the plinth above the door of the workshop? It would be a wonderful advertisement, everyone passing would see it and realize how talented you are. It’s too lovely to be destroyed or hidden in the workroom.’

‘Too dangerous. If it fell on you or me, it would kill us.’

‘Brace it with strong rope from behind. Setting it up can’t be a difficult job for someone like you.’

‘It’s a nice idea. It isn’t as though anyone around here is likely to buy it. Certainly not now my reputation is in tatters.

Although what has a brief moment all those years ago got to do with my work here?'

'Nothing, dear. Nothing at all, and the accusation was a lie, wasn't it?'

He glanced at her but said nothing.

'It's so long ago. My first grandchild and I've never seen her. Now another grandchild lost to me.'

Matt was staring into space, visualizing the fairy statue above the entrance for everyone to admire. They might dislike him but they'd have to admit that the fairy statue was a fine piece of work.

He spent the rest of the day working out the stresses and making a frame on which to fasten it. Then he arranged for a contractor to come and lift it into place and to check the safety of his supports. By the end of the week it would be on display and if anyone wanted to buy it the price had doubled.

* * *

At Ian's suggestion Faith wrote another letter to the people called Green. As before, she addressed it to Beautiful Homes. She wrote more fully, listing every address she remembered, with names of foster-parents and children's homes together with approximate dates. She waited every day for the postman to call, but weeks passed and there was no reply. She followed the letter with a third, three for luck, as Olive promised. But there was no response to that one either. Time to forget the dream about what she might have had and settle for the good things in her life, like good friends, a home and a pleasant enough way of earning her keep.

* * *

In London, the young woman from Beautiful Homes fingered the letter from Faith. It wasn't possible. Her sister *couldn't* have found them! Not after all these years. Her mother's change of name, her own legal adoption by her stepfather, it had all helped to cover their tracks. If that shabby individual with the Welsh accent was her sister she would die of shame. Slowly she tore the letter into shreds and fed it into the fire.

CHAPTER TEN

Olive had built a new life for herself after moving into the caravan. There were several cottages close by and she quickly made herself known. Within weeks she had become a friend to everyone, collecting shopping, running messages, while gathering a surprising number of customers for her catalogue and her Christmas Club. A couple of the farm cats visited regularly and she felt a part of the small community. She filled the days happily and regularly called to see Faith and her four lodgers.

The police had no evidence regarding the housebreaking and theft of seventy-four pounds and she hoped her sons had been truthful when they promised there would be no more illegal behaviour. If they settled and earned their money she would be content. The caravan wasn't ideal but there was more space than when three of them squashed into Faith's back room.

As well as making her weekly collection she would pop in and beg a cup of tea at No 3 some evenings and gather the latest news. Working in the baker's shop, Faith was beginning to know the neighbourhood well and Olive encouraged her to talk. Olive's newsgathering was unbeatable and she often knew what was happening before the people concerned.

'I saw Mr and Mrs Gretorex this morning,' she told Faith in a loud whisper one Sunday morning. 'Walking across the field they were, wandering aimlessly it seemed, crossing the field where there's a building site marked out. They just stood and stared for a while then walked back along the lane.'

'They go out every morning and come back after lunch,' Faith told her. 'Then they go out again most evenings.'

'Secretive they are. Funny really, most people are only too happy to talk about themselves, but they manage never to answer a question and avoid telling us anything about who they are or what they're doing in one small room.'

'Sometimes I think they're hiding a tragedy, something that happened that they can't talk about even to friends.'

'D'you think they were building a house and the builder cheated them? Or they lost their money and had to abandon the place? Poor dears if that happened. To lose a dream is the saddest thing.'

'What's your dream, Olive?' Faith asked softly.

'Me? I don't have any now, except the hope that my boys will get good jobs and settle down. That's no dream; that requires a miracle!' She changed the subject and talked of other people she had met.

Her gossip was never unkind, just hearing about a situation where she could help would send her around to the house in question and offer assistance. She fed cats while the owners were away, walked dogs when the owner found it difficult; she did a bit of cleaning when someone was ill and refused payment, but usually found herself another customer. She didn't earn a lot of money but she didn't need much.

Faith thought about Mr and Mrs Gretorex, whose Christian names were never used. She knew no more about them than on the day they moved in; as Olive said, they avoided answering questions and gave no hint about future plans. On impulse she caught the bus and went to see Olive. 'Come for a walk and show me where the unfinished house is. I have to admit I'm curious.'

Olive led her across fields and a short walk along a narrow, rarely used lane, then pointed into a field. Boundaries were marked with posts and wire and the area inside the wire was covered with piles of sand and gravel and broken cement bags. After making sure there was no one about they ducked under the wire and walked around the area.

Footings had been dug and filled with cement but it was obvious nothing had been done for a very long time. Children had played in the sand, spreading it into untidy scattered patches. The unused bags of cement were solid, having been rained on and dried many times. Chocolate and sweet-wrappers grew like flowers in areas where sandcastles stood, these and amateurish dens, made of corrugated iron and wood, were evidence of the children who occasionally colonized the place.

'It's very strange.' Olive whispered as though afraid of disturbing ghosts.

'What could this place mean to them? They must have other strands to their lives. No one lives fifty or so years without leaving a mark. Yet there have been no visitors and they rarely receive any post.'

Olive's post went to the farm and she called one morning to find a letter waiting for her from her sons. They were moving into a better flat and they invited her to come and visit. 'I confess we'd be glad of your help to sort it out as it's a bit of a mess,' the letter went on. 'We've made a start on the cleaning and bought wallpaper and paint, but we'd be very pleased if you could give us some advice.'

She showed the letter to one of her neighbours. 'Advice?' she said. 'Scrubbing more like!' She was smiling happily; they needed her, no matter what the reason, and that was good to know.

She stepped off the bus later that day and scrabbled in her bag to find the letter. It was Wednesday and Faith was sure to be at home. As she approached the gate she stopped. Someone was in the garden, a woman was walking round to the back of the house, her crouched attitude suggesting she didn't want to be seen. Silently Olive followed.

As the figure stopped and turned she recognized her. 'Hello, Gwenllian. Come back to apologize to Faith, have you? Want your old room back?'

Gwenllian began to run but Olive stood in her way. 'Or are you hoping to ruin the garden again?'

'Get out of my way. I just wanted a word with Faith, to tell her to stop spreading poison about Matt.'

'She stopped that a long time ago, and anyway it's the newspapers you want to complain to, not Faith.' Olive allowed the woman to pass, then followed her back to the gate closing it behind her and watching until she had turned the corner towards the railway station. Then she knocked on the door.

It was opened by Faith who invited her in. 'That Gwenllian Hughes was snooping around your garden,' Olive announced as she put down her basket and gathered teacups from the dresser. 'Cup of tea?' she asked unnecessarily, reaching for the kettle. 'I brought some cake.'

'What was she doing here? Surely she doesn't want to come hack as a lodger?'

'That's what I asked.' Olive laughed. 'Don't worry, I saw her off for you.'

'What did she say?'

'Only that you should stop spreading poison about Matt.'

'There *has* been more talk, although it hasn't come from me this time. Customers have mentioned that a woman is telling people she was attacked when she and Matt were becoming a bit more than friends, but no one believes her. It has nothing to do with me. Thank goodness.'

'I can't help feeling a bit sorry for him, mind,' Olive admitted. 'What he did was a long time ago and there's always a doubt when it's one person's word against another's.'

Faith felt the familiar surge of guilt and she was glad when Olive produced the letter and explained that she was once more going to London.

'While you're there, if you see the person with my name, will you try to get more details?' she asked.

Adding three spoonfuls of sugar to her tea, Olive promised to find out all she could.

Faith wondered about the visit of Matt's cousin. She hadn't knocked the door, so what could she have wanted? Could she have been responsible for the damage in the house at Christmas? And the ruined garden? It seemed unlikely, but she had been very upset when she had realized that Faith was the one who had revived Matt's troubles.

Guilt settled more heavily on her as she collected her purse and shopping bag and set off to the butcher's. When she heard the scream for a moment she was disorientated and unsure where the sound came from. Then she saw a young woman lying on the pavement. She ran to her as saw her begin to rise. The woman was shaken but seemed not to be seriously hurt.

'Come back with me, I don't live far away.' Faith gathered the woman's shopping, which had fallen across the road and helped her to No 3.

'What happened?' Faith asked.

'Silly of me, I tried to outrun a bicycle and had to jump for the kerb. I missed it,' she said sheepishly.

'Is there anyone I can call? There's a phone at the end of the road.'

'No, my daughter is at school. Thank you, but I'm all right now. Please don't bother yourself. I'll be fine.' She kept trying to get up and Faith coaxed her back into the chair to finish washing away the dirt from her scratches.

'I don't want you to leave before you drink a cup of tea. Now, are you sure there's no one I can get in touch with?'

'No, there's only my daughter, no one else.'

Faith was curious. What about the husband? Or surely there was a neighbour at least? She looked at the woman as she handed her a towel to rub herself dry. She looked undernourished. Her clothes were worn with too much laundering, her shoes were at least a size too large, the probable cause of the fall, she surmised. There was a shyness and lack of confidence clearly apparent in the woman's demeanour. She kept trying to leave, apology in her eyes as she tried to escape, not wanting to be further nuisance.

Faith gave her a fresh pad of cotton wool and some medicated cream to clean her face. She placed a mirror beside her then put the kettle to boil and set a tray. Gradually she persuaded the woman to talk. 'You might be feeling stiff and sore for a while. Is there someone at home to look after you?'

'No, but I'll be all right,' the young woman assured her. 'I live with my daughter, and anyway, I'm on my way to work.'

'Where do you work? I'll walk with you.'

'I'm an alteration hand in a ladies' dress shop. The shop closes on Wednesday but I go in and deal with the urgent orders. Thank you, but I have to go or I'll be late.' She sounded breathless, unable to relax, she looked as though she would dash for the door at any moment. Her brown eyes were wide, too large in her thin face and Faith felt genuine concern. A real scaredy-cat, she decided sadly.

When the woman eventually gave her name it was a complete surprise.

'You're Ethel Holland?' Surely this wasn't the bold temptress, the fine actress who lied in court when Matt was accused of assaulting her?

The woman felt rather than saw the reaction. She got up and gathered her things. 'I see you've heard of me,' she said in a low voice.

'You might have heard of *me*,' Faith replied. They stared at each other and it was Faith who broke the silence. 'Matt Hewitt?' The woman hung her head.

'I'm Faith Pryor. I had a child,' Faith said, 'and walked away from her. You were braver than I.'

'You walked away from Matt's child?'

'No.' Faith swiftly remembered to continue the lie. 'She wasn't Matt's daughter. We almost married but I didn't want him to be involved in her future after hearing what he did and that was why I had to walk away from her.'

'But she *was* Matt's child?'

Again Faith denied it but the woman was staring at her, looking right into her heart.

'I have to go now,' she said. 'I always meet Claire, my daughter, from school even though she's twelve.'

'Please,' Faith said, 'come and see me again. I work at the bakery but I'm here most of the time apart from that.'

Ethel Holland nodded, thanked her for her help and hurried away. Faith didn't think she would see her again. Someone else who finds it hard to make friends, she thought, then realized that for herself that was no longer true.

Her lodgers were friends, the neighbours too, and Olive Monk, who had forgiven her for forcing her and her sons to leave, and Winnie and Paul and their boys. Then there was Ian, who she still hoped would one day be more than a friend. No, for her, life was full and happy. She wondered whether she could help the sad Ethel Holland, whose life had been ruined by Matt, by introducing her into the circle of people who had made her own life so happy. Warm, caring people who would give friendship and ask nothing in return.

Ian called later that day and she told him about meeting Ethel Holland. 'She's so sad and frightened. I learned that she and her daughter live in two rooms and seem to avoid contact with any but the most essential people. I couldn't possibly see her as someone who had tempted and teased someone like Matt.'

When they had discussed Ethel and her daughter for a while, Ian said, 'I have to go, I have a couple more calls to make. D'you fancy going for a drive on Sunday afternoon? We could find somewhere to have tea?'

They made arrangements and he left a few minutes later, but a shout made her run after him. He pointed in disbelief at his car. All the tyres of his car were flat. An inspection revealed they had been slashed.

Again the police were called and again they promised to do what they could. Faith told them about her unseen visitor and they spoke to Olive, but a week later they had nothing to report.

Faith saw Ethel Holland again when she called to thank her for her help, bringing a small posy of flowers. Her daughter, Claire, was with her and it was then that Faith realized with a shock that Carol had two granddaughters, neither of whom she knew.

'I'm not the only one to suffer the loss of a family,' she told Kitty and Gareth as guilt once again overwhelmed her, knowing she was at least partly responsible. 'There must be many people with the same dream as me.'

'Don't give up hope, miracles do happen,' Kitty said, hugging her affectionately.

'Not for Carol they won't.'

* * *

Olive went to London and at once became happily involved in the refurbishment of her sons' flat. They had little money and what they did have, Olive spent on paint and cleaning materials. As Faith had done, she scoured the second-hand shops and visited two jumble sales and with a little imagination made the place habitable. 'Comfortable chaos', was how she described it on a postcard to Faith.

As she was putting the card through the post box she remembered her promise to try and find out more about the Green family and their possible connection with the Pryors.

Smartening herself up was not easy, and she rubbed the dust off her shoes and put on the warm coat which she had previously lent to Faith, and set off. Beautiful Homes looked uninviting. Self-consciously, she went in and began looking at the display of glass and china, until the woman described by Faith came out of the office. Loudly, so that anyone sitting in the adjoining office might hear, Olive asked, 'I'm looking for someone called Pryor. Anyone here with that name, is there?'

The woman approached more rapidly, urging her towards the door. 'Sorry, madam, the name is Green. There's no one of that name here.' That Welsh accent again, and, unbelievably, the same coat! 'May I suggest you ask at the library? Or the post office?'

Refusing to be hustled out, Olive moved aside then slowly walked around the expensive displays, admiring but without envy. 'This stuff is very fancy, isn't it?' she said, again loudly.

An older woman came out from the office. She walked moving her hip painfully and using a walking-stick. She wore a deaf aid in one ear.

'Hello,' Olive said cheerfully. 'D'you know anyone called Pryor?' Raising her voice she said again, 'Faith Pryor?'

'Please don't worry my mother! As you can see, she's far from well.'

Olive's sharp eyes were staring at the newcomer, whose face was frozen with shock. Then she turned to the younger one. 'You wouldn't be Joy, by any chance, would you? Joy Pryor?'

'It's all right, Mother, this lady is just leaving.' Refusing to let her stay a moment longer, she pushed Olive out of the shop and locked the door. She went to her mother and with an arm around her led her back to the office. 'It's all right, Mother. She's a madwoman. I had to tell her to leave. You never know what they'll do next.'

'I couldn't hear what she was saying. Nothing to do with Faith, was it?'

'I'm sorry, Mother, but she was talking a lot of nonsense. There's no hope of finding Faith after all this time, we both know that. Now, shall I get you a cup of tea and we can go over the illustrations for the new range of picnic ware. It certainly looks good. I think the white with the green and yellow trim, what do you think?' Gradually she coaxed her mother out of her distress and involved her in business talk.

* * *

It was more than a week later when Olive called to see Faith and when she did she was unsure what to tell her. Raising her hopes on little more than a suspicion would be unkind, but the chance of her finding her family was too important not to give her the information, vague as it might be. Eventually she decided to tell her exactly what had happened and the little that had been said.

'But if this woman is my sister, then my mother is . . . But she can't be alive. She'd have found me. What makes you think the woman is my sister? Do you think she looks like me? And the mother, is there any family resemblance?'

Regretfully, Olive shook her head. 'They're hiding something, though, I'm sure of that. The young one anyway: I had her really rattled. The older woman seemed ill and the bossy daughter was overprotective. Oh, I don't know, I just have a feeling that they do know the name. Go up why don't you? Dress a bit smart and walk in as though you're likely to buy. That way you might get a look at the mother.'

'I was one year old when I saw her last, what good will it do for me to see her? I can hardly expect to recognize her, can I? Besides, I've been there before, and I'll be shown the door immediately.'

'Go in there and make a fuss. Don't whisper, shout a bit. That's what I did and it brought the mother out of the office. Get that far and you're likely to learn something, even if it isn't what you want to hear.'

* * *

Faith wanted to grab a few things and go to London at once but practicalities calmed her. She had a job and she couldn't leave without making arrangements with Mrs Palmer. If she did what Olive suggested and dressed smartly, to look as little as possible as she had on her previous visit, she would need some money and she didn't have much savings.

Mrs Gretorex had just bought a suit for a wedding and she offered to lend it to her. It was blue silk in an extravagant full-skirted design and fitted her perfectly. After buying a cheeky little hat and some high-heeled shoes with matching handbag that cost a frightening amount, she felt capable of walking into the place as a prospective customer. With luck she might not be recognized immediately. Having time to look around might give her the confidence to do as Olive had suggested and make a very loud fuss.

She discussed it with Ian, who seemed amused by the escapade, and also with Vivienne, who treated her to some expensive stockings and lent her a beautiful rhinestone necklace to complete the outfit. Taking Mrs Palmer into her confidence she asked for a few days to go to London and set her mind at rest. 'I honestly don't think the people can be connected with me. If they were they wouldn't have ushered Olive away, they'd have wanted to find out more. Their longing to find me must be as strong as mine.'

'So you want to go so you can put it out of your mind, not with any hope of a happy outcome?' Mrs Palmer asked.

'I could be back the same day. I'll work in the bakery to make up the hours if you wish.'

'No need for that. Go on Tuesday, we aren't so busy as Monday. Get the truth, and if you do meet up with members of your family. I'll expect an invitation to the celebration party.'

Faith hugged her. 'Thank you. You're so kind.' Laughingly, she told her employer about the eclectic outfit she would wear. To which Mrs Palmer responded by offering her the loan of an umbrella!

* * *

The train journey to London seemed endless. She went into a hotel for coffee and to freshen up before making her way to Beautiful Homes again. Her footsteps slowed as she neared the imposing facade and she had a strong desire to forget the whole thing and go back to Paddington and the train back to South Wales. Instead she pulled her shoulders back and down, held her head high, arranged what she hoped was a haughty expression on her face and walked through the door.

'How may I help you, madam?' the assistant asked politely.

'I wish to see the owner,' Faith said, but her voice wasn't loud and the assistant looked doubtful. More loudly this time, remembering Olive's advice. Faith threw everything into one big effort and, very loudly, demanded to talk to Joy.

Wearing a startled expression, white-faced under the carefully applied make-up, the woman she had spoken to on her previous visit stepped out of the office. Behind her was an older woman, who Faith presumed was the woman's mother.

'You are Joy Pryor,' Faith said. Not a question but a statement. The older woman pushed forward and stared. 'I'm Faith. I believe we are sisters,' Faith went on, still in a very loud voice.

'Go and take your break now, Miss Taylor,' the young woman instructed sharply and glancing at her watch the assistant walked through the office and disappeared.

'What nonsense is it this time?' she asked, having recognized her visitor. 'There is no one here called Joy. I don't know what your idea is but I won't have my mother upset.'

Disappointment and disbelief stunned Faith. 'You must be Joy,' she said stupidly.

'Please leave at once.' As the young woman tried to guide her towards the door, Faith pushed her aside and in one final attempt stepped toward the older woman. 'My name is Pryor, Faith Mary Pryor. I was born in 1938.' She glared at the woman, who stared back wordlessly, then collapsed. Faith caught her before she fell to the floor.

Together, Faith and the woman she still believed must be her sister, helped the woman into the office. When the recovering woman spoke it was to Faith.

'I searched everywhere for my daughter. She was evacuated, you see, and after we were bombed I was ill for a very long time.'

'Don't say anything more,' her daughter warned. 'If she is who she says, she'll have a lot of questions to answer before we believe her.'

Faith was conscious of utter weariness. It was as though she had run for miles and had used up all her strength. 'Could

I have a cup of tea, d'you think?' she asked. The daughter called through to someone beyond the office and asked for a tray of tea for three people.

A customer entered. Calmly, the daughter went to attend to her. When the girl brought the tea she handed the customer over to the young assistant, saying she would be available if there were any queries. Then she came back in and glared at Faith.

'What makes you believe you're my sister?' she demanded. 'You've come here twice and upset my mother, so come on. Let's have your story, shall we?'

Determined not to be made to look small, remembering Olive's advice to speak loudly, she told them briefly about her childhood. About the various homes she'd had, a little about the misery of having no one to care about her, although she made light of the actual deprivation of some of her lonely years. 'I was given no information about my family, only that I had a sister Joy and that my family were from London,' she said in conclusion. 'You are Joy, you must be.'

The young woman shook her head. 'My name isn't Joy, it's Verity. Verity Green.'

'Then why all this? Why did you react so vehemently when I asked about Joy Pryor?'

The older woman struggled up to reach for a cup of tea. She stared at Faith for a long time, then smiled. 'I searched for you. I tried everywhere, travelled miles, followed the slightest clue, but no one knew where you'd gone. I later learned that you were registered — for a while at least — in the name of the people who fostered you and that meant the trail was lost,' She named a couple of the families who had cared for Faith but knew nothing about the children's homes or the later names and addresses.

Faith reached out and touched the woman's hand. 'I have searched for you, but everywhere I tried ended with disappointment. Why are you called Green? Did you remarry? Do I have a stepfather?'

'Not so fast,' Verity said sharply. 'We have no proof you are anything to do with us.'

'Yes. Your father was killed just days after you and Joy were sent away.'

'I was told that — when I was much older, of course. I'm sorry.'

'It's all right. I remarried but Roger died a year ago.'

'Stop this, you're upsetting my mother.'

'It's all right, Verity dear.'

'I only know I have a sister, Joy. I can't believe I'll be meeting her after all the years of waiting and hoping. I didn't know about Verity.'

'It does seem as though a miracle has happened,' the older woman said, 'and we've found each other after all these years.'

'Don't be taken in, Mother,' the daughter warned. 'This might be a dishonest ploy to get a share of the business.'

Faith was shocked. Of all the imagined greetings she had imagined, to be accused of dishonesty was not one of them. She stood and pulled her jacket around her. 'I'll leave you to think about that,' she said sharply. 'You can make enquiries about me and although there are some things I've done which I regret, you won't find anything to uphold such a suspicion!' Her hands were trembling as she fished in her handbag and brought out a piece of paper, which she handed to the woman who might be her mother. 'Here is my address and the name of the shop where I work. Incidentally I'm a qualified teacher but at present I sell bread and cakes in a local shop.'

When Verity tried to take the paper Faith snatched it away. 'No! While we're considering dishonesty, let's make sure this gets to the right person this time, shall we?' She put it into the older woman's hand, holding it in both of her own, staring into the woman's eyes, searching for some recognition.

* * *

On the journey home she was glad to have a carriage to herself. Tears were near the surface as she went through all that had happened. Who was Verity? How did she fit into the story? A stepdaughter? She wasn't sure of very much but she did know her sister was called Joy. So if the woman was her mother, where was Joy?

If the family called Green owned the business she could understand a little suspicion on the part of Verity, but could the business be why the younger woman had been so adamant that the story was untrue? Did she really think I've made up this involved story to be able to claim a share in their business? she asked herself. All I want is to know I belong somewhere, that I'm a part of a family. I don't plan to walk away from all my friends and integrate into a group of strangers. Running away is the past. Staying with people who are important to me, that's the present and future.

She went first to talk to Winnie. 'I'll have to go to London again. Until we've discussed everything that's happened neither of us can be sure, but, Winnie, I do feel sure. I really believe I've found my mother and maybe a sister; or even two. I'll have to take a few days off and spend a weekend visiting them.'

'Perhaps I can take your place in the baker's shop while you go. It's really important for you to sort this out, I have worked in shops before and if Mrs Palmer agrees. I could do a few days to see whether I suit. I'd be glad to get out of the house for a few hours and this would be a start.'

'Are you sure you're well enough?'

'I'm feeling fine.'

Mrs Gretorex and her husband were out when she got in, and it was Kitty and Gareth who were the next to listen to her story. Repeating it for Mrs Gretorex and yet again to a very excited Olive made her less confident. Then at the shop the next day Mrs Palmer was curious and asked a lot of questions. When the story was told, she said it sounded hopeful. 'Who is Verity?' she asked.

'I didn't quite understand. She's either a stepsister, whose father was Roger Green, or a child born soon after I was evacuated.'

'I can understand your sister's suspicion, mind. It sounds like a successful business and if you're the lost daughter you'd probably be entitled to a share of it. Perhaps, though, she's anxious because your mother has been disappointed more than once and even after so long, another disappointment would be distressing. Your sister — if that's who she is — is not afraid of losing part of the business but is protecting her.'

'I was so shocked. I expected her to be as hopeful as I'd have been if she'd approached me, not treat me like a villain.'

'Write to her, give any information you can remember, and your mother — if that's who she is — will be able to see if it fits with anything she's learned.'

'Thank you for letting me go. I'm very grateful, Mrs Palmer.'

'Don't worry, I want a favour in return,' was the reply. 'I've decided to visit my son and daughter-in-law in Bath for a few days. Can you manage if we find a part-time assistant for you?'

'Of course. I'll be glad to help. When d'you plan to go?'

'As soon as we can find someone suitable.'

They went through a list of possibles but none was available and it wasn't until much later that Faith remembered Winnie. 'It's just in the mornings I'll need help, things are quieter during the afternoon. If she could come between nine and three, or even one, I'll manage perfectly.' Negotiations took place and, with Paul working mornings and the three children at school, it was arranged.

Mrs Palmer left on Thursday evening and planned to stay until the following Wednesday. Faith started an hour earlier in the mornings and she and Winnie worked together until three, when Winnie left to meet the children. To Faith's surprise, Paul then arrived and helped clean the shop while she checked the till and delivered the money to the bank. He then walked her back to No 3.

She would have managed; the tasks weren't difficult but she was glad of his help, and surprised at the ease with which they all worked together: herself, Winnie and Paul fitting into the routine without a hitch. On Saturday there were a few cakes left, and she gave them to Paul to take home for Jack, Bill and Polly. He kissed her cheek, insisting the salute was from the children.

* * *

After discussing her possible family with Ian and Vivienne, Faith wrote to Mrs Green telling her in detail everything she remembered about her childhood. Names of foster-parents and of the homes where she had stayed were all written down, although dates were understandably vague. She waited a long, never-ending week and she still hadn't received a reply. Then at last, at the end of June, a letter came. Faith stared at it, afraid to open it and have a dream shattered. She decided to wait until Ian called that evening. But he was away from home when she phoned, so she went to see Winnie.

Paul answered the door and he looked relieved to see her. 'It's Winnie, she's been taken ill. I've been trying to find someone to come and let you know. Can you stay while I go with her to the hospital?'

Faith removed her coat, thrust the still unopened letter into her bag. 'Where are the children? I'll see Winnie first so she can tell me what I need to know, then I'll look after them. That's the best way I can help. Isn't it?'

'You're an angel,' Paul said, sighing with relief. He kissed her lightly adding, 'That's from the children.'

Once the children were fed and settled for the night she pulled out the letter, staring at the envelope, afraid to read what was inside. She was still staring at it when Paul came home.

'Winnie's all right but they want to keep her in for a few days to make sure,' he said.

They discussed the sudden chest pains that Winnie had been suffering for a while, each reassuring the other, then Paul asked about the envelope. He watched as she opened it.

'It's from the woman who might be my mother,' she told him. Then, after reading it twice, she said. 'The sister I remember, called Joy, lives in Newport and has a daughter.'

'Joy? Then it must be true. Against all the odds you've found your family. Your mother, your sister Joy and Verity, a sister you didn't know existed.'

She looked up at Paul and said, 'Joy would like to visit. All three of them, and also my mother and Verity.'

'How d'you feel about that? Seeing them on your home ground would be better than visiting that classy shop again, wouldn't it?'

'Not a shop, Beautiful Homes is an upmarket design centre,' she said with a smile.

'Even worse. See them in your home.'

'I don't have room for them to stay.'

'They can afford a decent hotel if the family own "Beautiful Homes",' he joked, miming quotes with his fingers.

When she reached home she wrote a reply. Two days later there was confirmation. Verity and her mother would call at No 3 the following Sunday. Joy and her husband and daughter would be with them. Not three but five relatives to face. It was a frightening prospect. Would they like her? Would she like them? Visions of the pompous Verity shattered most of her hope of a happy occasion.

Trying to put the proposed reunion out of her mind, the next day she went to see Winnie and found her friend happily ensconced in her home once more. 'Just a scare, indigestion most likely,' she said cheerfully. 'Thanks for helping Paul with the children.'

'That was a pleasure,' she said truthfully. 'Now, while I'm here can I do something?' A pile of ironing sat on a kitchen chair and without saying more, she put up the ironing board and prepared to tackle it. Winnie didn't argue. 'I do find it a bit tiring to stand too long,' she admitted. Faith looked at her and wondered if Winnie had told her the truth, and there really wasn't anything to worry about.

On reaching home she looked at her small table. There was no possibility of getting an extra five people around that in comfort and manage to eat. Specially as Verity was one of the five! Christmas had been different, they had been friends who thought it added to the fun. It would have to be a hotel. A pity, though; Paul had been right and home ground would have helped her to cope.

Kitty solved the problem for her. She and Gareth were going out. A picnic, they insisted, would be perfect for them, and if it rained they'd find a bus stop in which to shelter.

'Mr Gretorex will be away this weekend, visiting his family,' Mrs Gretorex told her, 'and I can eat at a hotel.'

'But I can't send you away!'

'No arguments' Kitty said firmly. 'You mustn't upset me, I'm soon to be a mother!'

Faith wondered why Mrs Gretorex wasn't going with her husband, but Mrs Gretorex wasn't the sort to explain.

The shopping was done and the meal planned. Ian and Vivienne promised to call at three o'clock in case things weren't going well and Faith needed rescuing. The house was made as neat and welcoming as she could make it. She had done all she could, the rest was up to the fates.

At 12.30 on that Sunday everything was ready, the roasting joint and the potatoes around it looked perfect. She'd had no doubt what to cook, everyone liked a roast. She turned everything down, added coal to the fire, dusted the furniture unnecessarily, then went outside and watched at the gate for their arrival.

A large car arrived and the people she longed to see, yet dreaded to face, walked up the path. The woman who might be her mother, and Verity. She opened the door and faced the first problem. How should she greet them? A handshake, a polite hug? Or should she just stand and allow them to file past like customers booked for Sunday lunch at a small café?

They shook hands.

The second problem was that Verity didn't eat meat. If anyone was going to be difficult today, Faith had guessed it would be Verity.

'Omelette?' Faith asked brightly.

Before they had removed their coats, another car drove up and a young woman with her husband and daughter stepped out. The first shock was to see how much alike Joy and Faith were. With a couple of years between them they wore their hair in a similar style, their clothes were in the same subdued shades and their eyes revealed the same excitement as they approached, hugged each other and kissed.

'Joy?' Faith said breathlessly.

'I'm Joy, this is my husband, and our daughter. Helen Mary.' She looked quizzically at Faith. 'My middle name and yours.'

'Then you really are my sister?'

'So it seems. Today we'll find out for certain.' Faith shook hands with Joy's husband Simon, then bent down to greet the little girl. 'Hello, Helen Mary, come on in, the others are here.' Simon was smiling at her, then looking at his wife. 'Peas in a pod. No doubt about it,' he said.

Faith felt her heart racing making her feel breathless and she wondered how she would survive without bursting into tears. She concentrated on making the little girl feel at home and as soon as she began to set out the meal, she felt better able to cope.

The meal was a success, apart from the slight inconvenience of cooking an omelette for Verity, who also refused the dessert, convinced the pastry on the apple pie had been made with animal fat. As Faith had guessed, Verity repeatedly managed to disrupt the otherwise pleasant gathering.

'I was injured during an air raid,' her mother told Faith.

'Apparently she was unconscious, lying across me to protect me,' Joy added.

'I was very confused for months, and for a long time after that I believed you had been with us and had been killed in that same raid. So it was a long time before I started to search for you.'

'It doesn't mean you're the daughter miraculously returned, though. There's such confusion over names, and people moved so much, you could be anyone.' Verity glanced a warning at her mother.

'Why was Joy with you? I thought she had been evacuated at the same time as me?'

'I had a message telling me she had scarlet fever and, as soon as she was convalescent, I brought her home.'

'If you'd been together you'd have known that.' Verity said.

'We were promised a place together, at least, that was what I was told later, but we were separated. I don't think I saw Joy after that first day.'

'Surely someone would have told you?'

'I was one year old.'

'Not for ever! You'd have been told when you were old enough to understand, surely?'

'I remember being told I no longer had a daddy but I chose not to believe it and even after all this time I sort of hoped he'd come back one day.'

'Yet you didn't ask about your sister? How odd.'

'Of course I asked. I've never stopped trying to find her!' Conversations were repeatedly stopped by Verity who seemed determined to disprove her claim.

'I remember us being gathered in a church hall,' Joy said. 'You were sick and went away. That's my last memory of you.'

'You remember a sister,' Verity insisted. 'You can't possibly say this is the same person. This is a preliminary discussion only.'

'Discussion? I thought it was friends getting to know each other,' Faith said.

'It's far too early to think we might be friends, and nothing has been said to convince me we might be more.'

‘Look at them. The similarity is amazing, and did you know they both trained as teachers?’ Simon argued. Verity tightened her lips but didn’t reply.

At three o’clock there was a lull, no one willing to try again. Faith knew whatever she said would be criticized. She was relieved when a knock at the door announced the arrival of Ian and his mother.

Conversations widened; the subject of relationships was avoided and the rest of the afternoon was relaxed. Vivienne helped her make tea, Ian handed round plates of cakes and sandwiches and at 5.30 the visitors prepared to leave.

‘I have a question for you,’ Verity said as she picked up her handbag. ‘How did you and that other person who came to Beautiful Homes, manage to be wearing the same ghastly coat?’

Faith and Vivienne laughed but didn’t try to explain.

As the two cars drove away Faith turned to Ian and said, ‘I still don’t know who Verity is.’

‘Fingers crossed she isn’t another sister,’ he said. ‘She’s prickly beyond.’

A letter two days later confirmed that Verity was a sister, born after the death of their father. It also informed her that Verity was getting married in October and that she, Faith, was invited. She took the letter to show Winnie and to check on her friend’s recovery.

‘I’ll have to tell them about Matt and my abandoned baby,’ she said, when the letter had been reread. ‘They won’t want to know me once they know about that. This could be the end, just when I was feeling so hopeful.’

* * *

When the card came inviting her to Verity’s wedding, Faith knew it was time to tell her secret. It was tempting to do so in a letter, but instead, she travelled up to London on a Sunday morning, intending to travel back the same day. Aware of the distress of having to tell her new family about her daughter, Winnie at once offered to go with her.

'I know I can't help,' she said, 'but we can travel together and go somewhere to have a meal and make it a bit of a day out. No matter how the day ends you won't be on your own.'

Faith thanked her friend and gratefully accepted.

They left very early, intending to give themselves time for coffee somewhere before going to see Faith's mother and sister. She wrote to the woman whom she still hesitated to call Mother, explaining that she needed to talk about an aspect of her life not so far discussed. 'It sounded very mysterious but I didn't want to even hint about what I had to tell them,' Faith explained to Winnie. 'And I won't accept the wedding invitation until they know the full story.'

'They wouldn't turn away from you, no matter what you have to explain. After all the years of searching, your mother won't let you go now. I'm certain of that.'

'I wish I felt the same. I think Verity is the least keen to accept me. She and my mother have built that business and perhaps she's afraid I'll interfere or want a part of it.'

They had arranged to meet at a hotel where lunch was available. Faith was pleased. It would be easier to talk over a meal. When they reached the place and walked into the dining room her mother and Verity were already there and, sitting beside them, she was relieved to see her other sister, Joy. 'Thank goodness,' she whispered to Winnie. 'She'll make coping with Verity a bit easier.'

After introductions were made and the meal ordered, Faith waited with a beating heart for the first course to arrive. When at last the waitress went away, she said, 'I had a child and I gave her up for adoption.'

Verity dropped her fork to her plate and stared open-mouthed. Joy said nothing but sadness and sympathy were in her eyes. She reached towards Faith and touched her arm. Her mother just stared, but there was no anger, or even curiosity, just sadness in her expression too.

'You must have had a very strong reason,' her mother said. She continued to stare, awaiting further explanation.

Faith haltingly told her story, Joy adding a question when Faith turned to her, unsure of how to continue. Unlike all the other times when she had recited what had happened to make her decide to leave her daughter, this time it sounded weak, cowardly and extremely cruel to the father. She was becoming less and less sure she had made the right decision. She now seriously doubted whether her conviction that Matt was likely to encourage the development of his own weaknesses in his child was true. She became very hot and colour rose in her cheeks as her words became less and less confident.

As her words faltered and dried up, the others waited in silence. 'You might think I was cowardly,' she said, reading the expression on Verity's face, 'but in fact it took all my determination to walk away from my child. Whether you can believe it or not, it was an act of love. Allowing my little girl to grow up without knowing her father or being aware of his propensity for anger and hitting out, will give her the very best chance in life.'

Verity looked away, but her mother offered her hands to Faith, who took them and tearfully said, 'Thank you for listening. I'll understand if you walk away.'

'No, Faith. I want to sit here with you and talk. This matter is over and done with and there are so many other things we need to learn about each other.'

Verity added little to the conversation and the mood became more light-hearted as they shared amusing anecdotes and memories of less serious events. Joy filled them in on the arrangements for Verity's wedding and made sure Faith knew she was expected to attend. 'It will be the perfect opportunity to meet some of your relations,' she said, then added, 'although, there are a few we'd like to hide from you!'

Her mother insisted she was welcome to bring a friend. Ian came to her mind but she dismissed the idea of inviting him. She didn't think he'd be easy with the idea of 'meeting the family'. There were connotations of closeness in that which he obviously would not want.

When Faith and Winnie reached home they went to tell the Gretorexes and Kitty and Gareth all that had been said. The strain of the day faded away as Winnie assured her that Joy and her mother genuinely sounded sympathetic. 'From what you say I'd guess they want you to be a part of the family for always. I think you might have difficulty winning Verity over,' she admitted, 'but it's only a matter of time.'

'I have to buy something really smart for the wedding,' Faith gasped, 'and I haven't any money!'

'Don't worry, you can borrow Olive's coat!'

* * *

Ian's mother went with her when she looked in various shops for a suitable outfit. On two Wednesday afternoons, half-day closing at the bakery, they travelled to other towns where the half-day closing was on a different day. Each time they came home exhausted but without success. They eventually found the perfect outfit at a second-hand shop.

The lady who ran the clothing shop had built a name for herself by buying from wealthy houses in some of the surrounding villages and selling from her rather scruffy premises just off the main street in town. One Saturday, having finished early, Faith and Vivienne walked past it on their way home and stopped to look at the window display. Without much hope they walked in and the small, bright-eyed owner came out. Without preamble she asked, 'What's the occasion? Wedding? Dinner party? Theatre?'

'Oh, I've been invited to a wedding and . . .' She didn't finish explaining as the little woman had disappeared behind a curtain. She quickly reappeared carrying several outfits over her arm. 'These will suit your colouring. Just arrived, this one has, fit you a treat, you being a bit heavy, like.'

'Heavy?' Faith laughed. 'Heavy sounds even worse than overweight or plump!'

'Well, dear, you're no featherweight and what's wrong with that?'

Faith looked at other clothes on display but each time her hand was tapped gently and the woman shook her head as though telling off a naughty child. 'Wrong colour,' or 'wrong style,' she admonished.

She ushered Faith into a small fitting-room and helped her into the dress and jacket she had recommended. It was a sage-green, straight-skirted dress, with a jacket lined and trimmed in ivory silk. 'The woman was right,' Vivienne whispered 'It suits you and fits perfectly.'

'Stay there,' the owner instructed, 'I'll fetch the hat and shoes.'

In less than half an hour they walked out carrying all Faith needed for Verity's wedding and she was still laughing at the antics of the shop owner when she reached home.

She tried the outfit on for Kitty and Mrs Gretorex to see and before she had taken it off again Ian called.

'You look nice. Going somewhere special?' he asked.

'Not today, but I've been invited to my — my sister's wedding.' Deciding to risk asking him, she said, 'I was told I could invite a friend, but I don't think you'd like to spend hours with a lot of strangers, would you?'

'Was that an invitation? It sounded as though you wanted me to refuse.' He looked at her thoughtfully. 'You'd prefer I didn't go?'

'I just didn't want you to think I was presumptuous. I'd love to go with you.'

'Then it's arranged.' He held her hand and turned her round and round. 'Wow, if this is what you're wearing I'll have to wear my smartest suit.'

Over the following weeks Faith's excitement rose and fell like a wild tide. Ian was reassuring and promised her a wonderful day. 'If the company is poor we'll make an excuse and leave. Although I doubt whether even Verity would be difficult on her own wedding day.'

The wedding was a large one and for Faith that was a relief. A small crowd all curious about her, asking questions, sizing her up, some suspicious, others blatantly hostile, would have been difficult to manage. Some guests were introduced to her as various cousins and an uncle and a couple of aunts but she took in very little. People gathered in groups and talked, glancing her way from time to time, some smiling, others wearing a frown, and she wished she could overhear what was being said. From some expressions, it would not be flattering, specially, she noted, when they had just spoken to Verity.

'I'm not going to remember a thing,' she wailed to Ian when yet another group had introduced themselves, then moved on.

'This isn't an exam, it's an occasion to be enjoyed.' Ian had been at her side throughout the service and the lull that followed and sat beside her at the wedding breakfast. Amid the smiles, there was only Verity to spoil the day. She scowled whenever she passed Faith and smiled only briefly at Ian when they were introduced; after that she ignored him.

As they were about to leave they talked to someone who introduced himself as Uncle Dewi. He had obviously been watching the proceedings because he came up to Faith and said, 'Don't worry too much about young Verity. Afraid you've come to take half of the business, she is. She'll come round.'

'Why would she think that? It belongs to her and Joy and my mother. I've had nothing to do with building it up.'

'The money, see.'

'What money?'

'It was your grandmother's money that gave them a start and now you've been found, I suppose you'll be entitled to your share.'

'Please reassure Verity that I have no intention of interfering with Beautiful Homes and I don't need money from any of them.'

'I'd talk to your mother if I were you, she'll be able to explain better than I.'

On the journey home Faith and Ian talked about all they'd learned and their impressions of the newly discovered family.

‘Are you pleased with the way the day went?’ Ian asked.

‘I don’t expect to have a lot to do with them, they’re busy people and I live too far away for regular visits, but it will be good to have letters, and to remember birthdays and Christmases.’

He laughed. ‘I saw you scribbling notes into your diary. Birthdays and addresses no doubt.’

‘You and your mother, Winnie and Paul and the children will always be at the top of any list I make, but I am happy that there are people in the world who are my family.’

‘And I’m happy that you’re happy.’ He smiled. ‘Now, what about going somewhere to eat? The wedding breakfast was a long time ago.’

CHAPTER ELEVEN

Mr Gretorex went away alone on several occasions, starting with a weekend then extending his absence for three then four more days. Faith longed to ask if there was a troublesome reason for this but, as always, Mrs Gretorex evaded questions and changed the subject with expert ease, making it quite clear that her private life was just that: private.

Mrs Gretorex filled her time in the house, helping Faith by doing some cleaning and preparing food. When there was nothing more pressing to do she knitted and sewed clothes for Kitty and Gareth's baby. This delighted Kitty who wrapped them carefully in tissue paper and put them in a Moses basket she had bought ready for the new arrival. She brought them out to show any visitors to the house and when Mr Gretorex came home after an absence of almost a week, she showed him. To Kitty's embarrassment he brushed them aside with hardly a word.

It was obvious something was wrong and although she longed to help, Faith knew she had to wait and hope that eventually Mrs Gretorex would come to her. The rent was paid regularly and the Sunday lunch arrangements still brought them together once a week and no one said anything further when Mrs Gretorex was alone.

'Goes to the library a lot, she does,' Olive reported, 'and reads romances and historicals.'

'Has there been anything happening at the building site?' Faith asked.

Olive shook her head. 'I did see her sitting up there once. Heaven knows what she was thinking about, sitting there in the cold all alone. Worried I was, so I went back to the caravan and made a flask of tea, but when I got back she was gone.'

Kitty told them later that their house was almost finished and Faith looked sad. It seemed likely that Mr and Mrs Gretorex would be leaving soon. They were unhappy and if he wanted to live somewhere else, his wife would surely go with him. Kitty and Gareth would move into their new home and once their baby was born they wouldn't visit very often. She would be losing all her friends and it wasn't a happy thought. Thank goodness for Winnie and Olive. They were close by and hopefully that wouldn't change.

* * *

On Wednesday afternoon Faith called to see Winnie and suggested a walk around the lake and a cup of tea in the café. She looked at her friend as she slowed down on the slightest incline. She sat on every available seat and on garden walls and even talking made her breathless. It was clear she hadn't told them the truth about her illness. As they turned for home Faith was alarmed at how exhausted she appeared. Calling one day when she knew Winnie would be out, she asked Paul for the truth.

'She insists it's nothing but a recurring chest infection and she refuses to let me talk to the doctor.'

'Refuses to let you? Paul, you're her husband, of course you need to find out what's wrong.'

'I've tried and although he hints that things maybe worse than she's telling me, he won't break confidences.'

'Then remind him you have three children!'

'Would you look after them on Sunday? I thought I'd borrow a car and take her to the seaside. She'd like that. Somewhere quiet, down The Vale perhaps.'

'Of course, Paul. You really do have to make her face whatever's wrong with her and get the necessary treatment.'

'If we can have a day together, I'm hoping to persuade her to talk.'

To Faith's surprise, Ian offered to share the care of Jack, Bill and Polly and promised them a day to remember.

'If Winnie is seriously ill they'll miss out on lots of things, so if you agree, we can make a difference.'

'Agree? I'm thrilled that we'll do this together.' Then she glanced at him, had she sounded too sure of him? Would the word 'together' give him doubts and cause him to avoid seeing too much of her? She was fond of him and guessed he felt the same, but there was always a hesitation, a wordless warning to her not to expect too much of him.

'I thought we'd take them to Bristol Zoo, what d'you think?'

'They've never been there. That's a lovely idea. I'll pack a picnic and we can treat them to a meal on the way back. I'll check with Paul to make sure he agrees to us taking them so far away before I tell them.'

'Paul trusts you, doesn't he?'

'I hope so.'

'You make friends easily. He — and Winnie of course — is very fond of you.'

Was there some hidden comment in the words? She shrugged. Was she getting paranoid? But the hesitation before including Winnie sounded curious.

Both Winnie and Paul were happy for the children to go to Bristol Zoo and there was great excitement once the children were told. She was laughing as she closed the door on them and set off home. Still smiling she was startled when Matt's cousin Gwenllian appeared and at once complained.

'Happy are you? You've no right to happiness after ruining Matt's life,' she said.

Faith turned away and hurried along the lanes back to No 3, her expression solemn. She hadn't replied, there was nothing she could have said to placate the woman. She wore her anger proudly, like a badge, outrage threatening to burst out whenever an opportunity offered.

Faith sighed as she went inside. Gwenllian must grow tired of her campaign eventually. She began planning what she would make for the picnic and the smile returned.

* * *

Verity was curious about the man Faith had treated so badly. Imagine giving away his child after denying he was the father. What sort of a man was he that he could cause such vindictiveness? Their new sister was obviously not as angelic as she appeared. There could never be a strong enough reason for her to treat a man she had loved like that. Verity took a couple of days off and, after telling her mother she was going to spend a few days in the north searching for new suppliers for their china and glass, she made her way to Barry and began asking for the workshop of Matt Hewitt.

A wedding and a honeymoon hadn't distracted her from her determination to discredit Faith. There was a lot to lose. Besides, her new husband was away for three weeks on a sales trip in Belgium. With cats away the mice will play, she thought with a smile. A visit to this Matt Hewitt might be interesting.

He was easy to find as, besides his skills as a sculptor and designer of garden furniture, the notoriety of the long-ago court case and its recent revival, made his name well known to most of the residents of the town. She travelled by train, then a taxi dropped her at the corner of the road in which Matt's workshop was situated. She walked slowly along, studying the rather untidy yard with the workshop at the far end. Above the entrance to the workshop was a statue that at once caught her eye. It represented a fairy, with a smaller figure holding her hand. It was beautiful.

As she reached the gate Matt came out of the workshop. He looked up and waited for her to approach. She didn't know what she had expected: someone small and anxious to please? Covered in stone dust and wearing overalls? Certainly someone boring, if he'd been attracted to someone like Faith. But Matt startled her with his dark good looks and strong physique. He stared at her boldly as she smiled and walked towards him; his eyes were almost magnetic and she found it hard to look away.

Forcing herself back to her usual arrogant style, she said, 'I believe you make some high quality sculptures besides these, er, things,' she waved an arm disparagingly at the garden benches and gnomes and planters surrounding them. 'I do hope I haven't travelled this far to see these cheap items.'

'None of my work is cheap and I always make the best quality, even if it's a flower pot for a child. Now, will you tell me how I can help, I have work to do.'

Heavens. This wasn't what Verity had expected at all. What had Faith been thinking of, walking away from this man?

'I run a London shop specializing in the best of modern design,' she said, trying to recover her poise. 'I noticed the statue of the fairies above the door, can you tell me how much it costs and whether you have anything of a similar nature to show me?' All the time she was talking it was as though she was listening to someone else's voice, the man had so confused her.

'You'd better come in and look at my display,' he said. He turned away and walked into the workshop, assuming she would follow. Again she was surprised. Not much charm about him for all his magnetism.

It was only when he began talking about the various pieces that his voice softened. The work was mostly statues of beautiful women designed for elegant gardens, or statues of small children in beguiling poses. Outside were the small, popular ornaments for small back gardens, but in here was where he gained his pleasure. She touched a model of a child holding up a shallow basket in which water would attract wild birds, and he smiled at her obvious delight.

She said very little, just allowed him to talk as he explained that some of the ideas came from poetry, or books he had loved as a child. 'Some of my happiest memories are from when I was young,' he said. When she left she had arranged to buy three statues for a startlingly high price and, having seen photographs of some of his previous work, promised to return for more.

'It has been such a pleasure meeting you,' she said. 'An artist with the heart of a poet.'

'Please come again,' he said. 'It's wonderful talking to someone who understands.' He laughed after she had stepped into her taxi, and went to tell his mother. Fingering the cheque, he kissed it and said, 'Idiotic woman. It's so easy to win them over with a bit of flattery and a hint of a tormented soul.'

When the statues were delivered Verity's mother was doubtful, but to their surprise they were sold within two weeks. Verity offered to go back to see if there were any more available.

'He'll probably have a book of sketches,' her mother said. 'Look through it and order what you think we can sell. Your choices were exactly right so I'll leave it to you. Although perhaps I could go and meet him sometime. It's always good to have some details about the artist to give the buyer. Makes it more personal.'

When she asked Verity how she had heard of the man, Verity was vague. 'Word of mouth, you know how it is. That's why I didn't say anything in case he was a disappointment.'

She wrote to Matt and told him when to expect her. When she arrived, he was in a smart suit. 'I thought we could talk over lunch,' he said. 'Then we'll come back and you can see the few quality items I have for sale. I'll bring my sketch book, so you won't be bored,' he said with a quirk of an eyebrow.

There was nothing pretentious about his choice of venue; in fact Verity at first thought it was some kind of joke.

They ate at a small café near the newsagent's shop and the choice was what to have with chips. Verity wasn't impressed but she ate a little of the fishcakes and baked beans. The place was full and very noisy, making conversation impossible and she concentrated on looking through the sketch book.

The variety showed his willingness to create small pieces as well as large imposing ones like the fairies over his door. There were concrete gnomes and small animals, which she guessed were regular sales; some illustrations showed them painted. She tore up a paper napkin and marked several pages before they finished the dark-brown tea and left.

Apart from the nude designed to sit beside a garden pond, the statues were suitable for any situation. She noticed for the first time the fine busts of Romanesque men set on plinths. They represented years of work in between making the cheaper items that sold easily to local people and the occasional tourist who managed to find the place. And he had doubted they would ever sell. He set the prices high and Verity agreed without discussion. The nude to sit beside a pond was going to be a centrepiece for their window display.

'Do you have to go back immediately?' he asked when the business was done.

She looked at him and smiled. 'Do you have dinner in mind at another greasy spoon?'

'My mother will have a meal ready and you're welcome to share it.'

She knew she ought to leave and get the train she had planned to take but instead she found herself agreeing to share their meal. Newly wed or not, it was difficult to refuse this man.

Carol fussed a lot — obviously flustered by their elegant, somewhat haughty visitor with her upper-class voice — anxious to please, but Matt seemed quite relaxed, even when his mother brought on eggs and chips. Verity looked up and saw he was smiling.

'This looks lovely, Mrs Hewitt,' she said. 'I love chips, don't you?'

‘Would you like beans with it?’ Matt asked, his dark eyes sparkling with amusement.

Holding back laughter, she agreed that, ‘Baked beans would be perfect. It’s so long since I had any.’

They were laughing as Matt walked her to the bus stop, insisting that a taxi was a waste of money. He took her arm as they crossed the road and slid his hand down until he was holding hers. At the railway station he pulled her towards him and kissed her. ‘Thanks,’ he said. ‘Today has been good.’

Her heart was racing as the train moved off. She looked back at the platform expecting him to be waiting for a final wave, but he was gone.

It wasn’t until the new order had arrived and her mother was pleased with her purchases that Verity told her who the sculptor was.

‘These were made by the man Faith ran from? Why didn’t you tell me? This could be most embarrassing.’

‘That’s why I said nothing. I wanted to see for myself who he was. We only have Faith’s version of what happened and you need all the facts before you can judge.’

‘And what have you decided? That Faith is lying to us?’

‘There are always two sides, Mother, that’s all I’ll say. Why don’t you come and meet him?’

‘One day maybe, but not yet. Be careful, Verity. In this instance hearing one side is enough to convince me that he’s a dangerous man.’

* * *

Joy and her husband visited No 3 the following week. It was Sunday afternoon, Faith was alone in the house and she welcomed them with delight. The day was dull but they wandered around and admired the garden then sat in the overcrowded living room.

Simon was an architect and he talked about the work he was engaged in. ‘Joy and I met in college,’ he said.

On being told that both Joy and Verity had been to art college to study design, Faith waved an arm around the cluttered room. 'Do you fancy practising your skills by telling me what to do to improve this room?' she asked with a laugh.

Joy said, 'I decided to teach, so Simon is the best to advise on design, although it looks a comfortable and friendly room and I can't think how you could improve it.' Faith smiled encouragingly at Simon.

'Well — it is a very comfortable and welcoming room, but there's an awful lot of furniture in here if you really want my opinion. All these big armchairs against the walls are not the best idea. It's only an illusion but it makes a room appear larger if you can see into the corners. And colour, changing this crimson and using a lighter colour will also give the impression of more space, as will avoiding putting heavy furniture like that couch in front of the window, blocking the light. But there, I expect you know all this.'

The door opened at that moment and there was a chorus of shouts as Jack, Bill and Polly burst in followed by Paul. 'Sorry, Faith, we didn't know you had visitors,' he apologized. 'Come on you three, we'll call another day.'

'Nonsense, Paul. Sit down and I'll find drinks for you all.' She heard the door open again and asked, 'Is Winnie with you?'

'No. We came out so Winnie can have a rest,' Paul explained.

Kitty and Gareth walked in and were encouraged to stay. Ten minutes later, Mrs Gretorex arrived with her husband. Introductions were made and before Faith had supplied them with lemonade, a neighbour called with some Brussels sprouts from their garden.

The seats were full, the children found stools and Simon laughed. 'I take back all I said about redesigning this room,' he said. 'Better if you talk to someone about building an extension!'

That was the first of many visits by Joy and Simon, and Faith knew they would get even closer as time passed. She heard from her mother by letter but there was no word from Verity. She had no idea that her younger sister had been to see Matt and would have been alarmed if she had.

Winnie's condition continued to cause alarm and she spent several more days in hospital. Apart from the hours in the shop, much of Faith's time was spent caring for the three children. Ian called often and she valued his support.

One evening Ian and Faith were about to eat a meal she had prepared when Paul arrived. It was clear from his expression that something was seriously wrong.

'Faith, I hate landing this on you, but can you come and stay the night with the kids? Winnie is in hospital and she is quite ill. I want to be there.'

'Where are the children now?' she asked.

'Outside, in the car.'

'Bring them in,' Ian said. 'We'll take them back later and Faith can put them to bed and stay. That way they'll think it's an evening out and not a panic.'

'Thank you.' Paul ushered the children in and, abandoning her meal, Faith found food for them and produced drawing paper and pencils to amuse them for the time before bed. Ian put aside his meal too and they concentrated on entertaining and calming the three anxious children.

It was four days before Winnie came home, pale and subdued. Ian was away on one of his long trips so Faith was on her own. She slept at Paul and Winnie's house and sent the children off to school before going to the shop. Mrs Palmer willingly allowed her to leave early to meet the children from school. Just as the shop was closing for lunch each day, Ian rang to ask for the latest news. It was a great comfort to know he shared her concerns. On Friday she was able to tell him that Winnie was home and she was no longer needed. She missed him and looked forward to his return the following afternoon.

As soon as the shop closed at four, she went straight to see Winnie and as Paul was seeing her out he hugged her and kissed her rather emotionally. She pulled away, embarrassed, and at that moment Paul looked up and said, 'Hi, Ian. Back from your travels, I see. Your Faith has been marvellous.'

Ian stood with a hand on the gate not attempting to come inside. 'Mrs Palmer told me where you'd be,' he said and he avoided looking at her.

'I just called to see Winnie, to reassure myself she's all right.'

'D'you want a lift back? I haven't been home yet and Mum will wonder where I am.'

'Thank you.' She poked her head through the gap of the door and called 'Goodbye,' to Winnie and the children. Aware of the colour rising in her cheeks, she slid into the car and said. 'Paul sometimes kisses my cheek and insists it's from the children,' she said. It sounded weak.

She chattered about her week but there was little response from Ian. Irritation began to rise. He had never so much as kissed her, at least not with any feeling, so how could he be upset about the peck from Paul? Only this time, she admitted, it had been more than a peck. His joy at having Winnie home had given the wrong impression altogether. She decided to ignore Ian's subdued mood and chattered on as though she hadn't noticed.

* * *

Olive found the darkness along the lonely lanes a trial as she returned to her caravan in the farmer's field. She hid her fears when her sons visited, joking about bumping into the occasional tree and getting lost in the wrong field. She rarely met anyone after darkness had fallen, and when she did the person always called out to reassure her, their country eyes coping better with the poor light than hers.

Both of her sons seemed settled and wrote to her regularly to tell her about their jobs. With growing confidence she put the fear of another call from the police out of her mind. It seemed that life was going to be all right. She was content living in the cosy caravan and was happy with the friends she had made in the cottages close by. Dealing with orders from her catalogue had also widened her group of friends and increased her feeling of belonging and being valued.

She wasn't aware that her sons had guessed that she was less than happy walking through the dark hedge-lined lanes at night and that they were discussing how best to deal with it.

'Pity is, I think she loves living there and, apart from the problem of walking in the intense darkness of night time in the country, she is happy.'

'Then we have to think of a way to make things better.'

* * *

Faith received a letter from her mother telling her they would visit on the following Sunday and Faith was very excited. Joy and Simon had called several times and it seemed she really was being treated as a member of the family, although she still felt less than confident in their presence. Instead of squeezing them around the small table, she booked lunch at The Ship, the large hotel near the old harbour. She invited Ian and his mother, needing someone to support her, mainly because of Verity's continuing doubts.

'Why not put up the Christmas trimmings?' Ian suggested. 'I know it's early but I don't expect they'll come again before Christmas and you can invite them back for tea before they leave.'

'It's only November. Besides, I don't think I want to decorate this year,' she said. 'Remember what happened last time?'

'A whole year has passed and even anger like Gwenllian's has to fade after so long.'

'I don't feel able to, sorry.'

'Flowers then?'

'Flowers would be lovely.'

'We'll go to the market together and choose, shall we?'

* * *

Faith's mother, with Verity and her husband Gregory, were being driven down by a friend and they expected to arrive at one o'clock, but, persuaded by Verity, they set out earlier and went first to see Matt. Verity knocked on the door and her mother stayed in the car. Carol opened the door, then called her son. 'Matt? Look who's here! It's Miss Green to see you.'

Matt snatched the door open and glared but his eyes softened immediately on seeing Verity. 'Sorry, for a moment I thought it would be . . .'

'My sister?' she offered.

'Come in.' He opened the door wide but she looked back to the gate.

'My mother's with me. She wanted to meet you as we've sold so much of your work.'

'Will she come in too?'

'Just as long as you don't offer us sausages and baked beans.' She saw the smile crease his face and beckoned to her mother to join them.

Introductions were made and Matt showed his visitors around his workshop. Verity's mother particularly liked the small fragile flowers he had sculpted and painted that he took out of the kiln. 'These are popular gifts for youngster to give their mothers,' he said. 'I charge less than I should when a child wants to buy a gift.'

Matt and Verity had been exchanging glances even when he was talking to her mother and when her mother prepared to leave, Verity said, 'Perhaps I'll stay a moment longer, Mother. I'm sure Matt will take me to Faith's when I've discussed our latest orders.'

Doubtfully, her mother left with Gregory, and Verity walked back into the workshop. At once she turned to Matt and he walked towards her, his arms open wide. He held her close and she was soon lost in his kiss. 'I've wanted to do that since the moment you first walked in,' he whispered. Then they kissed again. This time it was Carol's voice calling him that made them break apart. 'When can I see you again,' Matt whispered urgently.

‘It’s difficult. I live in London and it isn’t easy for me to come here,’ she said.

They walked back to the door of the house and Matt called, ‘I’m taking Verity to join her mother, back in a few minutes.’ With his hand holding hers, turning frequently to stare into her eyes, they walked the short distance to the van. He brushed the dust from the seat ineffectually before she got in, then he drove her to the end of Railway Cottages.

‘You really know how to treat a girl,’ she said in her most haughty voice. ‘Chips and beans, twice! Now a ride in a filthy van.’

‘Not too proud to accept, though,’ he said, and there was something that was not quite a smile in his dark eyes.

She didn’t get out, hoping to persuade him to talk about the affair with her newly discovered sister. ‘I’m sorry about the trouble you had with Faith. She must be a very hard person to steal your child. It was yours, wasn’t it?’

‘She was my child, yes. I’ll never see her though, thanks to your so-called sister.’

‘You don’t believe she’s who she purports to be?’

‘Purports,’ he mused. ‘Now there’s a fine word. Sounds better than saying she’s lying I suppose.’

‘Why d’you think she did it?’

‘I was accused of attacking a girl when I was younger. The girl convinced me she was older than her true age, and she did all the running. Because of that unfortunate incident, Faith convinced herself I’m evil and not fit to be a father. I’ll never forgive her, never.’

‘I’m sorry if talking about it upsets you,’ Verity said touching his arm, making smoothing movements. Almost mechanically he told his story, then he reached out and kissed her again. ‘You’d better go, both our mothers will be looking for us. We can’t disobey our mothers, can we?’

She turned as she stepped out of the van, shouting in alarm as the distance to the ground was greater than she had expected. He leaned across, pulled the door closed and drove away.

He had none of the social graces, that was for sure, but somehow she didn't consider them important. Matt Hewitt was certainly an intriguing man. A pity about the name, she couldn't imagine being called Mrs Hewitt. Anyone with ambition needed someone who sounded important, someone with a stylish manner and a hyphenated name. She was Mrs Gregory Ormsby-Grantham, that was partly why she had married him.

Faith noticed Verity's bright eyes and raised colour when she walked in, and wondered where the driver had taken her. Perhaps he was more than just their driver? The visit was a success, although Faith found Verity vague. She rarely joined in the conversation, sometimes being startled out of a daydream when someone attracted her attention.

When she was told of the visit to Matt and the arrangement to buy some of his better pieces she became worried. Surely it wasn't he who had given Verity that special glow?

'It's none of my business,' she said to her mother, 'but it isn't wise for Verity to deal with Matt.'

'Oh I don't think there's any worry there, I've met him and he's definitely not her type. Sophistication and lots of money is more Verity's idea of the ideal man and she's found that in Gregory. They've only been married a few weeks.'

'Well, wherever she's been, someone made her eyes sparkle, and whatever else he is, Matt Hewitt is a very attractive man.'

* * *

'I don't think you should see that man again,' Verity's mother warned when they were in the showroom the following day.

'You don't mean that driver?' Verity looked amused.

'You know who I mean. Matt seems charming enough but remember what Faith told us about him. Don't get mixed up with someone who could be dangerous, Verity. A mistake with a man like that is certain to end in real trouble.'

'He told me his version of what happened, and it was far removed from hers.'

'Of course. It's bound to be different. It's natural to put ourselves in the best possible light.'

'Did you know Faith has earned the nickname of the Runaway?'

'That's an odd name.'

'When things get difficult she moves away, runs away from everything and starts again a long way off. She forgets friends and responsibilities and moves on. What more of a problem is there than a child and no husband?'

'They had planned to marry, and would have if he hadn't had an accident.'

'He *offered* to marry her, to give the child a name. She couldn't cope so she lived up to her nickname and ran away.'

'What makes you think his story is the true one? Beware of an intriguing man with charm and looks. Your flirting days are over, Verity, your loyalty is to your husband. Having a bit of fun can lead to trouble you won't enjoy.'

Charm? Scruffy café and a ride in a filthy van without help getting out? Hardly a gentleman. But her mother was right about the looks. Since they returned she had spent more time than she should have thinking of ways to arrange another visit.

'You saw the delicate flower plaques he's made? And the small models of young animals? How could a man filled with anger produce such delicate work?'

'We're all a mixture of good and bad. Just don't presume his good qualities necessarily outweigh the rest.'

* * *

Paul called at No 3 one evening. Ian was there and he excused the intrusion before telling them that the news on Winnie's health was more serious than they had hoped.

'Her heart is not working as it should and she's gradually getting weaker.' he said. His voice was strained and he looked ill. 'I wondered if I could ask you to help with the children when things get bad? I'm managing now, with the neighbours taking them to school and minding them when things are difficult. But they love coming here and if I can ask, just sometimes, make it their special treat, it would be such a relief.'

Faith frowned. 'Of course. Why haven't you asked for my help over the last weeks? I've been to see Winnie and she's assured me everything is fine.'

'Pretence, I suppose. Telling you the true situation makes it real.'

She frowned. 'I won't go more regularly now I know, best I carry on normally until you tell me I need to do more. But please, Paul, we can make things better for the children if we keep in touch. Don't keep the truth from me.'

When he'd gone, Ian said. 'You know, you can include me in that offer. I like those three and I think Christmas, particularly, should be a good one.'

'Thank you.' She leaned across and kissed him.

'Is that from you or the children?' he asked.

'From me, Ian. Definitely from me to you.' She moved slightly and he put an arm around her and slowly kissed her again.

* * *

With winter approaching, work on the garden was over after a couple of weekends spent clearing up and building bonfires. In late November Kitty and Gareth Robbins told her they were moving out. It was a disappointment but also, Faith insisted, a cause for celebration.

The house they had bought was not far away. A mid-terrace with a long back garden. The baby was due in a few weeks and as they'd be so busy, Gareth joked that he'd ordered a double load of cement to cover it.

'Actually, it's rather pretty, mostly lawn, with small flower-beds, mature trees and shrubs and it's been well cared for,' Kitty explained.

'So we don't have to bring our tools and muscles on our first visit?' Faith said. 'Thank goodness for that. I was hoping gardening was over until the spring.' She laughed but there was no laughter in her heart. She would miss them dreadfully.

Life settled into a slower pace as the days grew shorter and the temperature dropped. The flurry of visits from her new family had faded to letters rather than arrangements to meet. The first Christmas card was from her mother and it included an invitation to spend the whole of the holiday with them.

This caused Faith a few problems. Much as she longed to be in London to share the occasion, she didn't want to spend Christmas without Ian. He could hardly leave his mother alone, and besides, there were still Mr and Mrs Gretorex to consider. And Olive Monk couldn't be left alone in that lonely caravan. She explained all this to Ian's mother.

'Winnie will need help too. Paul can't make Christmas happen without Winnie's help and she's too ill to cope. The children won't understand if things aren't what they expect.'

'Your heart is bigger than your house,' Vivienne said with a laugh. 'I can imagine you hiring the local church hall and still not fitting everyone in!'

'At least I can ask Olive to stay for a couple of nights; now the Robinses are leaving there'll be two empty rooms.'

Ian came later and she showed him the invitation. 'I can't go,' she said before he commented.

'The first Christmas since you found them and you won't go?'

'The truth is, they're still strangers. I'd rather be here with you and Olive and the Gretorexes. The other reason for not going is Winnie. I think we're needed to make sure that Jack, Bill and Polly have a good time.'

'A good time with a full house will help you forget last year too, so it's good you've decided to stay.'

'I suspect it was Matt's cousin and she seems to have given up trying to punish me for leaving Matt and my daughter. Thank goodness.'

'Don't be too sure. She's still full of resentment towards you.'

'Oh!' she suddenly shouted and Ian looked up in alarm.

'What is it?'

'I've just thought. I'll have to send presents for them all! What could I possibly buy that would please them?'

'Something small and beautifully made. We'll go to the gift shop where they sell locally crafted trinkets. You're sure to find something to suit the occasion.' He looked at her for a moment, then took out a Christmas card. 'I had an interesting greeting too,' he said.

She read it aloud. 'Happy Christmas, Ian, with love as always from your Tessa.'

'My mother met Tessa the other day and was told that Tessa and Nick are no longer together. How d'you feel about that?'

'Nick's probably been cheating on her.'

'As she did with me.'

'Has this raised once dead feelings for her?' She tried to look calm but dreaded his reply.

'It's made me realize I can't stay in that house. I bought it and planned to live there with Tessa and until I get out, her ghost will follow me around. I have never felt at peace there. Not like you do here.'

'What if she wants to come back to you, will that make a difference?'

'I thought love would be for ever, so no, she can never put it right.'

Faith's sigh was audible.

* * *

Kitty and Gareth came down from their room one day, carrying a huge bunch of flowers, and at once Faith's heart sank. They were moving out. They stood in front of her like a deputation, faces solemn, eyes subdued.

'What is it? Is this a formal goodbye?' Faith tried to smile.

'The truth is, Faith, we wondered if we could stay for a few more weeks.'

Kitty looked at her husband who coughed and said, 'Kitty isn't happy moving into a house far away from people she knows. It's a terrible cheek, we know that, but can we stay? With our parents so far away, she'd be far happier and feel much safer staying here with you.'

Faith jumped up and hugged them both. 'Yes please, I'd love it if you stayed. This is your home for as long as you want.'

* * *

Vivienne and Faith were shopping in Cardiff. They both had a list of people for whom they needed gifts and by five o'clock they had almost completed their purchases. Faith had bought presents for Jack, Bill and Polly, plus some cologne and some beautifully wrapped sweets for Winnie. Their baskets were full and packages were sliding about under their arms. It was time to head for home.

Packets of wrapping paper, silver and gold tape, extra ribbons and some baubles for the tree became almost impossible to carry and they were laughing as they stepped off the train and walked towards No 3.

Paul was waiting at the door with the children.

'Don't look!' Faith called. 'Shut your eyes until I've put your presents out of sight. I don't want to spoil the surprises!'

There was a scramble as Faith and Vivienne sorted out which of the packages belonged to whom and the gifts were taken upstairs, then Faith put the kettle on. 'Tea and some leftover cakes from the shop, right?'

'It seems likely that Winnie will be coming home in a couple of days,' Paul told them. 'It will be such a relief to have her here again. Even if she has to stay in bed, just knowing she's there. The children have missed her so much.'

* * *

A week before Christmas, Vivienne told Faith that she had seen Verity.

'Surely not? If she came here she'd have called, unless I was out when she came?'

'I don't want to upset you, Faith, but I don't think it was you she came to see.'

'She doesn't know anyone else. She wouldn't visit strangers.'

'She was with Matt and from what I saw they were definitely not strangers.'

'Matt? What could Verity have in common with Matt?'

'Whatever his problems, Matt's a handsome man. Besides, from what I heard at the newsagent's they are doing business together. Verity and your mother are buying more of his work to sell in their shop in London.'

'D'you think I should say something? At least tell, my — my mother how dangerous he is? Perhaps she doesn't know about these visits? I have warned her but she chose not to believe me. And what about Verity's husband? He's sure to find out. She can't be my sister! She's vain and utterly stupid!'

'Verity doesn't believe you, or maybe she likes playing with danger.'

'I still sometimes wonder whether I was wrong to give my daughter away. What if there was no danger and I deprived the man of a child for no reason except my own unfounded fears.' She looked so sad that Vivienne hugged her. 'One day your instincts will be proved correct. Just wait and see.'

'I hope no one gets hurt in proving it,' Faith replied, thinking of Verity.

She thought about it for some time, then, taking the notebook into which she had written her mother's phone number she went to the phone box on the corner.

'I don't know whether you want to hear this,' she began. 'It's about Verity.'

'You've heard the foolish girl has been visiting Matt Hewitt?'

'Yes, and I know she doesn't believe me, but he is a dangerous man. I thought I should tell you, but as you already know, I'm sorry if I'm interfering. I hope she doesn't get hurt by him, that's all.'

'Thank you for phoning, dear. I share your concern, although, it's unlikely she'll be amused by him for long. Her tastes run to more elegant men.'

'Like her poor husband?'

'As you say, like her poor husband. Matt Hewitt is such a crude and common, worldly man.'

Faith came off the phone feeling embarrassed, inadequate, someone audacious who was trying to mix with people out of her league. Someone she had been considering marrying was suitable for her but he was far below Verity's expectations, wasn't that what her mother had meant?

When Joy came laden with presents a few days before Christmas Day, Faith told her she had warned their mother about Verity's visits to Matt.

'She's very sure of herself and if things get unpleasant she'll walk away. She's always enjoyed having men admiring her, a gold ring on her finger won't change her. Put her out of your mind, have a wonderful Christmas,' Joy urged.

* * *

Despite Winnie's illness. Christmas was a cheerful time for Faith. There were cards from the newly discovered aunts and uncles and cousins. Letters came from her mother and Verity thanking her for the presents and promising to visit soon. Faith wasn't sure she wanted them to. Weren't they just being kind to the peasants in the funny little house overlooking the railway station?

Vivienne came on Christmas Eve and helped with the preparations. Ian came with his mother mid-morning the following day and they all fussed over a very pregnant Kitty. With Olive Monk and Mr and Mrs Gretorex joining them the table threatened to collapse and a second table was borrowed from neighbours to accommodate them all.

Olive stayed for three days, telling them of the fun she'd had paying out the Christmas savings and totting up her earnings from the catalogue. She helped to prepare food when Faith went back to work on the 27th.

Mr Gretorex stayed for the whole of the holiday period but Faith could see that their previous attempts at putting on a brave face were no longer possible. Unable to ignore it any longer, she sat Mrs Gretorex down with a cup of tea when her husband was out and asked, 'What is the matter, dear? Talk about it, that's much better than holding it all inside.'

Speaking in a low monotonous voice, Mrs Gretorex said. 'We had a son and he died. Since then we've been trying to rebuild our lives but it's impossible. These past few months we have been blaming each other, and we've drifted further and further apart.'

'I'm so sorry, but why haven't you told me? In all the months you've lived here, why couldn't you trust me?'

'It isn't easy to talk about it.'

'Olive told me you were building a house. Why isn't it finished? Surely a fresh start in a new place is what you both need?'

'It was for him you see. He was injured in a road accident and we designed a bungalow specially for him, but before the footings were in he — he passed away. After that there seemed no point in finishing it.'

Faith thought for a moment, then, risking an accusation of interfering, she said. 'I believe you should finish building the house.'

'It's too late. It was for our son.'

'Then finish it for him. See an end to it, walk through its rooms, remember how well you planned it. Grieving is an essential part of a loss as terrible as yours but it needs to end or nothing changes. Finish the house, let your son rest.'

'It won't be easy to persuade my husband.'

'Perhaps he's thinking the same about you.' She watched as expressions of despair and hope flittered across the sad face, then went on, 'I'd be very interested in seeing it and hearing you explain how you designed it. Even if your son didn't see it, it was still a labour of love. May I go there with you one day?'

'Not today, dear. Thank you but I'll go on my own today. Perhaps in a day or so I'll be able to show you. It's a beautiful place.'

'Please. I'd love you to show me, tell me how it was planned.'

When Mr Gretorex came in half an hour later, Faith casually mentioned that his wife was at the building plot. 'There's a bus in fifteen minutes that will take you as far as the farm.' she said. 'You could walk home together.'

* * *

Olive was walking across the field and saw Mrs Gretorex sitting on a pile of wood, wrapped in a shawl. 'She must be frozen, poor dab,' she muttered and hurried back to the caravan to make a flask of tea and bring her old coat. When she returned to the sad scene, she saw that there were two people there. Mr Gretorex had taken off his overcoat and had wrapped it around his wife's shoulders and held it in place with a comforting arm. Quietly, Olive crept back to the caravan, fingers tightly crossed.

* * *

Paul brought the children on several occasions to allow Winnie to rest. The news of her varied from hopeful to cause for concern.

On the Sunday following the celebration, Faith and Ian went for a walk across the fields. It was dry and crisp and they remarked how fortunate they were to have fresh clean air while in London people were dying from the mixture of smoke and fog that was now named smog.

Being so close to Olive's caravan was too tempting and they knocked on the door to beg a cup of tea. A very loud bark was the response and a rosy-faced Olive opened the door. Struggling to hold the collar of an enormous dog, she invited them in.

'What about this for a present, eh? My boys were worried about me going out at night collecting, so they bought me a companion.' She looked at the dog and said firmly, 'Doris, say hello.' The hound gave a huge bark. 'Now sit, good girl.' The dog obeyed.

Tea was made but went cold as they were shown the dog's obedience training in the field. With some help from the farmer and a lot of encouragement by the dog's willingness to learn, Olive had the perfect companion.

When they returned to No 3, rosy-faced and happy, Paul was sitting on the doorstep.

Alarmed by his posture, Faith ran to him and he stood up and hugged her. 'My lovely Winnie died this morning,' he told them. 'Our three adorable children have lost their mother.'

Ian came to them and put an arm around them both. Was it his imagination, or was Paul pushing him aside? He pulled Faith away and placed a proprietary arm around her shoulder, 'We will do everything we can to help,' he said. 'Won't we?'

The slight emphasis on the *we* was not lost on Paul. Once again he pushed Ian aside and hugged Faith, whispering, 'Thank you, Faith, dear. We need you so much. All of us.'

CHAPTER TWELVE

The following days were so confusing that Faith couldn't remember their sequence. She looked after the children for several hours each day and took them back to their home once Paul had finished his tasks. There seemed to be so much for him to do, but Faith deliberately didn't ask to help. Better he dealt with everything himself; that all the arrangements were in his hands alone. One reason was to ensure that he couldn't berate himself later for not doing more. Another was to keep him busy, with less time to think.

With Paul's permission, she, Ian and Vivienne answered the children's questions when they wanted to talk about what had happened and tried to keep everything as normal when they did not. Faith's own grieving for her friend was kept until she was alone.

The funeral, on that cold, dark January day was a sombre affair. People lined the streets to mark the passing of the young mother. Paul was the last to arrive at the church and when the congregation looked back to see him entering the church, carrying Polly, with Jack and Bill beside him there was a murmur of sympathy.

Faith put on a bright face as she walked out of the church with Ian. She smiled encouragingly as she took the three children and walked them back to their house, ready to serve the food that caterers had provided.

The dreadful day passed, but weeks later Paul was still leaving the task of meeting the children from school and looking after them until he came home from work to Faith. Ian said nothing but Faith knew she had to persuade Paul to let go.

He habitually kissed her lightly when he arrived with the children and when he left to take them home. When his kiss became more than a peck she began to worry.

'Paul,' she said one evening when he had called to collect Jack, Bill and Polly, 'don't you think it's time you sorted out a permanent arrangement to look after this precious threesome? Mrs Palmer has been very kind, but I can't continue to take advantage and leave her to clean the shop every day while I go to the school.'

'You're not willing to look after them?' He looked surprised and she felt guilty. 'I thought you loved them.'

She almost relented but knew that would be wrong. It had already gone on too long. 'You know I do, but they're yours and it's you they need, not me. They don't complain about coming here each day but it's home they want. Bill especially, he keeps asking the time and how much longer before they can go home. They want their home and their father. I don't think they'll accept what has happened until they have a settled routine.'

'But I work shifts, and I've been working extra hours. How can I cope without you?'

It was hard but she stood firm. 'Sorry, Paul, but I need to make plans too. It can't go on like this.'

'Does it have to? I mean, can't you give up your job and come and live with us?'

For one, shameful moment she hesitated. A home and children and maybe Paul too one day was so much like her long-held dream, while a future with Ian seemed so remote. He seemed to like her company but showed no sign of ever wanting more. She shook her head and walked away. 'Come on, kids, time to go home.'

'I'll see you tomorrow,' he said as he gathered the children and their belongings. 'We can discuss it then.'

'Nothing to discuss, Paul.' Her voice was strong as she said calmly, 'I'll give you a little time, of course, a week, maybe two, but we both need you to find a solution.'

Ian called that evening and picked up a couple of toys left by the children. 'How much longer before Paul sorts out the help he needs?' he asked.

She was thankful then that she could answer honestly and tell him she had raised the subject just hours before. 'I said I needed to plan my own life and for the children's sake he has to do the same.'

'I'm glad. I feel very sorry for them, but you've done as much as he could reasonably expect. He can't believe you'll continue to give so much of your time indefinitely.'

'I think he did. He seemed shocked when I told him I needed an end to my responsibilities.'

'He accepted it though?'

'Well, he said we'll discuss it again tomorrow. Give him time to think about it and he'll find a way of coping.'

'As long as it doesn't include you.' He looked at her strangely.

'It won't.'

* * *

When Ian was dropping his mother off at the shops the following day, he saw Paul walking towards the council offices. He got out and met him at the steps. 'How are things?' he asked. 'Is everything sorted now?'

'I still have a few things to do, but thanks to Faith everything is settling into place.'

'She's a remarkable person, but even she has to say no sometimes,' Ian said.

'Say no?' Paul looked surprised. 'It won't come to that. I've asked her to move in and look after us all. She can rent

No 3 and come and be a part of our family, the children will have stability. It's the perfect solution.'

Ian was too stunned to say more than. 'See you . . .'

He walked back to the car and didn't notice Matt walking towards him with Faith's sister Verity.

* * *

'Ian looks lost in thundery thoughts,' Matt remarked as they passed without any acknowledgement. 'Perhaps he's finally found out what a bitch Faith really is.'

'That's my sister you're talking about,' Verity said with a laugh. 'My dear, long-lost sister who thinks she can walk into a fortune.'

'Forget about her and come back to the workshop. I've some new ideas I want you to see.'

Vivienne watched as the couple crossed the road and got into Matt's van parked quite near Ian's. How could such a smart and obviously wealthy woman be attracted to someone like Matt Hewitt? The hint of danger? The rumours of a violent past? She shivered as the van drove away, the young woman snuggling close to the driver. Perhaps she didn't know? Should she warn her? No. Best not.

Someone else had seen the couple getting into the van. Matt's mother Carol also looked anxious. She too wondered whether she should warn the girl. Pretend as he might in front of others, she knew very well how quickly irritation could turn her son's mood to full-blown anger. If only she could get the girl on her own and tell her the full extent of Matt's police record. She'd have to be careful; if Matt found out he'd be furious. He insisted that all he needed was a chance, and maybe he thought Verity was the one to give it to him.

Verity had been staying at a nearby hotel, travelling around the South Wales area buying Welsh blankets, lovespoons and other quality craft items. She had been seeing a lot of Matt, who sometimes drove her and sometimes met her in the evening to eat out or go to the theatre or to a concert.

When she was leaving, Carol suggested the young woman might catch a later train. 'We could have lunch and take a walk along one of the local beaches, relax and get some sea air before you go back to London.'

'No, she has to get the ten o'clock train,' Matt insisted, 'And I have to go and pick up some supplies.'

'But an hour or two won't make any difference.'

Matt interrupted, irritation hardening his tone. 'Mam, she runs a business and she has to get back.' More softly, glancing at Verity, he added, 'Any time off she can manage I want her to save for when I'm here.'

'All right, dear. I just thought it would be nice for Verity and I to spend a few hours getting to know each other.' She gave a childish pout. 'You monopolize her completely when she comes. Can't you spare an hour or two?'

'It's all right, Matt,' Verity said. 'I'll stay. I'll just phone my mother to tell her I'll be a bit later getting home.'

Carol didn't feel safe talking about Matt at the house. It was as though the house was eavesdropping and he would hear the echoes and know what she had done. Instead she made coffee and led Verity into the garden behind the workshop.

Matt was curious. There had been an unusual insistence in the way his mother asked Verity to stay. Why did she want to talk to her while he was out of the way? Suspicion brought a frown to his face. Surely she wouldn't tell Verity about his sometimes uncontrollable temper? That was all it was, a sudden rage that he immediately regretted. He eased his foot off the accelerator, touched the brake and the vehicle slowed to a stop. Pulling on the handbrake, shutting down the engine he jumped from the cab and walked swiftly back to the workshop.

Carol felt traitorous, and tension was banging in her throat as she began to talk about Matt's temper. It was a risk, even though Matt was nowhere around. There was a chance that Verity wouldn't believe her and she might even tell Matt what had been said. 'My son is a wonderful, talented man, but like many artists, he does have a dark side,' she said.

Verity laughed. 'Oh how dramatic that sounds. If you're going to tell me about the girl who supposedly had his child after he'd assaulted her, then I already know the full story and accept Matt's version.'

'Perhaps you shouldn't.'

Verity stared at her. 'Are you saying you don't believe him? What sort of a mother are you? Don't you feel any loyalty towards your son?'

'I love my son, but that doesn't blind me to his problems.'

'You think he assaulted that girl and she had his child? Surely he'd have wanted to be involved with the child if he were the father. He would love to have a child and that alone convinces me he was innocent. He'd never behave as though she didn't exist if she were his.'

Carol bent her head, undecided whether or not to go on. She could see from the stubborn expression on the girl's face that she wouldn't be easily convinced. There was a real danger that she'd go straight to Matt and tell him everything she had said and the probable result of that was too frightening to contemplate.

'You don't have to tell me this,' Verity said. 'I'm not about to take your son from you. I have a husband and I only came here to buy a few new lines for our business. I've finished here and next month I'll probably be in Cornwall to see what remains from the Newlyn school of design.'

'I think you're playing with him and he doesn't take kindly to being an amusement.'

'I think I'd better go.' Verity stood and began to walk towards the house.

Carol pulled up her sleeves and showed her where old bruises, yellow and purple, were visible on both upper arms. 'These were from the last time he lost his temper with me,' she said quietly. 'I've also suffered a broken arm and a dislocated shoulder.'

'Nonsense,' Verity said, but with less certainty. 'You're making it up.'

'He loved Faith, so she was safe. He wanted to protect her and he would never have harmed her. Never. Even when she stole his child and ran away. But his feelings for you aren't love. When you anger him he'll lose his temper as he always does. Anger and frustration are emotions he can't control. Please, don't be there when he gets angry.' She stared at the young woman, willing her to believe. 'Verity, I want you to stay away, I know my son and I'm afraid for you.'

'I think I'll go now.' Verity's voice was hardly more than a whisper. Tearfully, Carol followed her into the house.

Against the wall of the yard, hidden by a stack of stones and piles of cement bags, Matt stood, his neck muscles taut, his eyes glittering with rage. He waited until the two women left the house, Carol carrying Verity's small travel case and heading for the station, then he walked to where he had left the van and went to find his cousin, Gwenllian. He needed sympathy, a way of dissipating his anger.

Gwenllian was at home and welcomed him inside. 'You look upset, Matt. Is there something wrong?'

'My mother has been persuading Verity to stay away from me. Told her I was guilty of attacking Ethel Holland and showed her bruises that she insists were made by me.'

'All this trouble is down to Faith. Everything was fine until she came along. They call her the Runaway; pity she doesn't disappear again. People will soon forget once she's out of the way.'

'It wasn't her fault. It's all down to my temper. Gwen, should I go back to the doctor, see someone who can help me?'

'You don't need that sort of help!' she exclaimed. 'Come on, Matt, you've never hit your mother, she was making it up to get rid of Verity. She's getting on and she's afraid of you leaving her on her own. That's all this is.'

'You're right, I've never hit her, but I grip too tightly and I've swung her around and she's tripped and fallen.

Twice she's been seriously hurt, so you're wrong, it is down to me. I just can't hold back anger when someone crosses me.'

'I'll never believe that's true. Faith caused all this by bringing up the story of Ethel Holland. Once she leaves, runs away — that's what she does, causes mayhem then runs away — everything will go back to how it was before you met her. There was no trouble in your life before she came.'

'Faith won't leave. She owns a house and that makes running away less easy to do.'

'She's seeing a lot of that Paul James since he's been widowed. She's probably planning to forget Ian Day and move in with him.'

'A ready-made family, that should appeal to her,' he said bitterly. 'She's obviously forgotten our daughter.'

'There must be a way to make her leave. We ought to make up a few rumours of our own, Matt. Make things unpleasant for her until she lives up to her nickname. A house can be sold. It shouldn't be too hard to remind a few people about her abandoning her child.'

'My child too, whatever she says, and I don't want that talked about, it's painful enough without having everyone treating it like a story from the Sunday papers!'

'Sorry, Matt. I should have thought about that.'

* * *

A child was on someone else's mind that afternoon. Kitty was sitting in Faith's living room and beside her, looking seriously worried, was Gareth, who was thumbing, unseeing, through a book given to them by a helpful nurse. 'I think we should go to the hospital now,' he said. 'The contractions are getting far too close. Will you be all right while I go to the phone-box and order a taxi?'

'Shouldn't we wait a while longer? It's probably a false alarm. Olive said most people think it's on the way long before it arrives.'

'Darling, I'm as frightened as you. But if it's too soon, well it's better than leaving it too long. I don't want my daughter born in a taxi!'

The door opened and Kitty gave a sigh of relief. 'Faith? Is that you? I think I'm about to give birth?'

'Not here, I hope!' Faith said, as cheerfully as she could.

'Thank goodness you're here,' Gareth said. 'Will you stay while I go and get a taxi?'

'No need,' a voice called and Ian came in smiling. 'Come on, the car's outside and we'll soon be there.'

Faith wrapped Kitty in a blanket even though she was far from cold. Ian went ahead and opened the car door, then waited until Kitty and Gareth were comfortable before getting in himself. 'Come on, you'd better come as well,' he said to Faith. So, after scribbling a note and carrying only the key, she jumped in. Slowly, calmly Ian drove to the hospital where they sat and waited patiently for news.

After checking with the nurses, they drove home, had something to eat, then returned to their place on the uncomfortable seat in the dark-green-tiled corridor to wait some more. It was almost eleven o'clock when an excited Gareth found them.

'It's a girl! We have a daughter, six pounds and fifteen ounces and she's beautiful and Kitty was wonderful and everything is perfect.' He blurted the news without a pause.

When he had calmed down and told them everything for the fifth time they went back to No 3. Olive was there and Mr and Mrs Gretorex. The news was reported all over again and in the kitchen, making the inevitable tea, Faith confided in Ian that the only sad note was the thought that now they would be leaving her and moving into their own home.

* * *

Paul advertised for help and had several replies. He asked Faith to read the applications and to sit in on the interviews and she agreed.

'Are you sure that's a good idea?' Ian asked when she told him. 'I think he still believes you'll go on helping him; perhaps moving in is the best solution.'

She stared at him, a frown darkening her brow. 'Are you telling me I should?'

'I can't tell you what to do, Faith. You make your own decisions.'

'Moving in to look after Paul and the children is not one of them!' She spoke sharply, hurt and confused by his remark. Did he really care so little for her that he could see that as a solution to Paul's problem?

Staring at her intently, he said, 'Tell him you won't do it, then. Tell him you can't be involved in what should be his decisions.'

'I admit I want to help for the sake of Winnie and the children, but I know you're right. Paul has to deal with his life his way. I said I'd go and I will, but will you come with me?' She reached for her coat. He nodded and they went out together.

Paul opened the door and stood back for them to go inside, but Faith stayed on the step. 'Paul, I've been thinking about this help you need, and—'

'And you'll help?' he interrupted.

'No, I'm not free to help any longer and I really think it's best for you to choose the person to look after Jack, Bill and Polly.'

'You're abandoning us?'

'Hardly that. I want to keep in touch with the children, I love them very much, but you have to build your new life, making your own decisions.'

'And is this *your* decision, Faith?' He looked at Ian then back at her.

'Yes. My decision.'

Ian said 'Goodnight,' as he put a proprietary arm on Faith's shoulder and led her away but Paul didn't respond.

Later that night, after Ian had gone home, Paul knocked the door and walked in.

‘Paul? Is something wrong? The children?’

‘A neighbour is with them. I wanted to warn you not to wait for Ian to make up his mind. Come and look after us; he doesn’t want more than casual friendship and I can offer you more, much more. Don’t waste years waiting for him to make up his mind.’

Swallowing that unpalatable truth she told him to stop talking in that way. ‘Winnie was my friend and it isn’t very long since we lost her.’

‘You know there was something between us, even before Winnie died, and now we don’t have to pretend any longer.’

Faith stood up and went to the door. ‘Time to leave,’ she said firmly. ‘And for both our sakes I think we should forget you called here this evening.’

‘Won’t you at least think about it before making a decision we’ll both regret?’

‘My decision is made and I know it’s the right one. Now go and please don’t mention this conversation again.’

She phoned Ian and told him what had happened. ‘I should have seen this coming, but I didn’t,’ she said.

‘He shouldn’t mention it again, but if he does, we’ll talk to him, together.’

‘I’ll miss the children.’

‘Once Paul has started rebuilding his life you’ll see them again, we both will.’

She settled to sleep an hour later warmed by Ian’s words; they implied a closeness. Her future was shining just a little bit more because of it.

* * *

Ian was getting his samples into the back of his car when he saw Tessa walking towards him. He stopped what he was doing and waited as she approached.

‘Do you want to see me?’

‘Yes, but if you’re busy I can come another time.’

‘Now will do.’ He didn’t want to arrange meetings, it was so easy for life to become complicated. Besides, she looked as though she had been crying and was in need of a moment of his time.

'I wanted to tell you I'm sorry. Every time I look at this house I daydream about living here with you. I was a fool to be taken in by Nick's flattery and charm.'

'I'm sorry, Tessa, but what d'you want me to do? We can't go back, even if we wanted to.'

'I do want to, that's the problem. Nick and I are no longer happy with each other. He's seeing other women. Ian, I'm so unhappy.' Tears ran down her cheeks from reddened eyes.

Familiarity tempted him in a brief moment of recognition. The girl he'd known since schooldays, a loving friend whom he had helped through every problem, large and small ever since. It would be so easy to offer her the familiar comfort of his arms. He saw a movement at the periphery of his sight and knew his mother was watching. Thoughts were disturbed, then a vision of Faith filled his mind and he knew that she was his future, not Tessa, who had left once and possibly would again.

'I've moved on,' he said. 'My life is full and I'm happy. If you and Nick are having problems you have to work through them.'

Vivienne had seen Tessa from the window and she opened the door and called, 'Don't be late for your appointment, Ian. Tessa, have you time for a cup of tea?'

Thankfully Ian drove off. Tessa ran in and hugged his mother.

Vivienne listened as Tessa told her of the frequent quarrels she had with Nick.

'What do you quarrel about, dear? Money? Choice of entertainment? Once you identify the problem you're halfway to fixing it.'

'I don't think so. He's been seeing other women. A girl who works in the bar of his local is his latest.'

'You're sure?'

'I'm sure.'

'You went with him when he was engaged to Faith,' Vivienne reminded her softly, 'and you were going to marry my son. You might have guessed it would happen again. That's often the case.'

'I realized my mistake soon after Nick and I ran off. I really loved Ian and Nick turned my head. A kind of madness I think, looking back.'

'Too late now, dear. Ian is happy, and you and Nick will sort yourselves out, I'm sure. Drink your tea and I'll walk part of the way home with you.'

'It's a lovely house, isn't it?'

'It's big for just the two of us, but it will be a lovely home when Ian furnishes it to suit himself and whoever he brings here as his wife.'

'That won't be me.'

'No, dear. It won't be you.'

Vivienne was worried. Ian seemed afraid to commit to Faith even though he seemed to be very fond of her. Could he still want Tessa after all that had happened? Tessa was married and a messy divorce was not what she wanted for her son.

* * *

Tessa walked past the bus stop, heading for the beach. She wasn't in a hurry, a day off work to go to the doctor meant she could spend the rest of the day as she chose. The doctor had been so cheerful when he told her she was pregnant. How could he smile as though presenting a valued prize? Presume it was every woman's dream? She and Nick were no longer a couple, and the so-called marriage was a sham. She hadn't the right to his name, even though she called herself Tessa Harris, Mrs Nick Harris.

She didn't think her parents would be very pleased when she told them the truth and she desperately needed someone to talk to. Mrs Palmer's cake shop wasn't far away and she went in and asked Faith if they could have lunch together.

Surprise and curiosity persuaded Faith to agree and they went into a corner café and ordered eggs on toast and tea.

'Nick and I are not married,' Tessa announced as soon as the waitress had brought their meal. 'There was a mix-up when we got to the register office and, well, we came home and everyone just presumed we'd done what we'd planned.'

'That's easily remedied. You can arrange a ceremony and no one else need know. If you want someone to come with you, I'd be happy to and I'll keep your secret.'

'It isn't that simple. Nick has had affairs with at least three other women since our pretend marriage. Now I'm going to have a baby and he doesn't want it.'

'A baby? But he has to support you; whether the marriage is real or not isn't relevant.' Faith felt sickness surge through her as memories of walking away from her baby returned as real as if it had just happened. She closed her eyes and saw the tiny helpless child she had known for such a brief moment. She pushed her food aside and couldn't speak for a long time.

'He doesn't want it. My parents won't be able to face the truth. I don't know what to do.'

'It's probably the shock,' Faith said shakily. 'He'll come round. Most men want a child to carry on their name, don't they?'

'I want to end the lies and make the marriage real. He wants to tell the truth and end it.' She wiped away a tear angrily. 'You gave your baby away; I desperately want to keep mine.'

'So would I in your circumstances,' Faith said softly, the pain harsh and deep.

'I'm sorry, I only meant the circumstances *are* so different, yet the result could be the same. I could lose my child too.'

'An abortion? You couldn't do that. Think of the risk for yourself!'

'I lose Nick or I lose the baby. What a choice, eh?'

* * *

Faith didn't feel able to talk to Ian about what she had learned, but she trusted Vivienne. Ian was at home but she went to the house and invited herself for supper. 'My treat,' she said, 'I'm buying fish and chips for us all.'

While Ian sorted out the paperwork after his day, she walked to the fish-and-chip shop with Vivienne and told her everything Tessa had admitted.

'I think Ian should know,' Vivienne said, 'but I'm afraid he'll feel too much sympathy. I know he still has feelings for her. After all, they've known each other since the age of seven.'

'I'll leave it for you to decide,' Faith said. They hurried back with the food but neither woman had much appetite.

Tessa was in real trouble and now Faith knew she was free to marry. This could be the point at which Ian returned to his first love. Faith felt the familiar urgings again. She was going to lose Ian and she wanted to pack everything up and run away.

* * *

Paul called at No 3 and found Faith making pastry for some jam tarts. She wiped her hands free of flour and asked him what he wanted.

'Nothing,' he said. 'I want nothing, I just called to tell you I've found someone to look after Jack, Bill and Polly.'

'Good. I'm pleased. Things will slot into place now you have help.'

'You know her, I believe. She was a lodger here for a while.'

Faith stared at him willing him not to say the name she dreaded. Please, don't let it be Gwenllian.

'Gwenllian, a cousin of Matt Hewitt,' he confirmed. He gave a harsh laugh. 'She said you wouldn't be pleased. From the expression on your face she was right.'

'It's nothing to do with me. But I wish it was someone else. She isn't slow to rise to anger. Sadly it must be in the Hewitt family.' She almost told him she suspected Gwenllian of ruining her first Christmas at No 3 and possibly her garden as well, but without proof she dared not. 'We don't like each other but that's no reason for me to doubt her ability to care for the children. But watch her, Paul. Make sure the children are safe.'

'You can change my mind, if you'd only agree to help us.'

'Sorry, Paul. I can't.'

An hour later, as the jam tarts were cooling on a wire tray, the door opened and Gwenllian burst in. 'How dare you interfere!'

Startled, Faith dropped the last of the pastries onto the floor. 'What am I supposed to have done now?'

'Tried to persuade Paul not to employ me to look after his children. What d'you think I'll do? Beat them? Poison them?'

'I simply reminded Paul that, like your cousin Matt, you have a temper.' She gestured towards her with a hand to demonstrate the example Gwenllian was giving.

'You ruined Matt's life by pretending to love him then giving away his child. Now you're trying to ruin mine.'

'Matt ruined his own life, and if you aren't careful, you'll do the same.'

Faith was shaking when the woman had gone. She picked up the damaged tarts and threw them into the garden for the birds. She seemed to bring out the worst in people. So many had shown disapproval since she came to the town. It was Olive, who called later for her weekly collection who put Gwenllian's outburst into perspective.

'Gwenllian isn't a friend, she's made that clear, but Paul is. You stick up for friends and if that means upsetting someone who might harm them it's something you have to accept.' She reached to the dresser and took down a couple of cups and saucers. 'Now, what about me trying a couple of them tarts? Blackcurrant jam, is it? My favourite.' Smiling, Faith filled the kettle.

Some time later, Olive was calling at a house close to where Tessa and Nick lived in two small rooms. As she approached the back door she heard someone crying.

'Hello? Anyone home?' She pushed the door wide and stepped inside. Tessa was curled up on the couch wrapped in a blanket and obviously in pain. 'My dear girl, what's happened?'

'The baby, I think I'm losing it.'

'A baby? Oh you poor dear. Where's your Nick?'

'He said he'd go to the chemist and get me something for the pain but that was more than two hours ago and I didn't know what to do.'

Bustling around the distressed woman, Olive made a hot drink; then ran to the corner and phoned for an ambulance. Nick still hadn't appeared when the medics took Tessa away. Leaving a note for Nick, Olive went with her and waited until someone came to tell her that Tessa was going to be all right but had lost the baby.

The hospital wanted to keep Tessa in until the next day as a precaution. Olive bought a few things and took them back to the hospital, then went to the two rooms, where the note lay just as she had left it. Patiently, she sat and waited for Nick to come home. On her reckoning he had been out for at least seven hours, and had been well aware as he left that Tessa was ill.

When he did appear he smelled of perfume and his eyes were glazed with alcohol.

Wordlessly she handed him the note she had written earlier on which she had noted the time.

'She's lost the baby, you say? I'd better go and see her.'

'Not till you've washed and sobered up,' Olive said. 'Who was she this time? The woman from the greengrocer's, was it? Beryl Thomas? She never was fussy who she went out with.'

He seemed not to have heard. All his mind had picked up was the news that the baby was no longer a problem. 'She's definitely lost the baby?' Olive was sickened by his smile.

* * *

More than a week had passed when Ian saw Tessa. He was alarmed at how ill she looked. He invited her to a café where he ordered tea and cakes.

'You look a little tired,' he said. 'It's all right, you can talk to me. Faith told my mother and she told me that you and Nick are going to have a baby.' She looked startled and he went on, soothingly, 'She also told me that you and he are not really married, so I'm here if you want to talk about it. I'm sure there's nothing that can't be sorted.'

He obviously knew nothing about her emergency visit to the hospital, so she hotly denied that she was expecting a child or that she and Nick were not legally married.

'Faith is spreading rumours again. It's what she does best, isn't it, Ian? First about Nick being a cheat, then Matt, now me. I am definitely not expecting a child. And do you really think I'd be living with Nick and calling myself his wife if it weren't true?'

Humiliated by his embarrassing mistake, he paid for the snack and left her there, after apologizing and promising to tell Faith and his mother they were wrong.

Tessa went home along the back lanes, hoping to avoid meeting people while she was unable to control her tears.

* * *

Ian rarely felt real anger, disappointment was his usual response to unkindness or misbehaviour, but today he was more than disappointed. He had been humiliated and so had Tessa. When he went into the baker's shop just as it was closing. Faith could see he had something on his mind. He waited while she collected her things, then, as they walked to the car he said, 'Where did you hear that Tessa was expecting a baby?'

'She told me herself. I told your mother but I didn't think you'd want to know. Why do you ask?'

'It isn't true. I've just seen her and when I mentioned it, she was very upset. It isn't true that she and Nick aren't legally married either. Why spread such stories?'

'Ian, Tessa came here and we had lunch together. She was upset and told me that she and Nick weren't married and she was carrying his child. A child he didn't want. Now why should she tell me that if it weren't true?'

'She denied telling you anything of the sort.'

'Then you have to decide who to believe, Tessa or me.' They had reached the car but she didn't get in. She stared at him for a moment, hurt and disbelief in her eyes. 'This is the end, Ian. Without trust there's nothing worth holding on to. Goodbye.'

'Wait, I have to think about this.'

'No you don't. Your mind was made up the moment Tessa said her piece. I believed her when she said she and Nick didn't marry, so she's still free for you to make everything right.'

She forced herself not to run and even though the temptation to turn and run back to him was almost overwhelming, she kept on walking until she had closed the door of No 3 behind her.

The following day she would make an appointment with a solicitor and an estate agent and start preparing to move. She loved Ian but he could never love her. She was unlovable. Friendships, yes, but never love. Paul needed her and hadn't even pretended to love her. Even her recently found sister Verity disliked her, regretting the day she had found them. Joy was kind but no more than she'd be to a stranger. She had to leave. There wasn't an alternative.

Paul would cope and Ian would go back to Tessa, live with her here in this town. She would meet them often and the pain would never leave her. Running away was the only thing to do.

She made appointments for later in the week and every time she thought of starting again it was like a wound to the heart. She was cheered by a letter from her sister Joy telling her she was coming for the weekend. Preparing food, making sure the bedroom was as comfortable as she could make it took her mind from her misery.

* * *

Joy came on Friday afternoon and on Saturday Mrs Palmer told her she could leave early. At half past two she and Joy caught the train into Cardiff for some shopping. During the journey Faith told her sister that she was moving.

'You're a wild goose, always on the move. Are you sure it's the right thing to do?' Joy asked. 'Why don't you let the house and come to stay with us for a while? Making a decision too fast isn't a wise thing to do. Parting from Ian is enough to cope with for the moment. You might find after a while that your life settles and you're happiest here where you have friends, and a job you like.'

'That's the other reason I want yet another fresh start. I do enjoy working for Mrs Palmer but I'm a teacher and I want to run a nursery for three- and-four-year-olds. If I can find a house suitable to convert into a day nursery with accommodation for myself, in a suitable location, then I don't mind where I live. There are some advantages to being a wild goose.'

'Is Verity a part of the reason? I know she hasn't been exactly welcoming.'

'She thinks I've searched for you for some ulterior motive, that I want to claim some inheritance. Well, I don't.'

'The money to start the business came from our grandmother, you see, and in the will the money was to be shared between the three of us. We had given up all hope of finding you. So you turning up like that was a shock.'

'Get a solicitor to draw up the form stating I want nothing from you and I'll sign it.'

'There's no need for that and anyway, our mother would never agree. Just be patient. Verity will soon realize how happy your arrival has made our mother.'

* * *

Faith and Joy had been invited to visit Kitty, Gareth and their new baby at the hospital on Sunday, so when a small boy came with a message asking Faith to go to the workshop where Matt had something special to show her, she shook her head and declined. 'Matt is the last person I want to see,' she whispered to Joy.

'Why don't I go instead?' Joy said. 'I can tell him you're busy. I don't know Kitty and Gareth, they're your friends.'

'There's no need for either of us to go. Matt isn't a part of my life.'

'But it is odd and I am curious,' Joy admitted.

* * *

Olive was catching up on her collections and when she called on Vivienne, Ian was there. This was one of the houses where she was usually offered refreshments and she sank into a chair. 'Terribly sad about poor Tessa, wasn't it?' she began.

'What about Tessa? She isn't ill, is she?' Ian asked.

'Not ill, but losing the baby like that was very distressing, specially as that Nick was out as usual. Knowing she was ill he disappeared for seven hours! Can you believe that? I got a taxi and went with her to the hospital.'

Getting into her stride she was interrupted by Ian asking, 'She was expecting a baby?'

'Yes, and Nick didn't want it. D'you know he couldn't disguise his relief when I told him she'd lost it, poor little mite.'

Ian reached for his coat. 'I have to go out.'

'You're not going to see Tessa, are you?' Vivienne asked.

'No, I need to see Faith. I owe her an apology.'

Ian went to No 3 and asked Mrs Gretorex where he could find Faith.

'I think she's gone to see Matt. A young lad called and said Matt wanted to see her. I'm not sure of the reason, but I heard the young boy say something about Matt having something to show her and she and Joy went straight out.'

'Thank you.' Ian wasn't sure what to do. If Faith was talking to Matt he couldn't burst in on a conversation. He turned away. He had been so stupid. Accusing her of lying, making her believe that Tessa was more important to him. Would she listen to him? He knew he had to try and put things right without delay. Turning again he walked towards Matt's workshop.

* * *

Wondering what Matt could possibly want, Faith left Joy at the corner of the road from where they could see the entrance to the yard. 'There's no van outside, that's curious,' Faith said.

The yard was empty when Joy reached the gate. She knocked on the door of the house but there was no reply. Curiously she went towards the workshop. Everywhere was completely silent as she walked across the yard, so quiet her footsteps seemed to echo. She stopped halfway to the workshop and looked around her. There had obviously been a mistake. She began to retrace her steps, then stood at the entrance and looked up the road for the sign of a van approaching.

Faith was about to get onto the bus when she stopped and turned away. She shouldn't have agreed to Joy going to see Matt. What could he want? And where was the van? Something was odd and she didn't trust Matt enough to ignore it. Increasing her walk to a run, she headed back to the yard.

Superficially, Joy and Faith were alike. Their height and build and even the way they dressed were similar. Only the colouring was different. The day was dull and as a fine drizzle was falling, Joy had pulled her hood over her head and when Ian saw her standing there in the distance, for a moment he thought it was Faith. He didn't call. He tried to decide what to say, the first words would be very important, his happiness depended on them.

Joy decided that Matt must be inside the office and she walked across the yard towards the entrance. Above the entrance stood the beautiful statue and behind it, Gwenllian was holding the ropes — twisted around a metal sign — that held it in place.

Joy stopped just a few yards away when she heard a sort of whimpering sound that seemed to be coming from the workshop. Standing just outside the doorway, she called, 'Is there anyone there?'

The sound was repeated and she was about to go inside when another noise above her made her stop directly under the statue, which seemed to be moving, rocking slightly on its plinth. Ian reached the gate at that moment and he gave a shouted warning. 'Faith! Look out! Run! She's up there!'

Joy hesitated and looked above the door, then the statue tottered more wildly and she was pushed aside and knocked to the ground by Ian. She rolled inside the doorway and as she tried to stand she lost her balance and tripped and fell. She lay directly beneath the tottering statue, stunned and confused.

Ian ran up the ladder that leaned against the overhanging porch. Then Faith appeared. She looked at Joy crouched near the doorway and then up to where Ian was struggling with Gwenllian. 'Get the police!' he shouted. Instead she climbed up to help Ian hold the statue in place. Joy then rose to her feet and walked, unsteadily on shaking legs, pressed tightly against the wall, to the house.

'The phone is in the office!' Faith shouted as she held onto the ropes beside Ian, while Gwenllian screamed and tried to push her over the edge.

Joy reached the phone on the office desk and dialled 999, then went out to stand near the workshop.

Grunts and groans filled the air interspersed with Gwenllian's screams. They hardly knew why they were trying to save the statue as they wrestled to get Gwenllian's hands off the ropes. The strength of the woman who had removed the heavy chain and replaced it with several loosely fastened ropes was terrifying. Releasing just two more half-hitches would cause the statue to fall; the real danger was that one of them would fall with it. Ian and Faith were unaware of the pain of the struggle, their concentration was on grabbing hold of Gwenllian.

Joy went back to where the ladder stood and climbed up, intending to add her strength to Ian's and Faith's and stop the statue from falling. She grabbed Gwenllian and tried to drag her away from the ropes but Gwenllian kicked her and she staggered back to the top of the ladder, lost her balance and hung over the edge. In spite of the chaotic situation Joy became aware again of the whimpering sounds and realized they were nearby. She picked herself up and went down the ladder.

She turned back as a cry from Faith made her look up to where a violent effort from the half-crazy Gwenllian had caused Faith to lose her balance and slip over the edge. To Joy's horror Faith was hanging by her hands, while Gwenllian tried to stamp on her fingers to make her fall.

In sheer panic Ian punched Gwenllian. She gave a small sigh and folded into a sitting position. Panting with the exertion, he tied the ropes around the hook that had held the statue in place. Then he ran down and helped Joy to rescue Faith by moving the ladder to allow her to descend. Then he held Faith as though he would never let her go.

Joy ran up the ladder on trembling legs and stood over the slowly recovering Gwenllian, holding a length of wood over her, as though it were a bat in the hands of a very determined cricketer.

When the police arrived Gwenllian was held with some of the rope she had used in her attempt to drop the statue on the woman below. When she had been told she had almost killed Joy, not Faith, all the fight had gone out of her.

'There's someone else in there.' Joy pointed at the workshop. 'I heard strange muffled sounds.'

Cautiously, one of the policemen went into the dark area and moments later carried out Matt's terrified mother. She was tied with parcel-tape and a rag had been placed inexpertly over her mouth, fastened with more of the same tape. Carol had managed to move it slightly by rubbing her face along the ground.

'It was a miracle she didn't suffocate,' one of the policemen told them as they comforted the terrified woman.

'Gwenllian Hughes?' Joy asked. 'Who is she and why did she want to kill me?'

'She didn't, she thought you were Faith.'

'Why did she want to kill Faith, then?'

'Because she believes I'm the cause of everything that is wrong in her life.' Faith said.

'I'm certain now that the wrecked garden and the ruin of my Christmas were down to Matt's mother, and Gwenllian felt it necessary to do something even worse, to show her support for Matt and convince Carol she had been right to do those terrible things. Only her ideas for revenge went too far.'

When Matt arrived home he ran to his distressed mother and demanded an explanation, glaring at Faith, obviously convinced she was responsible. He was horrified when he learned the truth.

'He's been to talk to the doctor and he's going to get help to control his temper,' Carol said tearfully, as the police led a subdued and frightened Gwenllian away.

'Something I should have done years ago, after I forced myself on Ethel Holland,' he said, admitting it for the first time.

Faith sobbed with relief. Walking away from the baby had been the right thing to do. Almost every night she dreamed of holding baby Dorothy in her arms even though that could never happen. She had given her away. And nothing could change that. Her daughter called someone else 'Mummy'. That was her punishment and it would last for the rest of her life.

Her thoughts then turned to Winnie's children, without their mother. She gasped. 'Ian! I have to tell Paul, he'll be expecting Gwenllian to meet the children from school!'

'I'll come with you.' Ian took her hand.

'I'll have to tell Gregory of Verity's part in all this,' Joy said quietly. 'Better than him hearing stories about his wife from the police.'

Carol was crying and being comforted by Matt. Looking around Faith likened it to a strange battleground; there was no blood, the wounds were invisible but they were life-threatening in their way.

Faith ran with Ian to the car; her thoughts were of the children, everything else was secondary. They met the children and took them home, where Paul was waiting. At first he thought it was some made-up story to discredit Gwenllian but when a policeman came and he realized they were telling the truth he collapsed into a chair.

Faith went next door to ask a neighbour to take the children for an hour and the kind lady promised to look after them until Paul had found someone suitable to take over their care. 'My children are grown up and it will be lovely to share someone else's little ones,' she told Faith.

Paul looked like a broken doll with the stuffing half-removed. Faith was aching with the need to help but she left him in the hands of the neighbour and the constable and walked away. This was for Paul to cope with. Much as she loved the children and wanted to help Winnie's family, it was better to give Paul the firm understanding that it was his problem and he must deal with it in his way.

* * *

Much later the friends were sitting in the garden of No 3, a bonfire burning, potatoes tucked into the edges. Ian and Mr Gretorex were taking turns to add fuel to the burning pile. Joy and Faith were sitting close together, aware of how easily the day could have ended in tragedy. Vivienne was making yet more tea in the kitchen and searching in the bags she had brought for more cakes.

'Before this awful day ends, I have to apologize, Faith,' Ian said. Joy got up and went to help Vivienne in the kitchen. 'I should have believed you. I realized today that I've been unable to let go of the years with Tessa. Afraid to admit to how much I feel for you. She walked away from me when I believed everything was perfect and I was afraid of it happening again, with you. Can you forgive me?'

'I have to admit I was seriously thinking of running away again, but Joy helped me to realize that would have been a mistake. It's here in Barry Town where I've been happiest, but I didn't think I could stay if it meant seeing you and Tessa happily together again.'

'Please, Faith, never run away again,' he pleaded.

'I will move, though. I want a house where I can open a nursery. I won't be moving very far, just to a house large enough for my plans.' She looked serious and went on. 'When I do I want to ask Ethel Holland to help. Like me she has had a sad life since the tragedy she suffered when she was little more than a child. People still blame the *woman* in these cases and she's had to live with that shame and *guilt* for so long. I want to help her realize her worth, give her confidence.'

'That's a wonderful idea. But don't think about moving away. What about my house? Didn't you say it would be a perfect place for a nursery school?'

She hesitated, not sure what he was offering. He put his arms around her and said, 'The house is large enough for lots of children, including ours.'

At once a picture of her tiny baby, a child she had abandoned, filled her heart with pain. 'I don't deserve to be happy,' she said shaking her head.

'Marry me, Faith. Our children will never make us forget your first-born,' he whispered. 'I'll make you so happy you'll never think of running, ever again.'

'I'm sorry, Ian, but it's too late. The time for loving is gone, swallowed up by your unhappiness and mine.'

'I know we'll be happy.'

'Too much has happened.'

'You could have the nursery school you dream of. A mother-in-law who'd be your friend. I love you, Faith.'

'Surely love shouldn't be so prosaic. It's all too convenient.'

They were all exhausted by the events of the past hours and he kissed her gently and left.

''Ere, what's been happening that I don't know about?' a voice called and Olive appeared, being dragged by the now enormous hound, Doris. 'I've just been to see Kitty and Gareth and that lovely baby of theirs, surrounded by unpacked boxes they are, but as happy as you'd wish for them. Then,' she went on, 'then, I met someone who knew someone, whose auntie knows a man whose son is a policeman. Tell me, what have I missed?' She listened to the story, punctuating it with lots of 'Well I never', and 'Who'd have believed that?' When it had all been explained she declared herself exhausted.

* * *

Faith didn't hear from Ian for several days and she told herself she had been right to refuse his proposal. He hadn't been sincere, it was a result of many things but not a passionate, undeniable love. The belief that she had been right to refuse him didn't make her happy. She knew that for herself, being married to Ian would have been the start of a wonderful life, but the love she felt for him was all-consuming, deep and unselfish and she wouldn't risk his unhappiness by accepting him while she doubted that it was best for him. If he still loved Tessa she wouldn't prevent them being together. Marrying Ian would have been so right for her but she was afraid Ian was proposing for all the wrong reasons. She was certain he still loved Tessa.

Her unhappy childhood, with her lonely search for her family and someone who cared, had damaged her emotionally. It was Ian who had taught her to love but how could she spend her life as second best to a memory of his first love?

He came to the house on the following Wednesday afternoon to find her forcing her fork into the hard ground in an attempt to plant some forgotten spring bulbs. There were dried leaves in her hair which had fallen from its clips after she had reached into a hedge to clear some dead grasses. There was dried earth on her cheek and mud on her hands.

He handed her an envelope and he was smiling. Something had changed, the look in his eyes was positive and filled with love, and with a rush of hope, she smiled back.

'Plans for turning the ground floor into a nursery,' he explained. 'I had an architect draw them up but they are only a starting point. You and he can discuss them and he'll make any changes you want.'

She opened them out on top of a wheelbarrow cautiously with the tips of grubby fingers and studied them, aware of him standing beside her, watching her and waiting for her reaction. 'Any conditions?' she asked, trying to stay calm. This was business, not a proposal.

'Two. First, that you buy all your equipment from me. Second, that you marry me.'

She turned towards him and as she began to ask about Tessa, he took her in his arms, mud and all.

Much later, with the house filled with its usual visitors and guests, Faith looked around her at the smiling faces, all enjoying sharing their happiness. Paul and the children were there, having called to tell them the neighbour was taking on the children full time, or at least for the hours during which Paul needed to work. Olive was chatting to Mr and Mrs Gretorex, whose bungalow, when completed, would mean they would be her near neighbours.

'We're so happy in our caravan home, aren't we, Doris?' Olive said, and the huge dog gave a growling reply, which Olive insisted meant, Yes.

They had all needed her for a while, Faith mused, but now their lives were settled and it was right for her to move on. Not to run away, she thought happily, but to move on, to a new and wonderful life.

THE END

ALSO BY GRACE THOMPSON

THE OWEN SISTERS FAMILY SAGAS
Book 1: GOODBYE TO DREAMS
Book 2: PAINT ON THE SMILES

STANDALONE NOVELS
THE END OF A JOURNEY
NOTHING IS FOREVER
GULL ISLAND
THE RUNAWAY

Thank you for reading this book.

If you enjoyed it please leave feedback on Amazon or Goodreads, and if there is anything we missed or you have a question about, then please get in touch. We appreciate you choosing our book.

Founded in 2014 in Shoreditch, London, we at Joffe Books pride ourselves on our history of innovative publishing. We were thrilled to be shortlisted for Independent Publisher of the Year at the British Book Awards.

www.joffebooks.com

We're very grateful to eagle-eyed readers who take the time to contact us. Please send any errors you find to corrections@joffebooks.com. We'll get them fixed ASAP.

Printed in Great Britain
by Amazon

13684333R00153